CN 6|23

KU-694-654

Alex Kava dedicated herself to writing in 1996, having had a successful career in PR and advertising. Praised by critics and fans alike, Alex Kava's Maggie O'Dell novels, *A Perfect Evil, Split Second, The Soul Catcher* and *A Necessary Evil*, have all been *New York Times* bestsellers as well as appearing on bestseller lists around the world.

Also available from

Alex
KAVA

BLACK FRIDAY

EXPOSED

WHITEWASH

A NECESSARY EVIL

ONE FALSE MOVE

AT THE STROKE OF MADNESS

THE SOUL CATCHER

SPLIT SECOND

A PERFECT EVIL

Alex
KAVA

Exposed

700032795940

All the characters in this book have no existence outside the imagination of the author, and have no relation whatsoever to anyone bearing the same name or names. They are not even distantly inspired by any individual known or unknown to the author, and all the incidents are pure invention.

All Rights Reserved including the right of reproduction in whole or in part in any form. This edition is published by arrangement with Harlequin Enterprises II B.V./S.à.r.l. The text of this publication or any part thereof may not be reproduced or transmitted in any form or by any means, electronic or mechanical, including photocopying, recording, storage in an information retrieval system, or otherwise, without the written permission of the publisher.

This book is sold subject to the condition that it shall not, by way of trade or otherwise, be lent, resold, hired out or otherwise circulated without the prior consent of the publisher in any form of binding or cover other than that in which it is published and without a similar condition including this condition being imposed on the subsequent purchaser.

Harlequin MIRA is a registered trademark of Harlequin Enterprises Limited, used under licence.

First published in Great Britain 2009. This edition 2012.
Harlequin MIRA, an imprint of Harlequin (UK) Limited,
Eton House, 18-24 Paradise Road,
Richmond, Surrey, TW9 1SR

© S.M. Kava 2008

ISBN 978 1 848 45170 4

60-0312

Harlequin's policy is to use papers that are natural, renewable and recyclable products and made from wood grown in sustainable forests. The logging and manufacturing processes conform to the legal environmental regulations of the country of origin.

Printed and bound by
CPI Group (UK) Ltd, Croydon, CR0 4YY

This one's for my friends who patiently endure my long absences and then make it feel as though no time at all has passed since our last visit.

Sharon Car
Marlene Haney
Patti El-Kachouti
Sandy Rockwood

ACKNOWLEDGEMENTS

I've often been given a hard time for my long acknowledgements, pages and pages thanking all the wonderful experts who answer questions, set me straight and allow me to nag and interrupt their daily lives. This time I'd be afraid to leave someone out because the list is long. So instead I decided to keep it simple. In a year that's asked more questions than provided answers, these are the three people who deserve this page.

To my team:

Deb Carlin, best friend and business manager extraordinaire, for keeping me centred, making sure my feet are firmly planted on the ground and seeing to it that this journey is a delight.

Amy Moore-Benson, friend and agent—we've been to hell and back. Thank you for being not only my advocate, but my champion as well.

Linda McFall—the new kid on the team—thank you for your patience, your expertise, your dedication and your humour. It's an absolute pleasure to have you as my editor.

CHAPTER
1

Lake Victoria
Uganda, Africa

Waheem was already bleeding when he boarded the crowded motorboat. He kept a bloodstained rag wadded up and pressed against his nose, hoping the other passengers wouldn't notice. Earlier the boat's owner, the man islanders called Pastor Roy, had helped Waheem load his rusted cage stuffed full of monkeys onto the last available space. But not even a mile from shore and Waheem noticed Pastor Roy glancing back and forth from his wife's tight smile to the blood now dripping down the front of Waheem's shirt. Pastor Roy looked like he regretted offering Waheem the last seat.

"Nosebleeds seem common on these islands," Pastor Roy said, almost a question, giving Waheem a chance to explain.

Waheem nodded like he had no idea what the man had

said. He understood English perfectly but pretended otherwise. There wouldn't be another charcoal or banana boat for two days, so he was grateful for his good fortune, grateful that Pastor Roy and his wife allowed him on board, especially with his cage of monkeys. But Waheem knew it would be a forty-minute trip from Buvuma Island to Jinja and he preferred silence to the pastor's chatter about Jesus. All the others had boarded first, so Waheem was stuck sitting up front, in salvation range. He didn't want to encourage the pastor to think he might save one more soul on the trip across the lake.

Besides, the others—a sad assortment of women and barefoot children and one blind old man—looked much more like they needed saving. Despite the bloody nose and the sudden throbbing pain inside his head, Waheem was young and strong and if things went as planned, he and his family would be rich, buying a shamba of their own instead of breaking their backs working for others.

"God is here," Pastor Roy called out, evidently not needing any encouragement. He steered the boat with one hand and waved the other at the islands surrounding them in the distance, beginning one of his sermons.

The other passengers all bowed their heads, almost an involuntary response to the man's voice. Perhaps they considered their reverence a small fee for passage on the pastor's boat. Waheem bowed his head, too, but watched from behind his blood-soaked rag, pretending to listen and trying to ignore the stink of monkey urine and the occasional spatter of his own warm blood dripping down his chin. He noticed the blind man's eyes, white blurry globes that darted back and forth while his wrinkled lips twitched, but there was only a mumbled hum, perhaps a prayer. A woman beside Waheem held tight the top of a burlap bag that moved on its own and smelled of wet chicken feathers. Everyone was quiet except for three little girls on the back of the boat who smiled and swayed. They were singing softly in a whispered chant. Even in their playfulness they were evidently aware that they shouldn't disturb the pastor's words.

"God hasn't forgotten you people," Pastor Roy continued, "and neither will I."

Waheem glanced at Pastor Roy's wife. She didn't seem to be paying any attention to her husband. She sat next to him at the front of the boat, rubbing her bare white arms with clear liquid from a plastic bottle, stopping every few seconds to pick tsetse flies from her silky, long hair.

"All of Lake Victoria's islands are filled with the outcasts, the poor, the criminals, the sick——" He paused and nodded at Waheem as if to differentiate his handicap from the rest of the list. "But I see only Jesus' children, waiting to be saved."

Waheem didn't correct the pastor. He didn't consider himself one of Buvuma's diseased outcasts, though there were plenty of them. It wasn't unusual to see someone sick or covered with lesions, open sores. The islands were a last resort for many. But not Waheem. He had never been sick a day in his life, at least not before the vomiting started last night.

It had gone on for hours. His stomach ached from the reminder. He didn't like thinking about the black vomit speckled with chunks of blood. He worried that he had thrown up pieces of his insides. That's what it felt like. Now his head throbbed and his nose wouldn't stop bleeding. He readjusted the rag, trying to find a spot that wasn't soiled. Blood dripped onto his dusty foot and he found himself staring at the pastor's shiny leather shoes. Waheem wondered how Pastor Roy expected to save anyone without getting his shoes dirty.

It didn't matter. Waheem cared only about getting his monkeys to Jinja in time to meet the American, a businessman dressed in equally shiny leather shoes. The man had promised Waheem a fortune. At least it was a fortune to Waheem. The American had agreed to pay him more money for each monkey than Waheem and his father could make in a whole year.

He wished he had been able to capture more, but it had taken almost two days to secure the three he had shoved together into the metal cage. To look at them now no one would believe the struggle he had gone through. Waheem knew from experience that monkeys had sharp teeth and if they wrapped their tails around a man's neck they could slash his face to shreds in a matter of minutes. He'd learned that much from the two short months he had worked for Okbar, the rich monkey trader from Jinja.

The job had been a good one, but there were nets and tranquilizer guns that Okbar had provided that made it seem simple. Waheem's main responsibility was to load up the sick monkeys the British veterinarian expelled out of the shipments; shipments that included hundreds of monkeys that would go onto a cargo plane destined for research labs in the United Kingdom and the United States.

The veterinarian thought Waheem loaded up the monkeys and took them away to be killed, but Okbar called that an "outrageous waste." So instead of killing the monkeys, Okbar instructed Waheem to take the poor sick ones to an island in Lake Victoria and set them free. Sometimes when Okbar came up short of monkeys for a shipment he had Waheem go out to the island and get a few of the sick ones. Oftentimes the veterinarian didn't even notice.

But now Okbar was gone. It had been months since anyone had seen him. Waheem wasn't sure where he had gone. One day his small, messy office in Jinja was empty, all the file cabinets, the metal desk, the tranquilizer guns and nets, everything gone. No one knew what had happened to Okbar. And Waheem was out of a job. He'd never forget the disappointment in his father's eyes. They would have to return to the fields and work long days to make up for the job that Waheem had lost.

Then one day the American showed up in Jinja, asking for Waheem, not Okbar, but Waheem. Somehow he knew about the monkeys that were taken to the island and those were the ones he wanted. He would pay the premium price. "But they must be the monkeys," he told Waheem, "from the island where you took the outcasts."

Waheem wasn't sure why anyone would want sick monkeys. He looked in at them now, hunched over, crowded together in the rusted, metal cage. Their noses were running and caked with green slime. Their faces were blank. They refused food and water. Still, Waheem avoided eye contact, knowing all too well what good aim a monkey, even a sick one, had when he decided to spit in your eye.

The monkeys must have sensed Waheem examining them because suddenly one grabbed the bars of the cage and started to screech. The noise didn't bother Waheem. He was used to it. It was normal compared to their eerie silence. But another monkey joined in and now Waheem saw the pastor's wife sit up and stare. There was no longer a tight smile on her perfect face. Waheem didn't think she looked frightened or concerned, but rather she looked disgusted. He worried the pastor might make him throw the cage overboard, or worse, make Waheem go overboard with them. Like most islanders he didn't know how to swim.

The throbbing in his head joined in with the monkeys' screeches and Waheem thought he could feel the boat rocking. His stomach threatened to spew up again. Only now did he realize the entire front of his shirt had blossomed into a huge red-and-black stain. And the bleeding continued. He could feel it inside his mouth, filling his throat. He swallowed and started coughing, trying to catch the chunks of blood but not quite successful. Some splattered the pastor's leather shoes.

Waheem's eyes darted around but avoided Pastor Roy.

Everyone was watching him. They would vote to throw him from the boat. He had seen them bow to the man's words. They would, no doubt, do whatever he asked. They were too far away from the islands. He'd never be able to stay afloat.

Suddenly the pastor's hand waved down at him and Waheem winced and jerked away. Only after he sat up and focused his eyes did he see that Pastor Roy was not getting ready to shove him overboard. Instead, the man was handing Waheem a white cloth, brilliant white with beautiful, decorative embroidery in the corner.

"Go ahead, take it," the pastor said in a soft voice, this not a sermon meant for any of the others. When Waheem didn't answer, Pastor Roy continued, "Yours is all used up." And he pointed to the dripping rag. "Go ahead, you need it more than I do."

Waheem's eyes darted around the small boat, all still watching, but none like the pastor's wife whose face had twisted into an angry scowl. Only, she no longer looked at Waheem. Her eyes, her anger now directed at her husband.

The rest of the trip was quiet except for the singsong chant of the little girls. Their voices lulled Waheem into a dreamlike state. At one point he thought he could hear his mother calling to him from the approaching shore. His vision became blurred and his ears filled with the sound of his own heartbeat.

He was weak and dizzy by the time the boat docked. This time Pastor Roy had to carry the cage for him while Waheem followed, stumbling through the crowds, women with baskets and burlap bags, men loitering and bicycles looping around them.

The pastor put down the cage and Waheem grunted his thanks, more a groan. But before the pastor turned to leave, Waheem dropped to his knees, choking and heaving, splattering the shiny leather shoes with black vomit. He reached to wipe his mouth and discovered blood dripping from his ears, and his throat already full again. He felt the pastor's hand on his shoulder and Waheem hardly recognized the voice calling for help. The calm authority that preached sermons had been replaced by a panicked screech.

Waheem's body jerked without warning. His arms thrashed and his legs flayed in the dirt, a seizure beyond his control. It was difficult to breathe. He gasped and choked, no longer able to swallow. Then he felt movement deep inside him. He could almost hear it, as if his insides were ripping apart. Blood seemed to pour out from everywhere. His brain registered no pain, only shock. The shock of seeing so much blood and realizing it was his own, seemed to override the pain.

A crowd gathered around him but they were a blur. Even the pastor's voice became a distant hum. Waheem could no longer see him. And he wasn't even conscious of the American businessman who slipped his gloved fingers around the handle of Waheem's rusted monkey cage and then simply walked away.

CHAPTER

2

Two months later
8:25 a.m.
Friday, September 28, 2007
Quantico, Virginia

Maggie O'Dell watched her boss, Assistant Director Cunningham, push up his glasses and examine the box of doughnuts sitting outside his office as if the decision might impact lives. It was the same intense look she saw him make when determining any decision, whether choosing a doughnut or running the Behavioral Science Unit. His serious poker face, despite the weathered lines in his forehead and around his intense eyes, remained unchanged. An index finger tapped his thin—almost nonexistent—upper lip.

He stood with a rod-straight back and feet set apart in the same stance he used to fire his Glock. A few minutes after eight in the morning and his well-pressed shirtsleeves were already rolled up, but meticulously and properly turned with cuffs tucked under. Lean and fit, he could eat the entire dozen and probably not notice it on his waistline. His salt-and-pepper hair was the only thing that hinted at his age. Maggie had heard rumors that he could bench-press fifty pounds more than what the recruits were doing despite being almost thirty years their senior. So it wasn't calories that affected his choice.

Maggie glanced down at herself. In many ways she had modeled her appearance after her boss. Creased trousers, a copper-colored suit that complemented her auburn hair and brown eyes but didn't distract or draw attention, a lock-n-load stance that conveyed confidence.

Sometimes she knew she overcompensated a bit. Old habits were hard to break. Ten years ago when Maggie made the transformation from forensic fellow to special agent her survival depended on her ability to blend in as much as possible with her male counterparts. No-nonsense hairstyle, very little makeup, tailored suits, but nothing formfitting. Of course, the FBI wasn't an agency that punished attractive women, but Maggie knew it certainly wasn't one that rewarded them, either.

Lately, however, she had noticed her suits were hanging a bit loosely on her. Not necessarily a result of that overcompensation, but perhaps from simple stress. Since July she had pushed her workout routine, going from a two-mile run to a three-mile then four, now five. Sometimes her legs cramped up, but she continued to push it. A few sore muscles were worth a clear head. That's what she told herself.

It wasn't all about stress, but rather an accumulation of things that had fogged up her mind the last several months. She had a logjam of files on her desk and one file in particular, a case from July, kept creeping back to the top of her stack: an unsolved murder in a restroom at Chicago's O'Hare International Airport. A priest stabbed through the heart. A priest named Father Michael Keller who had taken up plenty of space in Maggie's head for too many years.

Keller had been one of six priests who had been suspected of molesting young boys. Within four months all six priests had been murdered, all with the same MO. In July, Keller's murder was the last. Maggie knew for a fact that the killer had stopped killing, had promised to stop for good. Maggie told herself that if you make deals with killers you can't expect to keep a clear head.

That was the dark side of the fog. On the bright, or at least the flip side of the fog, there was something—or rather *someone* else who preoccupied too much of her mind. Someone named Nick Morrelli.

She snatched a chocolate-frosted doughnut out from under Cunningham and took a bite.

"Tully usually beats me to the chocolate ones," she said when Cunningham raised an eyebrow at her. But then he nodded as if that was explanation enough.

"By the way, where is he?" she asked. "He has court in an hour."

Normally she didn't keep tabs on her partner but if Tully wasn't there to testify then she would get stuck doing it, and for once she was taking off early. She actually had weekend plans. She and Detective Julia Racine had scheduled another road trip to Connecticut. Julia to see her father and Maggie to see a certain forensic anthropologist named Adam Bonzado, who showed some hope of taking Maggie's mind off the e-mails, the voice messages, the flowers and cards that a very persistent Nick Morrelli had been showering her with for the last five weeks.

"Court date's been changed," Cunningham said and Maggie had almost forgotten what they were talking about. It must have registered on her face, because Cunningham continued, "Tully had a family situation he needed to take care of."

Cunningham finally decided on a glazed cruller. Still examining the box's contents, he added, "You know how it is when kids get to be teenagers."

Maggie nodded, but actually she didn't know. Her family obligations extended as far as a white Labrador retriever named Harvey who was quite happy with two daily feedings, plenty of ear rubs and a place at the foot of her queen-size bed. Later this afternoon he'd be sprawled out and drooling on the leather backseat of Julia Racine's Saab, happy to be included.

She found herself wondering what Cunningham knew. She couldn't remember her boss ever being late because of a "family situation." After ten years of working alongside him

Maggie had no idea about the assistant director's family. There were no pictures on his clutter-free desk, nothing in his office to give any clues. She knew he was married, though she had never met his wife. Maggie didn't even know her name. It wasn't like they were invited to the same Christmas parties. Not that Maggie went to Christmas parties.

Cunningham kept his personal life exactly that— personal. And in many ways, Maggie had modeled her personal life after him, as well. There were no photos on her desk, either. During her divorce she never once mentioned any of it while on the job. Few colleagues knew she was married. She kept that part of her life separate. She had to. But her ex-husband, Greg, insisted it was some kind of proof, another reason for their divorce.

"How can you possibly love someone and keep such an important part of your life separate?"

She had no response. She couldn't explain it to him.

Sometimes she knew she wasn't even good at compartmentalizing. All she did know was that as someone who analyzed and profiled criminal behavior, someone who hunted down evil on a regular basis, who spent hours inside the minds of killers, she had to separate those portions of her life in order to remain whole. It sounded like a convenient oxymoron, separate and divide in order to remain whole.

She found herself wondering if Cunningham had to explain it to his wife. He obviously had been more successful at his explanation than Maggie had been at hers. One more reason she had adopted his nondisclosure habits.

No, Maggie didn't know Cunningham's wife's name or if he had children, what his favorite football team was or whether or not he believed in God. And actually she admired that about him. After all, the less people knew about you the less they could hurt you. It was one of a few ways to control collateral damage, something Maggie had learned the hard way. Something she had learned perhaps too well. Since her divorce she hadn't let anyone get close. No need to separate personal and professional if there was no personal.

"Wait." Cunningham grabbed Maggie's wrist, stopping her from taking a second bite.

He tossed his cruller on the counter and pointed inside the box. Maggie expected to see a cockroach or something as lethal. Instead, all she saw was the corner of a white envelope tucked on the bottom of the box. Through a doughnut hole she could make out bits of the block lettering. A box of doughnuts was a familiar congratulatory gift amongst the agents. That one should include a card and envelope didn't warrant this kind of reaction.

"Anyone know who brought in this box of doughnuts?" Cunningham asked loud enough to get everyone's attention but keeping the urgency Maggie saw in his eyes out of his voice.

There were a few shrugs and a couple of mumbled noes. They all went about their daily routine. This was not a shy bunch. Any one of them would take credit where it was due. But whoever had brought in the box had not stayed and that realization set the assistant director's left eye twitching.

Cunningham took a pen from his breast pocket and slipped it into a doughnut hole, lifting carefully to reveal the envelope. Maggie did think it suspicious someone would place a note at the bottom of the box where it would only be discovered after most of the doughnuts had been consumed. A sour taste filled her mouth. It was only one bite, she told herself. Then just as quickly wondered how many of her colleagues had already devoured several.

"Sometimes one of the other departments sends us down a box with a congratulations card," she made one last attempt, hoping her explanation would prove true.

"This doesn't look like a regular congratulations card." Cunningham pinched a corner of the envelope between his thumb and index finger.

"MR. F.B.I. MAN," was written in block printing across the middle of the envelope in what looked like a first grader's attempt at practicing capitalization.

Cunningham set it down on the counter gently as if it would shatter. Then he stepped back and looked around the room again. A few agents waited for the elevator. Cunningham's secretary, Anita, answered a ringing phone. No one noticed their boss, his darting eyes and the sweat on his upper lip the only signs of his growing panic.

"Anthrax?" Maggie asked quietly.

Cunningham shook his head. "It's not sealed. Flap is tucked."

The elevator dinged, drawing both their attention. But only a glance.

"It's too thin for explosives," Maggie said.

"There's nothing attached to the box, either."

She realized both of them were talking about this as if it were a harmless crossword puzzle.

"What about the doughnuts?" Maggie finally asked. That one bite felt like a lump in her stomach. "Could they have been poisoned?"

"Possibly."

Her mouth went dry. She wanted to believe their suspicions were unwarranted. It could be a prank between agents. That actually seemed more likely than a terrorist gaining access, not only to Quantico, but all the way down into the Behavioral Science Unit.

Once he made the decision, Cunningham took less than two seconds—maybe three—to untuck the flap, barely touching the envelope with a butter knife. Again pinching only a corner he was able to pull out the piece of paper inside. It was folded in half and each side was folded over about a quarter of an inch.

"Pharmacist fold," Maggie said and her stomach did another flip.

Cunningham nodded.

Before nifty plastic containers, pharmacists used to dispense drugs in plain white paper and fold over the sides to keep the pills or powder from falling out when you lifted them out of their envelope. Maggie recognized the fold, only because it was one of the lessons they had learned from the Anthrax Killer. Now she wondered if they had been too quick in simply opening the envelope.

Cunningham lifted the paper, keeping the folds intact, making a tent so they could see if there was anything inside. No powder, no residue. All Maggie saw was the same style block printing that was on the outside of the envelope. Again, reminding her of a child's handwriting.

Cunningham continued to use the end of his pen to open the note. The sentences were simple and short, one per line. Bold, capitalized letters shouted:

CALL ME GOD.

THERE WILL BE A CRASH TODAY.

At 13949 ELK GROVE

10:00 A.M.

I'D HATE FOR YOU TO MISS IT.

I AM GOD.

P.S. YOUR CHILDREN ARE NOT SAFE ANY-WHERE AT ANY TIME.

Cunningham looked at his watch, then at Maggie. With his voice steady and even, he said, "We'll need a bomb squad and a SWAT team. I'll meet you out front in fifteen." Then he turned and headed back to his office as casually as if this were an assignment he issued every day.

CHAPTER
3

Reston, Virginia

R. J. Tully slammed on his brakes, setting off a screeching chain reaction behind him. The Yukon driver who'd cut in front of him now waved a one-finger salute before realizing he'd have to stop for the changing traffic light.

"This is not my fault," Tully's daughter, Emma, said from the passenger seat. She was holding up her Starbucks latte with two hands, the protective spillproof lid intact, not a drip spilled.

Tully glanced at his own coffee where he had left it in the console's cup holder with the lid still off from when he had put in his cream. He hated drinking out of those spillproof lids. But maybe cleaning up the car's interior would be an incentive to use them. Coffee had splashed all over including the knee of his trousers.

"Why would this be your fault?" he asked her, but he kept his eyes on the Yukon driver who was staring at him in his rearview mirror. Was he goading Tully into a game of road rage? One of these days he'd love to pull out his FBI badge and wave it at an idiot like this. Especially now that the guy was stuck waiting for the red light just like the rest of the cars he had cut off.

Tully glanced at Emma when she didn't answer. She was staring out the passenger window, sipping her latte. "Why would you say that?" he asked again.

"You know, you're late for work because you have to drop me off." She shrugged without looking at him. "So you're in a hurry. But it's not *my* fault you're late."

"The idiot cut in front of me," Tully said, almost adding that this had nothing to do with him being in a hurry. And it certainly wasn't his fault, either. Thankfully he stopped himself. When had they gotten into playing the blame game? He and his ex-wife played it all the time, but only now did Tully realize he was taking on the same ritual with his daughter as if it were implanted in their genetic makeup, an involuntary reaction to outside stimuli.

"It's not your fault, sweet pea," Tully said. "You know I don't mind taking you to school. I'm glad to do it. I just need a bit more warning."

"Andrea got sick. You knew as soon as I knew." She shot him a look as if daring him to challenge her.

He didn't take the bait. Satisfied, Emma swiped at her long, blond hair that continually fell across her eyes. He stopped himself from saying anything.

"It's the style," she told Tully every time he nagged her about the habit. She had beautiful blue eyes. She shouldn't be hiding them. Though he didn't mention it now to avoid the eye-rolling and heavy sigh that usually followed his comments.

The light turned green. Tully eased his foot off the brake, slowing himself down. Maybe the knot in the back of his neck wasn't from the rude Yukon driver. Things had been tense between Emma and him. It was her senior year. She constantly reminded him how much stress she was under, yet all he saw was that she wanted to go have fun and hang out at the mall or the movies with her friends.

He grew frustrated with her cavalier attitude about studying, about her grades and yes, about college. And while he piled up college-recruitment catalogs on her bedroom desk she covered them with *Bride* and *Glamour* magazines, more excited about being her mother's maid of honor than landing an academic scholarship to the college of her choice.

She reminded him so much of Caroline sometimes. It didn't help that the older she got the more she looked like her mother, the fair skin, blond hair, the sapphire-blue eyes that knew almost instinctively how to manipulate him. The only thing she seemed to get from Tully was her tall, lanky figure.

He'd be glad when the wedding was over and done with. Only a week left. Perhaps he would survive. He didn't need Freud to remind him that his daughter's excitement about her mother's new marriage didn't just stick in his craw because she was ignoring her college plans.

Tully didn't begrudge Caroline getting married. This wasn't about their divorce. That had been years ago, so many years he had to stop and count them. No, it was the nagging feeling that he was losing his daughter to Caroline's new life.

Right after their divorce Caroline had sent Emma to live with him so that she could move on with no reminder of her past life. Or at least that's the way Tully played it over and over in his mind. Now everyone was excited about the wedding and just expected Tully to plod along as the ever-lasting bearer of stability. He hated that he was so reliable and dependable that to be anything else wasn't even a consideration.

He glanced at his watch. Reliable, dependable and late. It seemed to bother only him, especially the late part. Even when he called his boss, Assistant Director Cunningham, to leave a message that he would be late, he could hear Cunningham dismiss it, a bit of impatience in his voice that Tully would feel it necessary to call.

"It doesn't have to be this way," Emma said, bringing him back to his senses, back to the task at hand.

She'd flipped her hair back out of her eyes and was turned toward him, giving him that hopeful look of a little girl who wanted to make things right. They had been through a lot together in the last four years and she was right, it shouldn't result in this current state of animosity. Once again she was the wise one, setting him straight, reminding him what was really important. No, they didn't have to be arguing with each other and blaming each other. He welcomed a truce.

He sighed and smiled at her just as he pulled to the curb in front of her school. But before he could tell her she was right and that he loved her, she said, "I wouldn't have to depend on Andrea if you bought me my own car. It'd be so much easier."

So that's what this was about. Tully tried to keep the disappointment from his face while Emma pecked a kiss on his cheek. She scooted across the seat and was out the door, backpack in one hand, latte in the other, brushing aside any hopes he had of an actual truce.

CHAPTER
4

Elk Grove, Virginia

Maggie didn't like what she saw. The address in the note was in the middle of a quiet neighborhood of well-kept bungalows that were surrounded by huge oak trees and carefully manicured yards. The house owned by Anne B. Kellerman could be any house in any suburb in the country. Why had he chosen here?

A red bicycle with tassels on the handlebars was left in the driveway. Two houses down a gray-haired man raked leaves. A moving truck was parked at the end of the street where a woman paced the sidewalk, directing two men with a sofa.

No, Maggie didn't like it at all.

Why would anyone want to set off a bomb in a sleepy, suburban neighborhood? In the middle of the morning the only ones home were preschool children and their care-givers and a few retired people.

Is that what he meant by, YOUR CHILDREN ARE NOT SAFE ANYWHERE AT ANY TIME?

Perhaps the bomber wanted to make a statement, targeting the innocent, the vulnerable. Did he want them to know he had no limits, no qualms? That he could and would strike anywhere? After all, they might be able to beef up security at airports, in subways and train stations, but there was no way they could patrol every residential neighborhood in the D.C. area.

"I don't like this," Cunningham said.

They were curbside in a white panel van with an orange-and-blue plumbing logo that looked authentic, but inside, three FBI techs tapped at keyboards and watched wall monitors that showed four different angles of the house in question. The cameras relaying those angles were attached to the helmets of SWAT members getting into place. A duplicate van was parked behind them. A public-utility van was a block away, waiting with a bomb squad.

Maggie readjusted a purple-flowered jacket she'd never own, but that fit perfectly over the bulletproof vest. She had found it in one of BSU's closets that housed an odd assortment of potential disguises. Unlike her copper-colored suit jacket that said, "Warning, FBI agent knocking at your door," the purple flowers hopefully would get a "welcome" nod. That is, if no one noticed the bulge of her gun.

She readjusted her shoulder harness and the Smith &

Wesson in its holster. Other agents had updated years ago to Glocks, but Maggie stayed with her original service revolver. Situations like this she couldn't help thinking it didn't matter what kind of gun she used. The bulletproof vest wouldn't make much difference either, especially if they tripped an explosive device. Guys who sent invitations to law enforcement officers usually did so because they enjoyed blowing apart a few of them.

Cunningham had put in place as many precautions as he could. Unfortunately, a house-to-house evacuation was impossible. And they were running out of time.

Maggie glanced at her wristwatch: 9:46. Her eyes searched the neighborhood again—at least what she could see from the tinted back window.

He was probably here.

Watching. Waiting.

Maybe he had the detonator.

"What about the moving truck?" Maggie asked.

"Too obvious." Cunningham dismissed, without looking away from the monitors.

"Sometimes the ordinary becomes the invisible."

He glanced at her and for a second she thought it might be a mistake to quote his own words to him. His eyes darted back to the monitors but he fingered the miniature microphone clipped to his lapel and said into it, "Check the moving truck."

In a matter of seconds they watched an agent dressed in a tan jumpsuit with the same plumbing-company logo slip out the back of the van behind them. He approached the truck, checking the addresses on each house against a clipboard in his left hand. He was still talking to the truck's driver when Cunningham pointed to one of the other monitors, an impatient chess player anticipating the next move.

"Can we make out anything inside the house yet?" Cunningham asked the tech tapping the computer keys without a pause.

Maggie watched the moving truck, but glanced at the monitor that Cunningham was anxious to view. Somewhere behind the house in question, one of the SWAT-team members wore a helmet-mounted thermal imaging camera. The infrared-sensor technology could pick up body heat, distinguishing between a sofa and the person on the sofa. Hot objects appeared white, cool ones black. Anything above 392 degrees showed up in red. Firefighters used the cameras to find victims in smoked-filled buildings. Here they hoped to get a heads-up of how many people—whether victims, hostages or bombers—waited for them inside.

"Small heat source in the first room," the tech said, pointing at the screen as the first white mass glowed bright white. A few seconds later he was tapping the coordinates of the second heat source. "Maybe a bedroom. The person's lying down."

They waited, Cunningham leaned over the tech's shoulder, pushing up the bridge of his glasses. Maggie sat back where she could keep an eye on the other monitors and glance out at the moving truck. The agent waved a thank-you to the driver, but he walked around the open back of the truck, continuing his charade of checking addresses.

"Is that it?" Cunningham finally asked the tech. "Just two heat sources?"

"Looks that way."

Cunningham glanced out the window then looked to Maggie as he buttoned his jacket, a worn tweed borrowed from the same closet where Maggie found the purple-flowered one.

"Ready?" he asked as he grabbed a handful of campaign flyers and adjusted the Glock in his shoulder harness.

She nodded and scanned the neighborhood one last time.

"Ready," she said, then followed him out the back of the van.

CHAPTER
5

Washington, D.C.

Artie left the SUV in a public parking lot where the government-issued license plate would warrant little attention. He was a quick learner and he knew better than to get tripped up on a simple parking fine or traffic stop. Like Ted Bundy. The guy gets away with murder, escapes prison and then gets pulled over in a VW bug, driving after 1:00 a.m. on Davis Highway in Pensacola, Florida. An astute police officer thought the orange VW looked out of place and checked the license plate, discovering the car had been stolen in Tallahassee.

Artie knew stuff like that. Bits of trivia about killers. He also learned from it. He knew not to draw attention to himself. So he parked the SUV and walked. He didn't mind walking. He was in good shape, though he didn't work out.

Practically lived on fast food, switching from one kind to another. The hotel was only a few blocks away. He arrived as the tour bus was boarding. Perfect timing.

He had taken this tour of the Washington monuments a couple of times before. It was a great way to add to his collection. He could get DNA samples from people all across the country just by riding the ten-mile tour. Last time he had been lucky enough to confiscate a long red hair from a woman wearing a Seattle Seahawks sweatshirt.

The driver collected Artie's pass and he took an aisle seat across from a middle-aged couple. They said hello to him and immediately he pegged them from the Northeast, maybe New Hampshire. It was a game he played with himself, matching dialects to places.

"Where are you folks from?" he asked, friendly enough for a response.

"Hanover, New Hampshire," both said in unison.

He smiled and nodded, satisfied.

"How about yourself?"

"Atlanta," he chose this time, always using a city too big for anyone to expect him to know their aunt or cousin. Then he opened his tour brochure and closed the conversation. That was all he had really wanted, after all, was to prove himself right.

They took the hint but he could tell they would have liked to have asked more. He could morph himself into different characters. And he could be quite charming when he wanted to be. As a result, everyone seemed to enjoy talking to him. Sometimes he allowed it. It was good practice. Sometimes he could make up the lies faster than they could ask the questions. But he wasn't in the mood today. He had other things that required his focus.

He glanced at his watch. In a few minutes the FBI would be storming suburbia, expecting a crash, and he would be miles away. Artie believed the plan ingenious even though he didn't get to participate. He could imagine the routine. They would bring a SWAT team and a bomb squad, only they wouldn't be anywhere near prepared for what they'd find. They were such linear thinkers. The fact that they couldn't see that seemed just desserts for what was about to happen.

He slid his bulging backpack on the empty seat beside him. Usually it discouraged the stragglers, the tourists who thought they'd go on the tour alone and chat up other losers traveling by themselves. Speaking of losers, one was coming down the aisle now. He recognized the wandering eyes, looking, searching for one of its kind yet scurrying to find a seat. She wore a purple sweatshirt with embroidered butterflies and faded blue jeans and carried a huge, black purse, practically a saddlebag. Artie avoided eye contact when she looked his way, pulling open the brochure and pretending, once again, to be interested though he knew the route by heart.

She slid into the seat in front of him. In the reflection of the window he could see her pull the purse into her lap and start sifting through the contents. Soon he heard the *click-*

click of nail clippers, and found himself thinking it was the nervous energy of a straggler held in captivity.

How rude. Whatever happened to common manners? People brushed their hair in public, scratched their private areas, picked their noses and trimmed their fingernails. And of course, he actually loved it, because he had learned to use their bad habits to his advantage.

Artie grabbed a tissue from his backpack and accidentally dropped his brochure. As he picked it up with one hand, he took a swipe at the floor with the tissue cupped in his palm. He wadded it up and stuffed it in the book bag without anyone noticing the gestures or the fingernail clippings he had collected.

Then he sat back, pleased. The tour hadn't even begun and it was already quite successful, providing resources for the future. He glanced at his watch again. Yes, it was turning out to be a good day, a very good day.

CHAPTER
6

Elk Grove, Virginia

Maggie's hand stayed tucked inside her jacket, fingertips on the butt of her Smith & Wesson as the door opened. It had to be a mistake or a brilliant setup. The little girl who answered the door couldn't be much older than four, maybe five years old.

"Is your mom here?" Cunningham asked and Maggie didn't hear a trace of his surprise. Instead, his voice was gentle and soothing, like a man who had once been a father to a child this age.

Maggie's eyes searched the room beyond the doorway. A noisy TV was the main attraction, with pillows, dirty plates and discarded toys surrounding it. The place was a mess, but from neglect, not a hostage takeover.

The little girl looked neglected, too. Peanut butter and

jelly with crumbs stuck to the corners of her mouth. Her long hair was a tangle that she pushed out of her eyes to get a better look at them. She wore pink pajamas with stains where cartoon characters' faces used to be.

"Are you sellin' something?" Maggie could tell it was a question she was used to asking, well rehearsed and even with a dismissive frown.

"No, sweetie, we're not selling anything," Cunningham told her. "We just need to talk to your mom."

The little girl took a glance over her shoulder, a telling sign that the mother was, indeed, here.

"What's your name?" Cunningham asked while Maggie edged closer inside.

She could see two doors, one door was open, showing a bathroom. The door to the right was closed. From what she remembered on the computer monitor, the second heat source was on the other side.

"My name's Mary Louise, but I don't think I'm 'posed to talk to you."

The little girl was distracted and watching Maggie. She wasn't as smooth with children as Cunningham and somehow kids always sensed it. Just like dogs. Dogs always seemed to be able to pick out the one person who was uncomfortable being around them, then gravitated to that person as if trying to win her over. Dogs, Maggie could handle. Children, she didn't have a clue about.

She heard the whisper of one of the FBI techs in the microphone bud in her right ear, "Nine minutes," and she glanced back at Cunningham. He touched his ear to tell her he had heard, too. They were running out of time. Maggie's gut instinct told her they should snatch up the little girl and just leave.

"Is your mom asleep, Mary Louise?" Cunningham pointed at the closed door.

Mary Louise's eyes followed his hand as Maggie slipped behind her and into the room.

"She hasn't been feeling good," the little girl confessed. "And my tummy hurts."

"Oh, I'm sorry." Cunningham patted her on the head. The distraction worked. Now Mary Louise didn't even glance back at Maggie, who tiptoed across the room, her eyes taking in everything from the *People* magazines scattered on the coffee table to the M&Ms spilled on the carpet to the plastic crucifix hanging on the wall. She looked for wires. She listened over the TV cartoons for any buzzing or clicking. She even sniffed the air for sulfur.

"Maybe I can help you and your mom," Cunningham told the girl who stared up at him and nodded.

Maggie could see the girl was on the verge of tears, biting her lower lip to keep from crying. It was a gesture she recognized from her own childhood and she hated that adults were evidently still using that stupid ruse that "big girls don't cry."

But it was clear Cunningham had won the girl over. She reached up and took his hand. "I think she's really sick," Mary Louise said under a sniffle with a quick swipe at her nose. Then she started leading Cunningham to the closed door.

That's when Maggie heard another whisper in her ear, "Four minutes left."

CHAPTER

7

Quantico, Virginia

R. J. Tully couldn't believe he was missing out and all because Emma didn't have a ride to school. He didn't want to think she might have orchestrated the entire event just to convince him she needed her own car. He wasn't ready to believe his seventeen-year-old daughter could be that manipulative. And he certainly wasn't ready to give in. He hated the idea of her having her own car. A car was a huge responsibility. He had a job for three years—starting at age fifteen—before he was allowed, or rather, could afford his own car. A car was a level of independence he wasn't willing to grant Emma just yet. It should be something she earned. Although he wasn't sure what she'd need to do to prove herself worthy.

"How many doughnuts?" Keith Ganza's monotone brought Tully back to the FBI lab. Getting in late put him in charge of the evidence, so here he was in Ganza's glass-enclosed work space.

"I don't know," Tully said. "Does it make a difference?"

"It does if they've been tampered with." Ganza's skeletal frame with sloped shoulders was bent over the center counter as he dissected a glazed cruller.

Maybe there was something wrong with Tully because, tampered with or not, the cruller still made his mouth water. He'd had only coffee for breakfast, most of it spilled over the interior of his car, and lunch was a couple hours away. He glanced instead at a couple of white-coated scientists in the glass-enclosed labs across the hallway. Tully disliked his claustrophobic office, four floors below the earth back at BSU, but he knew he'd never be able to work here in the labs where your every movement could be observed. Each lab— the techno-term was "biovestibule"—really amounted to a glass cubicle, a sterile workstation surrounded by metal contraptions, test tubes in trays and microscopes attached to computers. The glazed cruller on Ganza's stainless-steel tray seemed out of place.

"Doughnut places don't deliver, do they?" Tully asked, thinking out loud.

Ganza looked up at him, pale blue eyes over half glasses that had slid to the end of a hawkish nose. He reminded Tully of a friendly version of a mad scientist or of a tall scarecrow wearing a Boston Red Sox baseball cap. The cap forced Ganza's thinning gray hair to stick straight out over wide-rim ears, adding to the overall picture. His lined and haggard face registered a perpetual frown, and now he shot Tully a look that said, "You've got to be kidding," but Ganza would never say that. He knew that ridiculous questions sometimes ended up cracking a few cases.

"There might be a place in the District that'll deliver, but out here to Quantico? I'd guess, no."

"We're going over everyone who came and went this morning. So far there's been no unusual activity," Tully said.

Tully noticed that the box was plain white cardboard with no logo imprinted anywhere outside or inside.

"From the note it sounds like the doughnuts were only a means to deliver the threat," Tully said, "rather than the actual threat."

"You never know." Ganza slid crumbs from the cruller into a test tube.

Ganza was a process machine, a scientist before a law officer. He didn't decide what needed to be done, he simply did it, discounting chance, luck or speculation. For Ganza, the evidence always told the story. It wasn't just props for a story or theory already in progress.

He poured a clear liquid into the test tube, capped it with a rubber stopper and began to agitate it. Tully watched him rock back and forth on the balls of his feet as he rocked the test tube, almost like someone would rock a baby to sleep. He tried not to think of Ichabod Crane doing the Robot or he might burst out laughing. That was the kind of morning he was having.

Tully's stomach growled and Ganza raised an eyebrow at

him. They caught each other glancing at the counter where the remaining doughnuts sat in their box.

"There's a tuna sandwich in the fridge. You're welcome to half," Ganza offered, nodding toward the refrigerator in the corner where Tully knew there were also lab specimens. Possibly bits and pieces of tissue and blood. It would all be contained, bagged or capped, even on a separate shelf, but still too close for Tully.

"No, thanks," he told the lab's director, trying to sound grateful instead of disgusted.

Tully had watched Ganza eat between tests and he had seen his partner Maggie O'Dell eat a breakfast sausage biscuit once during an autopsy. But Tully viewed it as his last bastion of civility that he wouldn't cross that line. There were so few in this business left to cross. At least, that's what he told others. Fact was, it made his skin crawl just a little to combine the idea of eating a meal with the blood and guts of a murder.

Tully was still thinking about his stomach when he picked up the two plastic bags, one containing the note, the other the envelope. He had used plain white paper sold anywhere from office supplies stores to Wal-Mart. The ink he used would, no doubt, test to be the same ink used in just about every ink pen. And the guy didn't seal the envelope, so no chance of saliva, no chance of DNA.

Tully had put in a call to George Sloane before joining Ganza. Sloane was Cunningham's choice documents guy ever since the anthrax case in fall 2001. Tully thought forensic document sleuthing was more luck than anything, but he didn't see any harm in letting Sloane play his magic. Of course, Tully realized that his thinking of Sloane's contribution as little more than voodoo was no different than what some people thought of criminal profiling. Both depended on recognizing behaviors of the criminal mind, which was never as predictable as any of them hoped.

Ganza had set aside the test tube and was poking around the box again. With long metal forceps he pinched what looked like microscopic pieces, and was putting them into a plastic evidence bag. He pushed up his glasses and dived the forceps in, suddenly getting excited.

"Might be his," Ganza said, showing Tully the half-inch black hair now clenched at the end of the forceps.

Tully caught himself before he winced. So much for craving any of those doughnuts.

Ganza placed the hair on a glass slide and slid it under a microscope. "Got enough of a root for DNA." He twisted the focus and swooped down to the eyepiece for a better look. "At first glance, I'd say he's not Caucasian."

"Also could be someone at the doughnut shop," Tully said.

Tully looked at the note and envelope again. "So how many people would know how to do an old-fashioned pharmaceutical fold like this?"

"He may have read about it somewhere. Could be showing off," Ganza answered.

Tully lifted the envelope and piece of paper higher so that the lab's fluorescent light shined through both. That's when he saw it, almost invisible in the corner on the back side of the envelope. Sometimes you didn't need a forensic documents expert to catch stuff like this.

"We might have something here," Tully said, continuing to hold the plastic bag to the light, waiting for Ganza to leave behind the microscope and come around the table.

"Son of a bitch," Ganza said before Tully could point out the subtle indentations on the envelope. "Bet he didn't plan on leaving that behind."

CHAPTER
8

Elk Grove, Virginia

Maggie tried to keep Mary Louise from seeing the Smith & Wesson gripped in her hand and down by her side. Cunningham moved the little girl to the corner behind him, shielding her from whatever they were about to find.

"Backup is at the front door," Maggie heard in the earbud. She avoided glancing over her shoulder. "Bomb squad is scanning outer perimeter. They're ready to go in. Are you coming out?"

Maggie looked to Cunningham.

"Negative," he said, barely audible while he smiled at Mary Louise. The little girl was chattering to him about eating a whole bag of M&Ms which she really, really loved and was probably the reason her tummy hurt.

Maggie knew they were out of time, yet Cunningham was

hesitating. She watched him scan the door frame again and again. Nothing looked out of place. Not on this side. Cunningham cocked his head as he listened for any sound behind the door. His right hand clutched the doorknob. His body kept close to the wall. His left hand stayed open and ready in front of Mary Louise like a traffic cop holding her back.

In an ambush situation they'd kick in the door, weapons drawn. But the threat of rigged explosives with hidden trip wires warranted slow and easy. Maggie knew they should let the bomb squad take it from here.

Cunningham wasn't budging. Another victim, Mary Louise's mother, was on the other side. If they picked up the little girl and ran, would it set off a panic? Was someone watching the house with a detonator, waiting for them to do exactly that?

"Ready?" he asked Maggie.

She wanted it over with. They had already wasted too much time. Yes, she nodded, and he eased the door open.

There was no click. No sizzle. No bang.

Nothing.

Except for an unnerving rasping sound. Someone inside the room was having trouble breathing.

Mary Louise swept past both of them while Cunningham grabbed and missed. She bounded up onto the bed where it looked like a pile of bedding had been dumped in the middle. The SWAT team swarmed the outside room, moving so quietly Maggie didn't even notice them brush behind her, already in the bedroom.

"Mommy, Mommy, someone came to help," Mary Louise sang out to the swaddled bundle.

Cunningham rushed over and he swooped the girl into his arms, cradling her close to his chest. But then he stopped dead in his tracks, and turned back to Maggie. There was a flicker of panic in his eyes, but his voice remained calm and soothing as he said, "There's blood."

A pause and another glance, then, "A lot of it."

Maggie came in closer. She could see only the woman's head, matted hair sticking to her forehead. She was gasping, almost a gurgle. Blood spurted from her mouth and nose onto a stained pillowcase. There was blood all over the bedding. But she couldn't see any external wounds.

Then Maggie remembered the note's warning. She realized it was too late. There was no bomb. There were no explosives.

"We may have expected the wrong kind of crash," Maggie said. Instead of relief, her stomach took a plunge.

"What are you talking about?" Cunningham tried to get a closer look while the little girl squirmed in his arms.

"Instead of a bomb squad we should have brought a hazmat team." She could feel everything around her grind to a halt. The bomb squad and SWAT team were frozen in place by her words.

That's when Mary Louise started throwing up. Her upset tummy spewed up red and green all over the front of Cunningham, spraying Maggie, too.

"Christ!" he muttered as he wiped vomit and spittle from his face.

CHAPTER
9

Quantico, Virginia

R. J. Tully watched Keith Ganza process the envelope with the indentation using an ESDA (Electronic Detection Apparatus). He remembered as a kid rubbing the side of a number-two pencil over indentations in a notepad to reveal what had been written on the page that used to be on top. He probably read how to do it in *Encyclopedia Brown*. He was crazy for those books when he was about nine or ten, long before he even knew what an FBI agent was or did. They had an influence. Made him realize how much he loved solving puzzles. If only Emma read something more than *Bride* and *Glamour*. He had no clue what she was interested in these days, although if text messaging became a career skill she'd have that mastered.

It amazed him how much that generation depended on computers. Kids knew how to access e-mail and create

MySpace profiles, but logic and ingenuity, even puzzle solving, were foreign concepts. As Tully watched Ganza he couldn't help but think that a lead pencil would do the trick and be quicker. At least they would have known already whether there was something to process. But the expensive equipment didn't destroy the evidence. And that was important.

Ganza adjusted the light on the ESDA. He had the envelope sandwiched between the metal bed and a Mylar overlay. When he was ready he'd pour a mixture of photocopier toner and tiny glass beads over the Mylar. The machine created an electric static charge with the glass beads scattering the toner and attaching it to the indented parts of the paper, almost like inking an embossed image. At least that's how Tully understood it. With the image visible they could then take a picture of it and enlarge it.

Sometimes the images appeared to be only scribbles. But this time it looked like they had more. The envelope had definitely been underneath a piece of paper that someone had written on, pressing hard enough to leave indentations. The solution almost seemed too easy. But even criminals, especially cocky ones, got sloppy. Could they be that lucky?

"You think it's his handwriting?" Tully asked, meaning the guy who left the bomb threat. "Or just some accident? Maybe someone at the bakery?"

"He'd never let the note out of his sight or put it in the doughnut box until he was ready to unload it." Ganza handled the transparency with gloved fingertips, placing it on a light box gently as though it would shatter.

He fidgeted with some buttons and suddenly the impression grew and darkened. There would be no further tests needed. The letters looked as if they had been jotted quickly, but they were easy to decipher. The note read:

> Call Nathan R.
> 7:00 p.m.

All the periods and the colon were especially indented from extra pressure.

Tully held up the plastic bag with the original note, trying to make an amateur handwriting comparison.

"Block printing, but not all caps like in the note," he said.

"Almost as if he didn't think he had to disguise this."

"Because he didn't think we'd ever see it."

Just then Ganza's cell phone started ringing. He yanked off his latex gloves and flipped the phone open while walking to the other side of the lab. Ganza barely said hello and Tully's cell phone started chiming like a Chinese dinner bell. He'd hit the button yesterday and accidentally changed his ring tone. The damn thing drove him crazy. He was constantly screwing up settings in his search for missed calls or voice messages. And now he'd have to make up with Emma long enough to get her to fix it.

"R. J. Tully," he said after three chimes.

"We've got a problem." He recognized Maggie O'Dell's voice without an introduction.

Before she could explain the problem, Ganza was rushing across the lab, his eyes locking onto Tully's. Into the phone he said, "We can be there as soon as I get packed up." To Tully, he said, "We've got to go now, before the military gets their hands on the evidence."

"Oh, good," Maggie said in his ear. "You're with Ganza."

"What's going on?" he asked, but Ganza was headed in the other direction again, gathering equipment, the cell phone still pressed to his ear, his long strides almost wobbly like he was hurrying along on stilts.

It was Maggie who finally answered, "We've got a real mess here."

CHAPTER
10

U.S. Army Medical Research Institute of Infectious Diseases
Fort Detrick, Maryland

Colonel Benjamin Platt, M.D., didn't question Commander Janklow's order. He was used to taking orders whether they included jumping out of an aircraft into the Persian Gulf while wearing full scuba gear or organizing a biocontainment team and heading out to suburbia. Although back in his jumping days he was a bit younger and much more idealistic. Still, he wouldn't question his orders. Instead, he hurried down the hallways, his stride confident, the heels of his spit-n-polish shoes clicking hard against the tiles, the only indication of nervous energy.

Platt wouldn't question the commander's orders, but he couldn't help wondering if the man might be blowing this situation out of proportion. New to his post with less than three months under his belt, Commander Jeremy Janklow was an outsider, a political appointment that most everyone viewed as a favor rather than a competent leader of USAMRIID (pronounced You-SAM-Rid), one of the most respected research facilities in the world. Platt worried that Janklow had spent too much of the last decade behind a desk. Was it possible the commander was simply looking for a crisis? A fire to put out that might boost his reputation?

One of the lab doors opened before Platt got to the end of the hallway and the stocky, bearded man who emerged waved Platt to the office next door. Neither said a word, not even a greeting, until they were inside and the door closed.

Michael McCathy slipped off his lab coat and exchanged it for a navy cardigan, cashmere and not a speck of dust on it. McCathy was older and bigger than Platt. Any signs of his long-ago days as a linebacker had been replaced by pale skin, sagging jowls, a slight paunch and tired deep-set eyes, magnified by wireless eyeglasses. Platt, on the other hand, was lean from a daily workout that included running five miles and a half hour of lifting weights. His summer tan was only now beginning to fade, his brown hair still lightened by hours in the sun coaching Little League and now soccer. Platt had a frenetic energy about him, almost a complete opposite to McCathy who always moved with slow and deliberate motions.

Even now McCathy was arranging his crisply pressed lab coat on a hanger, placing it on the coat tree in the corner as though he had all the time in the world. Platt watched

McCathy's methodical gestures, each grating on his nerves. The man was obsessive-compulsive about everything. He was egotistical, and annoying as hell. Platt could only take him in small doses. But the new commander, Janklow, thought McCathy was a genius and insisted he be included in this mission.

A law enforcement dropout, somehow McCathy had ended up at USAMRIID as a civilian microbiologist, a biohazard expert, apparently content to spend his days with test tubes and microscopes, concocting and speculating terrorist scenarios that might include biological warfare.

Platt and McCathy had little in common except for a shared fascination of biological agents, particularly viruses and filoviruses. Platt had held Lassa, a Level 4 virus, in his gloved hands while inside a makeshift medevac tent outside of Sierra Leone. McCathy had been a bioweapons inspector in Iraq who claimed to have seen and handled canisters filled with biological soup. He insisted there were hundreds more just waiting for a weapons delivery system. He and his team were the last ones that Saddam Hussein threw out before the war and their testimonies were part of the argument used to go to war. Platt respected the work McCathy had done. It didn't mean he liked the man.

"I thought you said your team would be in civilian clothes?" McCathy gave Platt's uniform an up-down glance like a disapproving headmaster.

"Civilian clothes and civilian vehicles, except for the panel truck." Platt tried to contain his impatience. He didn't need to explain himself to McCathy. It'd take him five minutes in the locker to change into jeans, a T-shirt and his leather bomber jacket. "They're almost ready at the loading dock. Do you have everything you need?"

McCathy nodded but now was taking off his rimless eyeglasses and cleaning them with absolutely no sense of urgency. "It'll be tight if we have to change in the truck. And slow going. Probably only one at a time with a two-man support team. You sure there isn't someplace on-site we could use for a staging area?"

Platt hated this, McCathy questioning him, second-guessing him. McCathy constantly reminded everyone that as a civilian he didn't have to take orders from anyone except his boss, the commander.

"It's residential," Platt explained, even though he'd already told McCathy this on the phone.

"What about a house next door?" McCathy asked, pulling a small bottle of disinfectant from his trouser pocket and squirting some in his hand.

"Orders are to not evacuate. We don't want a panic."

"You've got to be pulling my leg," McCathy said under his breath to emphasize his disgust. "What if it's something?"

"Then we'll be prepared to contain and isolate."

McCathy smiled at him and shook his head. "We both know that won't be enough if this ends up being anthrax or goddamn ricen."

"Evac team is on standby."

"Standby." McCathy repeated with another smile. No, this

was a smirk. And Platt recognized it and the tone. McCathy used it in meetings to show his disdain for authority and for rules in general. Platt wondered why McCathy would want to work at a military research lab. He carried himself like a man with some special entitlement, smug in his cashmere cardigan, as though he was the only one brilliant enough to see incompetence, and he seemed to see it running rampant all around him.

McCathy was older than Platt and had been at USAMRIID for much longer, reasons enough in the scientist's mind to dismiss Platt. Also, as a civilian, McCathy didn't have to adhere to a rank-and-file hierarchy. It didn't make a difference to him if Platt was a sergeant or a colonel. He still wasn't going to take orders from him. To top things off, McCathy had managed to draw the attention and favor of Commander Janklow.

None of that mattered to Platt. McCathy didn't intimidate him in the least. Platt had seen things and done things that would shock the fluorescent-skinned McCathy who, outside of his stint as a weapons inspector, was used to living in his sterilized, controlled lablike world. No, men like McCathy didn't intimidate Platt. They simply annoyed him. He was in charge of this mission and he wasn't going to be lured into a pissing contest, especially with someone like McCathy.

"I'll meet you on the dock in ten," he told McCathy and he didn't wait for a response.

CHAPTER
11

Elk Grove, Virginia

Maggie had a premed background only because once upon a time her father had encouraged her to become a medical doctor. However, after a sideswiped childhood that drop-kicked her into the role of caretaker for her alcoholic suicidal mother, Maggie discovered she was more interested in what made the mind tick rather than the heart.

Still, she studied premed out of a sense of obligation to her dead father. Eventually she ended up in psychology and then forensics. Her premed training allowed her to assist at autopsies and sometimes came in handy at crime scenes. This time it helped her recognize that Mary Louise and her mother had not been poisoned. Instead, they'd been exposed.

If the threat in the note proved true, that there was going to be a "crash," then Mary Louise and her mother had not only been exposed to some biological agent but it was now trying to live inside them. Maggie recognized the term, often used as "crash and bleed out" when military and medical personnel spoke about biological agents. The crash would come when the biological organism ended up destroying its host, and it usually did so from the inside out.

The SWAT team had recognized the term, as well. It had taken little to convince them to leave, even though they all wore gas masks and would have, most likely, been safe. At first Cunningham had ordered Maggie to leave with them. It didn't take long for her to see the realization in his eyes. There was a combination of regret and guilt, maybe a bit of fear when it finally hit him. He couldn't let her leave. He couldn't let either of them just walk out.

They agreed they had to stay out of the bedroom but only after a brief argument. Maggie knew Cunningham was right. They had no idea what they had walked into. Yet Maggie's medical training and her instinct clashed with common sense. What if there was something she could do for Mary Louise's mother? The woman's raspy breathing mixed with a rhythmic hiss and spray. It sounded like she was choking on her own blood and mucus. Maggie knew how to perform a field tracheotomy that would clear the woman's airway.

Cunningham's response was to order Maggie out of the room. When she started to challenge him, he stood between her and the sick woman and pointed toward the bedroom door. She had no choice but to turn around and leave. Cunningham wouldn't allow Maggie to help. Instead, he took

Mary Louise to the bathroom to clean her up and clean himself, as well. He stopped Maggie from even following them. She knew he was trying to protect her, a valiant but useless gesture. Maggie knew that it was probably too late. Mary Louise's vomit had sprayed her, too.

For some reason memories of her first crime scene came back to her. Perhaps because Cunningham had tried to protect her then, as well. She had just finished her training as an agent after a year as a forensic fellow at Quantico. It was in the middle of the summer, hot and humid, and the inside of the double-wide trailer must have been ten to fifteen degrees hotter. She had never seen so much blood sprayed everywhere: the walls of the trailer, the furniture, the plates left out on the kitchen counter. But it was the sour smell of rotting flesh and the buzzing of flies that stayed firmly implanted in her memory.

She had thrown up, contaminating the crime scene, a newbie losing it on her first case. But Assistant Director Cunningham, who had been so tough on her throughout her entire training—pushing her, questioning her, nagging her—kept one hand on her shoulder while she retched and choked and spit. He never once reprimanded or chastised her. Instead, in a low, quiet, steady and reassuring voice he said to her, "It happens to all of us at least once."

Now here in this little house in a quiet suburb that day seemed so long ago. Maggie looked around the living room, zoning out the laugh track and sound effects of TV cartoons.

How did he do it?

She let her eyes take in everything again, only this time

she tried to imagine a similar delivery system like the doughnut container. There were no pizza boxes, no take-out containers, no pastry boxes. He would have wanted it to be something ordinary, something disposable and most importantly, something unnoticeable.

There was much to learn about a killer from the victims he chose. So why did he choose Mary Louise and her mother? Maggie took in the contents of the room. The furniture was an eclectic combination: a particleboard bookcase, a flowered threadbare sofa and mismatched recliner, a braided rug and a brand-new flat-screen TV. The wooden coffee table with scuffed corners appeared to be the centerpiece of the family, holding the TV remote, a pair of reading glasses, dirty plates and mugs sitting in milk rings, crumpled potato chips, spilled bags of M&Ms, a coloring book and box of sixty-four crayons, some scattered and broken on the rug.

In the corner two stacks of magazines teetered next to a desk. A pile of mail—catalogs, envelopes and packages in various stages of opening—covered a writing desk; some of the pile had fallen onto the chair.

There were several pictures on the bookcase: Mary Louise at different ages, sometimes with her mother. One with an older couple, perhaps the child's grandparents. But there were none with a father and none with pictures that looked like a father had been cut out.

Mary Louise and her mother appeared ordinary and happy and harmless. And maybe that alone had been the sole reason for the killer to choose them.

Then something caught Maggie's eye. On the desk, sticking out of the lopsided pile of mail, was a six-by-nine manila envelope. She could see only the return address but it was enough to draw her attention. It was handwritten in block lettering, all caps, and it looked an awful lot like the lettering on the note she had just seen about an hour ago.

Maggie looked around the room again. Cunningham had already told her they would need to call in the nearest disease control and containment center. That meant Fort Detrick and that meant the Army would be taking over. Most likely they'd seal off the rooms—probably the entire house. Their first priority would be biocontainment and treatment of the occupants. Processing evidence would come later. Would they even know what to look for?

She found a box of large plastic bags with Ziploc seals in a kitchen cabinet. Back in the living room she lifted off the top pile of mail so she wouldn't have to tug the manila envelope out and risk smearing anything. Then carefully using only her fingertips she picked up the envelope by a corner and dropped it into plastic bags. She sealed it and dropped it into another plastic bag just to be safe.

She told herself she was saving the Army a bit of work. Of course they'd be grateful, but still, she tucked the double-bagged envelope into the back of her trouser's waistband, letting it lie smoothly against the small of her back. She pulled her shirt and jacket down over it, just in case they weren't so grateful.

CHAPTER
12

North Platte, Nebraska

Patsy Kowak tucked the package under her arm and examined the postage-due envelope. Roy, their mail carrier, would never hold back a piece of mail. He was good about that. But this was embarrassing. The return address was her son's office. Maybe that new assistant. Still there was no excuse. Almost two dollars due.

She slipped the envelope inside her denim jacket as she glanced down the long dirt driveway. No sense in upsetting her husband, Ward. As it was, they were barely speaking.

Patsy took in a gulp of the crisp morning air and tried to clear the tension from her mind. She listened to a distant train whistle and the cawing of crows on their way to feed in the fields. She loved this time of year. The river maples and cottonwoods that surrounded their ranch no longer hinted at fall, but were lit up with red and gold. She could smell smoke from their fireplace, a soothing scent of pine and walnut. Ward insisted it was too early to turn on the furnace, but he was good about getting the chill out of the house with an early-morning fire.

Yes, she loved this time of year and she loved her walks to the mailbox, a daily ritual that included filling her pockets with peppermints for Penny and Cedric. This morning she included apple slices for the duo. Ward grumbled about her spoiling and pampering the two horses who had long been retired, yet he was the one who brought home the three-pound bags of peppermints from Wal-Mart. Her gruff-and-tough rancher husband had a soft spot he rarely showed. It came out more often with their granddaughter, Regan, and sometimes with Patsy, and always with the animals. But hardly ever with their son, Conrad.

She shook her head remembering their latest argument about Conrad. It seemed to be the only thing they argued about anymore. The boy was a successful vice president of a large pharmaceutical company. He held a master's degree in business, owned his own condo, had access to the company's private jet, and yet, Ward Kowak would have none of it. Her husband's idea of success? Having something precious to pass on. Like this land. Like your good name.

His good name.

She shook her head at the reminder. It had only been the beginning when Conrad legally changed the spelling of his name from Kowak to Kovak. He said it was important that business associates pronounced his name correctly, and since the "w" is pronounced as a "v" sound in Polish, what did it really matter? That was their son's reasoning, his explanation. Their son with the master's degree and the VP after his newly spelled name. How could he not know something like that would hurt his father?

The name change had only been the tip of the iceberg. The sinking of the *Titanic* had come over the Fourth of July when Conrad announced he was getting married. Patsy couldn't have been happier. Conrad's younger sister had already been married for five years with a beautiful daughter, their angel, Regan. Even Ward softened to the boy, thinking—perhaps hoping— that it was finally a sign of Conrad maturing and settling down. That is, until they discovered the woman was fifteen years older than Conrad, divorced and already had a teenage child.

It didn't matter to Patsy. She just wanted her son to be happy. But Ward seemed to take it as another personal affront, yet another defiance by his son to somehow blacken the family name. Her husband was being childish and Patsy had told him so.

As she neared the house she found herself relieved that Ward's pickup was still gone. He muttered something over breakfast about having "some errands to run in town."

On her way up the steps she patted Festus, their old German shepherd, lounging in the patch of sunlight on the porch. The dog used to go with her on her walks to the mailbox. She didn't like to think about how much he was slowing down since his years measured her own.

As soon as Patsy came into the house she tossed the mail on the kitchen counter. Except for the package. She retrieved a pair of scissors from the junk drawer and slit open the brown padded envelope then slid the contents onto the counter.

No letter, not even a note. That was her son—Mr. Organization at work, but it didn't transfer to his personal life. He was always on the run, throwing things together at the last minute, even when he was trying to make a point. That had to be the case, since the last time they talked to Conrad, Patsy remembered Ward complaining about the hike in airline tickets as if that would be excuse enough to not attend the wedding. Money didn't matter to Ward, though Conrad believed it did. He had called his father "cheap," not understanding the difference between cheap and thrifty. This had to be Conrad's point. Why else would he send a Ziploc bag with what looked to Patsy like several hundred dollars in cash?

This was ridiculous. Her son was being just as childish as his father. She simply wouldn't allow this family feud. Instead, she'd have to stash the money somewhere so Ward wouldn't see it.

CHAPTER
13

Elk Grove, Virginia

It was too late.

Tully knew as soon as they turned onto the street. Even Ganza stopped chewing, a wad of tuna sandwich still stuffed in his mouth while he muttered, "Son of a bitch, they beat us here."

A guy with short cropped hair, an athletic frame and confident gestures waved the FBI's plumbing van away from the curb to make room for a white panel truck. Tully recognized the way the man moved, the way he held himself, a taut jawline, steady eyes that captured everything around him. He was a commanding presence and although he wore blue jeans and a leather bomber jacket, Tully knew this guy was a soldier.

"They're sending our lab techs home," Tully said, pulling his own car over to the side, a half block away.

Ganza threw his sandwich on the dashboard and started digging through his pockets. Tully stared at the sandwich crumbs scattered and falling all over his car. He remembered the coffee spills from that morning. It seemed like days ago instead of hours. Ganza was punching a phone number into his cell phone while Tully watched the soldier direct the panel truck up onto the lawn, guiding it as it backed all the way to the rear of the house. He bet this guy never had a half-eaten sandwich on the dashboard of his car or coffee stains on the upholstery.

"We're right outside," Ganza was saying into the phone. "They're sending away our van. What are we supposed to do?" Ganza's monotone didn't give away his urgency. He left that to his long, bony fingers, tapping the console between them.

Another white truck passed alongside them. This one had Virginia Water and Sewer printed in black on the sides. The truck was too white, too clean. From where Tully sat he noticed the tires showed little wear. Two men got out of the truck, dressed in white jumpsuits, logos on the pockets, polished black boots, not a speck of dirt. They started taking construction-crew sawhorses from the back and blocking off the street. Neighbors might believe the house in question had a water main break or a gas leak. That is if they didn't notice the clean boots and new tires. The old man raking his front yard stopped to watch, but Tully didn't think he looked alarmed or even interested. After a few minutes he went back to raking.

The FBI's plumbing van passed through the narrow opening between the sawhorses. It pulled up beside Tully's car and the driver's window of the van came down. Tully opened his window, too. The agent inside was familiar to Tully though he knew him only by sight and not by name. It didn't matter. He looked past Tully and over to Ganza when he said, "It's a military-slash-Homeland Security operation now. Nothing we can do about it."

"What about collecting evidence?" Ganza was still on the phone, responding to both the agent and whoever he had on the line. Tully wondered if it was possible Ganza had a direct line to the FBI director.

"Secure and protect," the agent said. "That's their priority. They're treating it like a terrorist threat, not a crime scene. And we're not invited to the party."

"But we've got two agents inside," Tully said, looking back at the house, realizing Maggie and Cunningham weren't with the SWAT team climbing into the second plumbing van. "They're still inside, right?" Tully glanced at the agent, who now looked away and rubbed at his jaw.

"Yeah, they're still inside. That's the reason Assistant Director Cunningham called in the troops." He glanced back at Tully and Ganza, who were quiet, staring and waiting though they already knew what they would hear. "They've both been exposed."

CHAPTER
14

Elk Grove, Virginia

Colonel Benjamin Platt understood that fifty percent of a biocontainment operation was containing the news. Commander Janklow had been quite clear. They were to take every precaution possible to keep the news media out and if that wasn't possible then Platt was to convince them this was a routine response to a routine request. He was not to use any "scary terms"—Janklow's words—that would incite a panic. Phrases like "crash and bleed," "lethal chain of transmission," "evacuation," "biohazard" or "contamination." And under no uncertain terms was he to ever use the term "exposed."

Truth was they had no idea if there was even a problem. Platt still had hopes that this was a knee-jerk reaction, someone getting a little too excited. After the anthrax scare in the fall of 2001 there had been hundreds of prank letters, attempts at fame or hopes of revenge. Platt knew there was a fifty-fifty chance this fit into that category. Somebody wanting his fifteen minutes of fame on the six-o'clock news.

Platt saw McCathy waiting for him at the back door of the panel truck, scratching his beard and frowning, tapping his foot to show his impatience. It was McCathy's turn to wait.

Finally satisfied that everything and everyone was in place, Platt knocked on the truck's back door. Within seconds a lock clicked and the metal door gave a high screech as it rolled up into its tracks. Platt had the truck backed to the rear door of the house, blocked by a privacy fence on one side and toolshed on the other. It'd be difficult for anyone to see inside the truck, and they'd have only three steps to get inside the house. The back door entered a small enclosed porch, then another door opened to the kitchen. Platt figured they'd be able to use it as a decon area when leaving.

McCathy started to climb into the truck but Platt stopped him.

"It's my mission, I go in first. You'll come in second."

McCathy nodded and stepped back. It wasn't a courtesy, it was a risk, and McCathy wouldn't argue. If anything McCathy looked relieved.

Two of Platt's sergeants, two of his best in the biohazard unit, waited inside the truck. He climbed up and pulled the thick plastic sheet down behind him to cover the open back. He started changing into the scrubs Sergeant Herandez handed him, though she averted her eyes as soon as he unbuckled his belt. She was young, he was her superior officer. In a few seconds he would be trusting her and Sergeant Landis with his life as they made certain he was sufficiently secured against a potential biological agent, and yet she seemed to be blushing at the sight of him in his skivvies. It almost made him smile.

Platt had hired twice as many women on his biohazard team than his predecessor at USAMRIID who had made it known that he didn't think women could or should work inside a hot zone because they'd panic or become hysterical. Platt knew better and ignored everything his predecessor taught him about women, but at times like this the differences surprised him, maybe even amused him. And Platt wasn't easily amused these days.

Landis held the Racal suit up, ready to help Platt into it. Unlike the blue space suits they used inside USAMRIID's Level 4 suites, the Racal suit was orange, bright orange and field designed with a battery-powered air supply that could last up to six hours.

Platt pulled on a double pair of rubber gloves and Herandez taped them to the sleeves of the suit while Landis taped Platt's boots to the legs, creating an airtight seal. The helmet, a clear, soft plastic bubble, was the final step and usually the telling one. Platt had watched men and women, brave soldiers, dedicated scientists, freak out in a space suit from claustrophobia, clawing their way out. Platt had spent thirty-six hours behind enemy lines in Afghanistan trapped inside a tank disabled by an IED (improvised explosive device), hoping someone other than the Taliban would find him while he treated his fellow soldiers, one with a gaping head wound, the other with half his arm blown off. There wasn't much that could compare to that. Entering hot zones in a cocoonlike space suit seemed like a cakewalk.

He waited while Hernandez and Landis double-checked his suit. Even before they switched on the electric blower Platt was sweating, trickles sliding down his back. The motor whirled and he heard the air sucking into the suit while it puffed out around him.

Herandez gave him a thumbs-up. It was difficult to talk over the sound of the electric blower. Platt waved a gloved hand at the tape and made a tearing motion. She nodded, understanding immediately, and started ripping off three-to-five-inch pieces then attached them one on top of the other to Platt's sleeve where he could easily reach. If there was a break in his suit he'd use the pieces to patch the hole before the suit lost pressure. Any kind of break or tear could render the suit useless in a hot zone.

It had been a while since Platt had done this in the field. The last time had been at the *Miami Herald* in 2001 when a letter addressed to JLo found its way to a photographer. The letter was filled with anthrax spores. The photographer died weeks later. Platt still had hopes that this wasn't anything close to anthrax. In fact, he'd be pleased with a hoax.

Finally he returned Herandez's thumbs-up. Waddling like a toddler learning to walk, he let the pair of sergeants help him out the back of the truck. He waited to get his balance. In three steps he was at the back door of the house and ready.

CHAPTER
15

Elk Grove, Virginia

When Maggie was a little girl she loved to watch old black-and-white horror movies. *The Creature from the Black Lagoon* was her favorite but she also loved Alfred Hitchcock and episodes of *The Twilight Zone*. As soon as she saw the man in the orange space suit walk through the kitchen door she almost expected to hear Rod Serling's voice narrating the bizarre scene.

Earlier, Cunningham had reluctantly made the call to the Army Research facility. It was either USAMRIID or the CDC, and USAMRIID was only about an hour away. Cunningham had given Director Frank of the FBI and Commander Janklow the basics, along with a layout of the residential area. All three men agreed extraordinary measures would be taken, including whatever it took to prevent a panic. Then Cunningham asked Maggie to unlock the back door to the kitchen and they waited.

They had been expecting a group from USAMRIID. Maggie had even watched the white panel truck back onto the lawn. She saw the construction crew block off the street. And yet, she wasn't sure what she had truly expected—men and women in gas masks, perhaps. Maybe surgical scrubs and gowns. But certainly not space suits.

It was just a precaution, she told herself. Of course, they had to take every precaution. But at the same time she told herself this, she also felt a bit sick to her stomach.

The man in the orange space suit didn't see her at first. It took full body movement to turn and look around. And he couldn't possibly hear her. His suit hissed and whirled to keep the pressurized air circulating. Maggie imagined it was even noisier inside the plastic bubble.

He moved slowly, deliberately, a moonwalk into the living room. The boots looked heavy. His arms stuck out, not able to rest against the puffed suit. He stood less than six feet away when he turned. She couldn't see his face through a fog of mist built up on the plastic helmet. With a gloved hand he pushed the plastic against his face and was able to smear the inside moisture away.

His eyes met hers. They were intense, dark brown and his brow was furrowed. He looked as if he was trying to decide what to say to her. The plastic started to fog up again and this time he slapped it against his face, causing a hiccup in his electric motor. The air pressure gasped, hesitated then started sucking air again. When he looked at Maggie a second time he attempted a shrug, as if to say he had no idea what had just happened. And then he did something Maggie never expected. He grinned at her. It was enough to break the tension and she actually laughed.

That's when Cunningham came into the room with Mary Louise close behind, close at his side. The little girl took one look at the spaceman and started to scream.

CHAPTER
16

Elk Grove, Virginia

Tully punched the number into his cell phone again. For security purposes he never saved numbers in his phone's memory. Or at least he wouldn't even if he knew how.

Still no answer.

After two rings it went to voice message again. He flipped the phone shut. Both Cunningham and Maggie had their phones turned off. He'd rather believe that than the alternative—the U.S. Army wasn't allowing them to answer.

It wasn't that Tully didn't respect the United States military…okay, that wasn't true. He didn't respect military officers, especially like the guy he had seen earlier, the one directing traffic, able to order and command with only a wave of a hand and a nod of the head. How many soldiers had that same officer sent to their deaths with as little as a wave of a hand or a nod of his head? Anytime Tully had worked with the military on previous operations the officers in charge took over and did so without apology or even much notice. They didn't play nice and usually they preferred to do so in secrecy. And as far as Tully could tell, they were doing the exact thing right here, right now.

Tully had moved his car to the other side of the street, still along the curb, but at an angle, so he could see between the panel truck and the back of the house. It was just a slice but enough to make out an orange field suit moving from the truck to the back door several minutes ago. And now he could see a second orange suit just blurred across the same path.

He glanced away to watch Ganza loping across the street from the construction crew, making his way back to Tully's car. Ganza wasn't much taller than Tully—maybe an inch or two—but he seemed to carry his height like it was a burden on his skeletal frame. His long, thin legs with knobby knees poking at sagging, brown trousers, skinny neck and sloped shoulders reminded Tully of a giraffe. Even his white lab coat—he hadn't bothered to leave it behind during their rush to the scene—looked like the spotted hide of a giraffe with gray-and-brown splotches where Ganza had attempted, unsuccessfully, to get out stains. When Tully first got divorced it had been a game for him to guess which men he met were married and which ones were single. Caroline would have never let him leave the house with a stain on his tie. Now stains would be a permanent part of his wardrobe if he didn't have women in his life—Maggie, Gwen, Emma—constantly wiping at his shirt cuffs, his tie, his jacket lapels. Tully guessed early on that Ganza had never been married. Not only that, he evidently didn't spend much time around women who even wiped at his stains.

Ganza opened the passenger door and slid in, slamming the door shut with more force than necessary. It was the most emotion Tully could remember the man ever displaying.

"Sons of bitches won't let us collect evidence," Ganza said in his trademark monotone, despite the slammed door. "They have to isolate and contain."

Tully could have told him that before Ganza bothered to show his ID and badge to the soldiers masquerading in construction-crew clothing.

"They're right, you know." He didn't glance over to see Ganza scowl at him. He didn't need to. He could feel it. "They can't risk more people getting exposed, if there is something in that house."

"I know that. But they'll destroy whatever evidence there is. They don't know what to look for." Ganza grabbed the half-eaten tuna sandwich from the dashboard. It had been sitting there since he left it, in the sun. He took a bite and another then said with his mouth still full, "I offered to gear up and collect it."

"You mean in one of their space suits?"

"Sure, why not?"

"You ever been in one before?" Tully asked.

"Can't be much different than a gas mask." But Ganza sat

back and gave Tully a long sideways look. "What? You've been in one?"

"Once. A long time ago," Tully said and left it at that.

He and Ganza weren't friends and Tully wasn't the type to share more than what was necessary, a trait Gwen Patterson constantly reminded him was—what were her words?—"rather annoying." Of course, she didn't like it. She was a psychologist by trade. She could get people to share their deep dark secrets. And if Tully wanted her to be a part of his personal life he would need to learn to share those deep dark secrets with her.

But Ganza...he didn't owe Ganza anything. Besides, Tully didn't like to be reminded of the four-hour episode that had been early on in his FBI training. It had been part of basic training back then—after all, 1982 was still the Cold War—that they should all spend several hours in a space suit, although the activity was more about breaking agents down than about biocontainment.

Tully saw something. He could see motion through the slice between the truck and the back of the house. He jerked forward, practically diving around the steering wheel to get a better look. He hoped he was mistaken. But if he wasn't, it looked as if they were taking someone out of the house and into the rear of the truck in a clear plastic body bag.

USAMRIID
Fort Detrick, Maryland

They called it "the Slammer," and Maggie knew about it only from rumor. She would have preferred to leave it that way.

The Slammer was actually a Biosafety Level 4 containment hospital, an isolation ward within USAMRIID at Fort Detrick. The Army used it for patients suspected of having an infectious disease or of being exposed to a biological agent. Those patients, until proven otherwise, were also suspected of being highly contagious.

For the most part, Maggie understood that the Slammer was used, or ready, primarily in case any one of USAMRIID's scientists was accidentally exposed in one of the research labs. USAMRIID housed frozen specimens of all kinds of nasty organisms, viruses and diseases. At one time during the

Cold War USAMRIID's chief assignment was to collect and design biological warfare. These days, as far as Maggie knew, it was solely dedicated to developing vaccines and controlling, or rather containing, any exposures or outbreaks. And after 9/11 and the anthrax scare that followed, it was also USAMRIID's job to come up with remedies for any terrorist threats that might include contaminations or deadly pathogens.

If one of their own pathologists or veterinarians or microbiologists got pricked with a contaminated needle or cut by a broken test tube or bitten by a lab monkey they had to be able to treat them. They wouldn't be able to transport them to an area hospital and risk further exposure or media. So they'd take them here, to their own hospital that they, themselves, had nicknamed the Slammer, because it was exactly that, a biological solitary confinement. Maggie realized that Assistant Director Cunningham probably had no idea that when he agreed to the Army taking control of the situation it meant committing himself and Maggie to the Slammer.

At first glance the rooms appeared to be ordinary hospital suites, if you didn't mind one of the walls being a full-glass viewing window and having double steel doors locked from the outside. Maggie suspected that she and Cunningham would each get their own room, their own solitary confinement. Mary Louise and her mother were also here somewhere. Maggie hoped they were together.

A woman in a blue space suit escorted Maggie to her

room through a series of staging areas. Each had thick heavy doors. Each slammed shut behind them, but it wasn't until the last door, when the air locks sucked in, sealing the door shut, that Maggie felt a panic begin. It started slowly, quietly, ticking in the back of her mind like a heartbeat, only a heartbeat that didn't seem to belong to her. The air was different inside this room. Different from the hallway. Different from the inner staging areas they had just passed through.

Maggie told herself it was just a slight bit of claustrophobia. She'd be fine. Maybe if she told them she had been stuffed into a freezer last year by a madman, they would sympathize and let her go?

Probably not.

To be fair, the panic had actually begun earlier back at Mary Louise's house. It started when Maggie watched the two orange spacemen take Mary Louise's mother out the back door of her suburban house sealed inside a sort of bubble stretcher, what almost looked to Maggie like a plastic body bag. That's when Maggie felt her skin go clammy and sweat trickle down her back. She worried they intended to take all of them out in plastic body bags and she knew she wouldn't last a minute inside. It didn't matter that the contraption had its own oxygen supply. She would panic. She would want to claw her way out. And she had already started to feel her heart racing and her breathing start to become labored. Yes, that was when the panic started.

The spaceman, who she later learned was Colonel Platt, must have seen the terror in Maggie's eyes. He had already had to settle a screaming child and load up a sick and bleeding woman. Had he been worried that he might have another person in hysterics, clawing her way out of his expensive contraption?

Later Maggie would learn they simply didn't have enough bubble stretchers for all of them, so Cunningham and Maggie ended up getting a decon shower in the kitchen. The spray misted their clothes, their skin, their hair but didn't soak through their clothes. Her plastic bag tucked up under the back of her shirt and coat remained safely in place and out of sight, damp and sticking to the sweat of her skin. She could still smell the bleach. It seemed to stay inside her lungs, stinging if she dared to take a deep breath.

"OVERNIGHT," the woman in the space suit yelled at Maggie over the hissing of her air blower. She handed Maggie a hospital gown that had been folded on the chair. "WE'LL NEED TO KEEP YOU OVERNIGHT."

Then she motioned for Maggie to sit up on the bed while she unwrapped a plastic tongue depressor and cotton swab. She set aside a sealed syringe. "I NEED TO TAKE A THROAT CULTURE AND THEN DRAW SOME BLOOD," she shouted, mouthing and exaggerating the words slowly in case Maggie still couldn't hear her. Then showing her a specimen cup she said, "AND I'LL NEED YOU TO FILL THIS."

Beyond the glass wall Maggie could see others watching. But the woman in the space suit must have misunderstood Maggie's misgivings and pointed to the corner where Maggie could see she, at least, had her own bathroom.

Still, she wondered if it was normal that she could hear her heart beat so loudly. How long had it been pounding this hard against her chest? There was no doubt now. This one, this heartbeat, did belong to her. She tried not to listen. She tilted her head back when the woman was ready, and opened her mouth, trying not to concentrate on not being able to swallow, to breathe, even if it was for a few seconds. The woman was good, experienced, fast. *Thank God*.

She bagged the swab then picked up the syringe. Maggie looked away while the needle pricked and sunk into her skin. She could see tubes and equipment along the other walls, a camera in the corner of the ceiling, monitors blinking and beeping even though they weren't attached to her yet.

The last time she was in a hospital room, shortly after the freezer incident, she remembered waking up, startled to find tubes and wires connected to her body, bags of fluids hanging above her, monitors bleeping out the rhythm of her heart-beat. She was told that another minute or two of hypother-mia and the freezer would have been her ice coffin.

They had drained all the blood out of her to warm up and then put back in. She wasn't sure how that was possible. She didn't like to think about it even with her medical back-ground. For weeks afterward she had nightmares about the procedure. Otherwise she remembered little about the entire ordeal, except for the cold, the panic, the claustro-phobia, all of which culminated in an overwhelming ex-haustion.

The woman in the space suit capped one tube of blood and

began to fill yet another, Maggie focused on the window. At least it wasn't a one-way view. She could see the faces on the other side. There were four, maybe five people, punching keyboards, watching monitors, computer screens. All were occupied except for one. One who must have just joined them because she hadn't noticed him until now.

He stood close to the window, watching her. Having someone she recognized calmed her even if he did have a furrowed brow and worried eyes. She released a sigh and realized it was almost as if she had been holding her breath.

She smiled at R. J. Tully and he gave her a stiff wave, his face lined with concern. She remembered the envelope, double-bagged and swaddled, carefully hidden within her neatly folded jacket. She'd have to find a way to get it to him. But for now she mouthed to him, because she knew he'd never be able to hear her through the thick wall of glass, "Harvey. Please check on Harvey."

He simply nodded.

CHAPTER
18

Reston, Virginia

Emma Tully pulled out the letter from the yellowed envelope. At first, the stack of envelopes that were gathered together with an orange rubber band had grabbed her attention because the top one, this one, had a twenty-cent stamp with a woman's picture: Ethel Barrymore. She'd never heard of Ethel Barrymore before. Perhaps she was Drew's grandmother? It didn't matter. What caught Emma's attention was that she couldn't believe stamps had ever been twenty cents.

She wondered if the stack of envelopes had long been forgotten. She had found them the last time she stayed at her mom's house in Cleveland. The bundled stack was stuffed in the back drawer of the guest-room bureau. Forgotten perhaps, but important enough to save. And her mom was definitely not the pack-rat type. The letters were even kept in chronological order. Again, not something her mom would do unless these were special.

Emma didn't know anyone who even wrote real letters anymore. This was a treat. Especially if Emma's suspicions were true. Were these old love letters her dad had written to her mom before they were married? That was like awesomely romantic. It was like taking a peek into a part of her own history.

She settled back into her pillows.

August 26, 1982
Dear Liney,
I got in last night around eight. Yes, safe and sound. You didn't need to worry. Although now I can admit I was a little rattled about flying. I know I told you it didn't bother me and I know I'm right about the odds of two major crashes happening within a couple months of each other. It's just not going to happen. But for a few minutes when I sat in the plane while we were still on the tarmac at O'Hare I did think about all those burning body parts blown all over that New Orleans neighborhood. I just told myself that I'm going to be the guy who investigates what went wrong.

You should see this place. Quantico's like a whole little town hidden inside a pine forest. I guess I expected military barracks or something.

I found my room at the dorm. Three guys to a room and they're not big rooms. But that's okay. The other guys don't seem too bad. Hey, we all want to be feebies, so we've got that in common.

It's funny, because almost immediately we assigned each other nicknames. That's not entirely true, "Razzy" came with his and thought we all needed one, so Reggie's J.B. because the guy eats jelly beans like his life depended on it. Seriously, he brought his own bag. I think it's a three-pounder. He says President Reagan eats them, too. I don't know if that's true or not. I picked up the latest Time *at the airport because they had an interview with Reagan. They didn't mention anything about jelly beans. Just about the recession and him riding horses with the queen. But hey, if he eats jelly beans that's kinda cool.*

Oh and my nickname—bet you'd never guess. It's Indy. Yeah, okay, obviously because I'm from Indiana. These guys have no clue where Indiana is, let alone Terre Haute.

I know I told you once that I hate nicknames. You remember that, right? Mostly because as a kid my dad called me "dimwit" or "klutz." Stupid stuff like that. But I don't mind this nickname. I actually like it. It reminds me of the movie, you know, Indiana Jones. That was the second movie we saw together last summer, remember? Of course you remember. How could you forget, right?

So anyway, I kind of like the idea of being associated with a guy who carries a whip and wins the girl with very little effort. That's definitely more my style than klutz. More my style than what my dad had in store for me. He was still going off on me this morning about deserting the family business. Hey,

*I even look a little like Harrison Ford, don't you think? Be-
sides, Indiana Jones, Indy, is definitely more in line with what
I have in mind for myself.*

*Yeah, Quantico is only the beginning of my brilliant ca-
reer. I've got big plans.*

Until next time.

Yours truly,

Indy

Emma pulled out the next one but stopped when she
heard the front door. Footsteps marched directly to her
bedroom. What now? She swooped up the letters and stuffed
them under her bedcovers, just as the knock came.

"Hey, sweet pea," her dad called. There was no anger. She
sighed in relief. "I have to do a favor for Maggie. You want
to go for a drive with me?"

Normally she'd groan and make some excuse. But tonight
she didn't mind. Maybe she was curious to see if she could
notice any trace of Indiana Jones.

CHAPTER
19

Razzy's
Downtown Pensacola, Florida

Rick Ragazzi closed out the cash register, slamming the tray, hoping his partner, his cousin Joey, would take the hint. He couldn't seem to get Joey to understand that this was a business not his private haven to entertain guests. Tonight Joey prepared crème brûlée, on the house, for a group of six who'd stopped by after the Saenger Theatre's evening production up the street. It would have been an okay gesture for a party of six who maybe had dropped several hundred bucks on dinner, but this group had ordered only coffee.

"What? No dessert?" Joey had joked, stopping at their table during his usual stroll to greet the guests while his kitchen staff cleaned up for the night. He asked their head waitress, Rita, to pour more coffee for the group while he headed back to the kitchen. Within minutes he returned, presenting his creation. He had them laughing and applauding. Cousin Joey, the chef, was no better than an actor, craving and demanding attention, then lapping up praise.

They were so different from each other that sometimes Rick wondered how they could be related. Of course, it was those differences that made them such good partners. Rick had the head for business. He was a numbers guy, an operations whiz. He had calculated salaries, overhead, product cost and was able to come up with a plan, complete with projections, net earnings and profit margin. But it wasn't because of his thrifty spending and efficient management that they were able to post a profit after only eight months in business. Even Rick knew it didn't matter how brilliant his business plan would be without his charming cousin, the award-winning chef. At twenty-four Joey was a culinary magician or at least, that was what *Gourmet* magazine had called him.

People came to the restaurant the first time out of curiosity. They returned over and over again because they liked the food. And that was all Joey. Rick made sure the staff was well trained, courteous and prompt. But he couldn't poach an egg or filet a piece of fish to save his soul. He looked down at his hands, nicks and cuts in various stages of healing. The most recent reminder was a cut on his index finger from attempting to help chop vegetables. Joey was definitely the talent, the product. Rick was simply the manager.

Their success got a boost from trendy spring breakers and summer tourists. Now came the tough part. They'd need to hold on until they entered the holiday season. September had already shown a slowing down. October would be the hardest. And just yesterday their main refrigerator, the expensive monster that Joey insisted they had to have, had started freaking out on them. Of course, the warranty expired last month and the repairman claimed it needed a whole new compressor—seven hundred dollars they hadn't planned for.

Rick watched Joey with his audience. It was hard to stay impatient with him. When they first started setting up the place Rick suggested they replace the kitchen wall with glass so diners could watch Joey perform. Turned out to be too expensive, so they put it off. Otherwise they would have done it. Rick was used to Joey being the center of attention. He really didn't mind. Sometimes he joined in and played Joey's straight man. As kids they actually did bits at family gatherings with Rick doing the setup and Joey getting the punch line. Everyone thought it was cute because Rick was a couple years older and bigger, a bit taller, back then.

As teenagers they were each other's best friend. During the summers they chased girls together on Pensacola Beach until Rick finally admitted he really didn't like girls all that much. Even that admission had been something they worked through together, with Joey being the first one to say it wasn't that big of a deal. It just meant less competition for him.

In college, Joey studied culinary arts, and Rick, business management. Opening a restaurant together seemed a no-brainer for both of them. But keeping it open would perhaps be a miracle. Especially since they had no silent partner, no rich beneficiary or obligated family members.

Rick's family wasn't interested and Joey refused to accept help from his father. Rick wasn't sure why Joey was being so stubborn. Uncle Vic, at least, wanted to help and unlike Rick's dad, Uncle Vic had never called Rick "a queer" or told the two they'd "never make it." Hard to believe the two men were brothers.

Rick had honored Joey's wishes. But Joey had no idea how much it cost to run things each month, each week. Rick knew their meager summer profit would never get them through a slow winter. If they had to close the doors any one of the area's restaurants would snatch up the opportunity to have Joey Ragazzi. But Rick? What would he do? Get a job at one of the local accounting firms?

Hell, this was his one chance. So when the envelope from Uncle Vic came about a week ago—to Rick, not Joey—he decided not to tell Joey, but not to send it back, either. Made sense. Even Uncle Vic understood his son wouldn't take his help, but maybe his cousin would. There was a thousand dollars in cash. Rick had counted it twice then put it back inside the sealed Ziploc plastic bag it came in.

He justified his secrecy by telling himself a thousand dollars wasn't enough to make or break them. It wasn't a big deal. And yet this week with the refrigerator compressor going out, a thousand dollars could change everything.

CHAPTER
20

Newburgh Heights, Virginia

R. J. Tully mashed cooked carrots into the stainless-steel bowl. He knew the routine and in case he forgot, Maggie had instructions on a laminated note card attached to the inside cupboard door. His partner rarely asked favors and the few times she had all involved taking care of Harvey.

He looked out the kitchen window at the white Lab catching the glow-in-the-dark Frisbee each time, no matter how wild of a throw Emma sent him. Tully shook his head. She'd never been good at athletics. Maybe his fault. Their father-daughter sports outings included a remote and recliners more often than a glove and a baseball.

He pushed up his already folded shirtsleeves and added dry dog food to the bowl. Then he stirred in the mess of carrots. He was glad he had stopped and picked up his daughter. She had a special connection with Maggie's dog, Harvey. He liked watching them together. Being with Harvey was one of the few times Emma let her guard down. She could run and laugh and be silly with the dog. Tully felt like he was seeing a snapshot in time, a time not that long ago, and it reminded him of that ache—half awe, half protectiveness. He used to get that feeling just looking at her when she was a baby and then a toddler. He'd catch himself watching her and shake his head in disbelief that he was a father of such a beautiful, smart and funny little girl.

"How about putting on a sweatshirt?" he yelled out the back door.

She ignored him. He expected it despite his reminiscing. He'd give them a few more minutes before he let Harvey know his dinner was ready.

Tully filled the water bowl and cleaned up the counter. The kitchen was huge. The house, the backyard, the property was huge, especially compared to Tully's two-bedroom bungalow in Reston. He understood Maggie had bought the place in this prestigious neighborhood with some sort of trust her father had left her. She kept the house nice and simple but classy with a few scattered pieces that made it feel like a home. The place seemed sparse, again, perhaps only compared to his messy, overflowing bungalow.

Still, he knew the house and décor had little to do with why Maggie had bought this property. The purchase had more to with the natural barrier of the river that ran behind the house and the privacy fence surrounding it along with the state-of-the-art security system.

Tully looked around the well-stocked kitchen and wondered if Maggie ever cooked. Her best friend, Gwen Patterson, was a gourmet cook, just one of her many talents that Tully appreciated. They'd sort of been seeing each other officially for several months. Though he wasn't quite sure if she'd agree their relationship was "official." They hadn't really declared it as such and he had no idea what criteria had to be met to make it official. Maybe it was just in his own mind. He hadn't been with another woman since his divorce from Caroline. Gwen thought he was doing her a favor by letting them take things slow. Tully let her believe the favor was one-sided. It seemed like the gentlemanly thing to do. Fact was, anything more serious scared the hell out of him.

"He's hungry." Emma came racing in with Harvey wagging behind her. She didn't wait for Tully. She grabbed the bowl off the counter and presented the food to Harvey, making him go to his designated eating place, telling him to sit and then setting the bowl down.

Yes, she sure did remind him of when she was little, bright eyes and lopsided grin, sitting on the floor next to the dog with knees up, one pink scar showing through the threadbare denim. She looked…happy. Amazing that a dog could do what a father couldn't.

"Is Maggie okay?" she asked.

The question surprised Tully. For one thing it was a grown-up question and he was reminiscing about his little girl. Also Emma rarely asked about anyone unless it somehow concerned her. She wasn't rude, she was just a teenager. That stage where everything and everyone in the world either didn't exist or existed only to revolve around them.

"She'll be okay," he said. And he knew that was true, despite her panic. Actually Maggie had been good at hiding her panic. No one else probably saw it. He almost wished he hadn't. It didn't seem natural to see Maggie vulnerable.

"So what's up with the special delivery?"

Emma pointed to the bouquet of flowers they had found wrapped neatly in tissue and left at Maggie's front door. It looked to Tully that the local florist knew exactly where to tuck them on the portico, safe from the wind and drive-by viewers, as if the florist was used to delivering to this address. Tully knew Maggie had been getting flowers at Quantico, too. And although she didn't explain or comment, he gathered that she wasn't too happy about the deliveries, but at the same time she didn't seem distressed.

Women. Sometimes Tully thought he'd never figure them out.

"A secret admirer," Tully told Emma.

"Oh, so she's not, like, sick and dying or something?"

"No. God no," Tully said before he caught himself. Then he smiled, trying to defuse any indication in his voice that might have said otherwise. He hoped that wasn't the case, that she was seriously sick. Of course that wasn't the case.

"You said she'd be gone overnight?" Emma wanted to know.

"Yeah, she'll be back tomorrow." He hoped that was true.

"We're not going to leave Harvey here by himself all night, are we?"

"He'll be okay, sweet pea. He's stayed here by himself before." But she didn't look convinced. She was petting him as he licked up the last remnants, orange bits of carrot stuck to the black part of his nose.

"If we take him with us it'll save us a trip in the morning to feed him."

She gave him that look, that "pretty-please" look.

"And tomorrow's Saturday," she said. "I'll stay home and watch him."

"What if your friends call?" He knew she hadn't thought this out. Emma? Home all day on a Saturday? Tully was sure it'd take more than a dog, even a dog she adored, to keep her from hanging out at the mall or going to a movie on a precious Saturday.

"I'll just tell them I can't. That we're doing a favor for a friend. They'll understand. That's what you do for friends, right?" She gave Harvey's neck a hug and the dog's tail thumped against the wall. "And Harvey and I are buds, right, Harvey? Besides, I don't have school on Monday either. Fall break, remember?"

He liked the idea of having Emma home, though he'd have to see her actually stay home for three days in order to believe it. Next weekend was the wedding and she'd be distracted and gone. But she was right. If they needed to come back it was a forty-minute drive from here to their home in

Reston. Tully was pretty sure Maggie would not be released tomorrow, probably not all weekend. He only hoped she didn't realize that.

"That's kinda cool," Emma said and Tully had no idea what she was talking about until she pointed to the flowers again. "It's sweet, you know, to have someone send you flowers." Then she sideswiped him with her follow-up, "Did you ever send flowers to Mom?"

Tully's cell phone interrupted before he could answer. *Saved.*

He shrugged an apology as he glanced at the phone number but it wasn't one he recognized.

"Agent Tully."

"So what do you have for me?" a man's voice bellowed.

"Excuse me?"

There was dead air for a few seconds then, "This is Sloane, for Christ's sake. You called me, remember?"

Tully had left a message for George Sloane earlier in the day. He hadn't worked with Sloane for a while and had almost forgotten about his brusque, rude "why are you bothering the mighty Oz?" manner.

"And I appreciate the quick call back," Tully said, getting in his own dig, although he already knew Sloane wouldn't catch it or acknowledge it. Actually it was a cheap dig, really sort of beneath Tully, but something about George Sloane always brought out the worst in Tully. "Assistant Director Cunningham would like your expert opinion on a special delivery we had this morning."

"So why isn't Cunningham calling?"

Tully suppressed a sigh and shook his head. It wasn't about protocol with Sloane. It was about entitlement. If prodded he would insist he was important enough to be asked by the top-level people, not a "grunt like Tully."

"He's a bit tied up right now," Tully said and was reminded that he hadn't been able to talk with his boss since morning. He had tried to see Cunningham at USAMRIID. They wouldn't allow it. Seeing Maggie was grudgingly allowed and even then as a sort of consolation prize. He hadn't been able to reach Cunningham by phone, either.

"How soon could you take a look?" Tully asked.

"I've got time right now."

"Tonight?" Tully saw Emma flinch at the word and wondered how many times he had left her to make her in-voluntarily flinch at the interruption. "Where are you?"

"Here at the university."

Tully watched Emma shove dog food into a plastic con-tainer. She was pretending to not listen in. "He'll need more than that, Em," he told her. She nodded and started search-ing the kitchen pantry.

"Oh, I see," Sloane said and Tully could hear the smirk. "You have a hot date. I understand."

"Emma is my daughter, George."

"Of course, your daughter, Emma. How old is she now? She must be in high school."

"This is her last year," Tully said and caught Emma rolling her eyes at him. She hated when he talked about her.

"I have a class at Quantico tomorrow morning at nine. My forensic documents for dummies in law enforcement. I can take a look at Cunningham's stuff before class while the retards are finding their seats."

Though Sloane was being his snide self Tully was surprised to have him compromising without a challenge. The two of them went back a lot of years and Tully could count on one hand the times George Sloane had cut him some slack. It felt like this time might be because of Emma.

"That'd work great. Thanks, George."

"I'll see you in the morning."

Tully closed his cell phone and turned to find Emma staring at him, waiting.

"I'm not going anywhere tonight except home with you, sweet pea," he told her.

She rolled her eyes like it didn't matter, but the smile was genuine. Harvey, however, was the one who got the hug.

"Help me shut off some of these lights."

Tully flipped the backyard switch and headed to the entryway to reset the complicated alarm system. He passed a side window and noticed a car parked up the street. He shut off the nearest light and backed up enough to glimpse out the window again, this time without being seen. In this neighborhood with circle drives and houses set back off the street no one parked on the street. Especially at this time of night.

CHAPTER
21

Artie heard the monkeys down the hall, screeching again. It was late and whoever was supposed to feed them had probably forgotten or figured no one would notice on a Friday night. *Assholes*. And no one *would* notice. No one ever came down here on weekend evenings. That was exactly why he was here. The place was quiet and he didn't have to worry about anyone walking in on him, wanting to know what he was doing.

He decided if the monkeys were still screeching when he was ready to leave he'd use his key card and at least throw them some biscuits. They were sneaky little bastards and Artie didn't like being around them. They reminded him of little old men with bright eyes and beards and they looked at him like they knew something he didn't know. He couldn't explain what it was that gave him the creeps. He didn't trust them but he did feel sorry for them. He couldn't imagine being stuck in a cage all day, depending on someone else.

Artie let the monkeys screech at his back as he walked all the way to the opposite end of the hall. The door had a metal sign attached that said: QUARANTINE in red letters. He used his key card and let himself in to the small deserted lab. No one used it anymore except for storage.

They used to keep sick, contaminated monkeys in here while they tested them. He wondered if they'd made the monkeys sick just so they could do their tests. That's what they were doing with the ones down at the other end of the hall. But the ones that occupied this little lab had been different. He wasn't sure how. No one talked about it. Probably because every single monkey ended up dying.

Ever since then, the lab remained unused, untouched. The monkeys' cages still lined up against one wall. It was as if whatever happened here was beyond repair. At least everything had been washed down and sterilized. The smell of bleach lingered, helped along by Artie's recent contributions. He thought it was silly that science-minded people, logical thinkers, would be superstitious.

That made him smile. He actually liked that people—even scientists—were so predictable. In fact, that was one of the things he could pretty much count on. It didn't matter what social class, what background and upbringing, what occupation, there were basic factors like greed and suspicion—even superstition—that everyone had a small dose of. Like it was engineered into human DNA. And Artie freely admitted that he included himself. Yeah, he was a little superstitious. It certainly didn't hurt to be a little. If he did something a certain way and good things happened, then he repeated those steps. Maybe that was more of a ritual than superstition.

He wrestled out of his gray hoodie and slung his backpack onto the long, narrow stainless-steel table that took up the middle of the room. Behind him were floor-to-ceiling cabinets. He wiped his sweaty palms on the front of his baggy T-shirt then twisted the combination of a padlock on one of the cabinets.

He began his ritual, taking out everything he needed: a gallon jug of bleach, latex gloves, a surgical mask, goggles, a tray of surgical utensils and a box of Ziploc plastic bags. From his backpack he pulled out a small box and snapped it open.

This was the part he still hated. He carefully removed the loaded syringe and took off the cap. He knew the vaccine was as good as liquid gold and worth a small fortune on the black market. At least that's what his mentor had said when he told Artie to use it sparingly. He clenched his teeth, made a fist and stuck the needle into his arm.

Artie put on the surgical mask and goggles, then two layers of latex gloves. He always put them on in the same order—call it superstition, ritual, whatever—it worked every time. Again from his backpack he brought out the plastic bag with fingernail clippings he had snatched from the tour-bus floor. He also laid out two mailing envelopes with the labels already attached. The block lettering looked per-fectly amateurish, almost childlike. Perhaps the person at

Benjamin Tasker Middle School who would receive one of the packages would even think that it was sent from a student.

Finally ready, Artie went to the old chest freezer that rumbled in the corner. He worked the combination to the padlock on its door. He swung open the lid and made himself look at the dead monkey wrapped in clear plastic, lying on its back with arms and legs flaying, locked in place and looking as if the monkey were trying to claw its way out. Artie avoided its eyes. Even frozen, the little bastard gave him the creeps. He grabbed a plastic bag from the side of the freezer and shut the lid, worked the padlock back into the handle, made the lock click.

He tossed the bag from hand to hand, a frozen glob, a Popsicle of blood and tissue. All he needed was a sliver.

CHAPTER
22

Newburgh Heights, Virginia

Tully climbed over a dark corner of Maggie's privacy fence without much effort or sound. He was tall, long-legged and still in good shape if you didn't count a bum knee. Of course it helped that there was an air conditioner unit he could use as a step up. On the other side he slinked down and let his eyes adjust to the darkness. He glanced back at Maggie's house and hoped Emma was following his instructions, packing Harvey's leash and toys and not looking out back to see what exactly her father thought he needed to check on.

Worrying about Emma reminded him of Caroline. When he first met Caroline she seemed enamored of his career choice. It wasn't until years after they were married and after Emma was born that Caroline pushed for him to get out of the field, stay home more, quit jumping fences and stop hunting killers.

"What about teaching?" she had asked over and over again.

Ironically, just as he managed to get the ultimate teaching job—or at least, Quantico was the ultimate FBI teaching job for him—Caroline decided she wanted a divorce. She had countered his travels with travels of her own as the CEO of a large advertising agency. And what he believed had been requests for the safety of their daughter—him getting out of the field and out of killers' radar—had really been some strange, selfish jealousy. She wanted the adventure and not the responsibilities that came with being a parent.

Instead, it was Tully who constantly worried that his job could and would put Emma in danger. She had been on the cusp before. Too close for comfort. And so was this.

Tully didn't like prowling around while Emma was only yards away. But if someone was watching Maggie's house Tully needed to find out why. Was it possible that the same guy who sent Maggie and Cunningham to the Kellerman house was now outside Maggie's home? Maybe Tully and Emma had interrupted his plans.

Tully kept to the outside fence line, staying in the shadows. The few streetlights were decorative ironwork with faint yellow globes, another perk of the prestigious neighborhood with expensive alarm systems and false security. Tully had already figured out the route he needed to take so he could approach the car from behind. Along the fence, beside the evergreens and directly out to the street, hidden the entire time by shadows and branches.

He tucked his hand inside his jacket, wrapping his fingers around the butt of his Glock. Then he stood up straight and walked casually past the last set of bushes, coming to the trunk of the car, rounding it quickly and pulling out his gun. He had his Glock pressed to the car window with his badge flapping beside it before the driver even looked up at him.

By the time the man rolled down the car window Tully was already shaking his head and holstering his weapon.

"What the hell are you doing, Morrelli?"

CHAPTER
23

Saturday, September 29
The Slammer

Midnight came and went but time dragged on. Maggie channel surfed. She asked for a novel, a newspaper or any current magazines, maybe a pen and notepad. The woman in the blue space suit said she'd see what she could find, but when she arrived again she had only another syringe to draw more blood.

The faces on the other side of the glass came and went, too. There were fewer as the night grew longer. They had taken her cell phone but allowed her access to a corded phone inside her room. They told her, without apology, that all her phone calls would be monitored then "reminded" her—though it sounded more like a reprimand than a reminder—that she was not to talk about what had happened or mention anything regarding her whereabouts. "Where-abouts," that's what the woman in the blue space suit called it.

Earlier Maggie had made two calls. The first she had to leave a voice message, knowing the call wouldn't be able to be returned. She told her friend, Gwen Patterson, that she'd be okay. "Talk to Tully," Maggie said, hating that it sounded so mysterious when she really just wanted to let her friend know that she shouldn't worry.

The second call was to Julia Racine and the detective picked up after only one ring. It was less than an hour before the two were supposed to leave for their weekend road trip to Connecticut.

"It's Maggie. Sorry, I'm not gonna be able to go."

"Bummer," was Racine's response.

She had expected the high-strung detective to throw a fit, at least show some disappointment. Maggie found herself disappointed, instead, that there was little reaction. The two of them weren't exactly friends. They were colleagues who had exchanged favors. No big deal. Okay, so the favors were sort of life-changing, the "you saved my mom so I saved your dad" kind of favor. Maybe a little bit of a big deal.

As a result Maggie had grown attached to Racine's father although his early-onset Alzheimer's sometimes prevented him from remembering their bond. The two women had been through a lot in a short time, brought together by killers and mutual incentives to bring those killers to justice. What had begun several years ago with animosity and distrust had dissolved into respect and understanding. Though to hear Racine, it was really no big deal.

"So you've got a big case or something?" the detective had asked.

"Something like that. I can't explain right now."

"Sure, I understand." Racine had almost cut Maggie off with her instant understanding. "Jill's been bugging me to spend more time with her anyway."

Maggie knew little about Racine's mysterious new lover, except that Racine sometimes called her G.I. Jill, so at least Maggie knew she was in the Army. At first Maggie thought that Racine kept her new lover a mystery because she had once been attracted to and rejected by Maggie. But they were beyond that. In many ways Racine reminded Maggie of herself. She kept her personal life private. That was all it was.

Maggie promised to touch base with Racine on Monday. Maybe the following weekend would work for another road trip. But when she hung up, Maggie couldn't shake the emptiness that settled in the pit of her stomach. She didn't have anyone else to call.

Though she had counted on seeing forensic anthropologist Adam Bonzado in Connecticut over the weekend she hadn't really made plans with him. That was sort of where they were right now. Casual, spontaneous, the "call me from the road" at the last minute, "oh, by the way, if you don't have anything going on this weekend …" Now she couldn't even call him to say she wasn't making the spontaneous road trip after all. It was supposed to be the grown-up, mature, no-strings kind of relationship she wanted, the ultimate nonre-lationship.

Then she found herself thinking about Nick Morrelli, again. Since her trip to Nebraska in July, Morrelli had been persistent in wanting to see her. Through rumors, she heard that he had called off his wedding engagement. Once upon a time Maggie's mother had accused Nick Morrelli of breaking up Maggie's marriage, which wasn't in the least bit true. However, now Maggie did feel responsible that Nick had broken off his engagement to pursue her.

She and Nick Morrelli had worked together on a case four years ago, the murders of two little boys and the kidnapping of Nick's nephew. Nothing had happened between them. There had been an attraction. Some sexual tension. But mostly the case had been emotionally and physically draining. How could you judge true feelings when you're running on adrenaline?

Worst of all was that she didn't feel elated about his canceled engagement or even his sudden pursuit. She didn't ask for this. She hadn't expected it and she certainly had not encouraged it.

For the moment Maggie tried to shove aside her personal life and concentrate on her present situation. She had asked the woman in the blue space suit how Mary Louise and her mother were. Her keeper, her informant, her link to the outside world said she didn't know. Maggie asked if she could see Mary Louise and was told, "I don't know." She asked several times to, at least, talk to Assistant Director Cunningham. Each time she was told he would not be available until morning. It seemed an odd thing to say, especially after a string of, "I don't knows."

There was another telephone alongside the wall of glass. This one had no dial, no buttons to push, and Maggie knew it was connected to the room next door, the room on the other side of the glass that was lined with blinking monitors, computer screens and other medical equipment. The phone was a communication system between the patient and the techs or doctors or whoever they were. Though none of them had attempted to communicate with her. In fact, they paid little attention to her and left the communications to the woman in the blue space suit.

Maggie thought about picking up the phone and de-manding to get an update. Then she calmed herself. It wouldn't help to antagonize her caretakers, her keepers, her wardens. She could get through the night. That's all she needed to do. Just get through this night.

Over the course of the evening the woman in the blue space suit had brought Maggie water but no food. Again, no apology, but at least an explanation. They would be taking blood and urine samples throughout the night, so they couldn't allow her to eat. Maggie asked what they were looking for. The woman hesitated, then said she didn't know. Maggie asked if they had narrowed it down.

Another pause while the woman simply shrugged. After some thought she yelled, "THOSE ARE QUESTIONS YOU WOULD NEED TO ASK COLONEL PLATT."

But when Maggie asked if the colonel would be stopping by soon to see her, the woman said she didn't know.

"Could you please tell him I'd like to see him?"

"OF COURSE," the woman shouted over her blower, but she answered this too quickly and Maggie wondered if Platt had gone home hours ago.

CHAPTER
24

Newburgh Heights, Virginia

"Somehow I never imagined you as a stalker, Morrelli." Tully was not pleased to see the Boston A.D.A.

"I brought Maggie some flowers. She wasn't home. I left them. Nothing strange about that."

"Was she expecting you?"

"No, she wasn't. Not that it's any of your business."

"You're sitting in a parked car outside her house. I'm checking on her house. It's my business."

It had been a long day. Tully wondered if he'd be reacting differently if Emma wasn't waiting for him just yards away. Something about needing to bring out his Glock while his daughter was in the vicinity set him on edge. He didn't like it and he wasn't about to let Morrelli off the hook for putting him in this position. Besides, if Morrelli was important enough to Maggie, wouldn't she have called him? Boston was about an eight-hour drive, an hour-and-a-half flight. Not exactly a spontaneous trip just to deliver flowers.

"So you dropped off the flowers," Tully said, leaning on the rental like he was ready for a long explanation. "Maggie's not here. Why are you still here?"

"I saw someone go inside her house. Thought maybe I should stick around and make sure it was okay."

Tully shook his head. Morrelli was good. Convincing. Classic good looks with an easy charm. No wonder he was an assistant D.A. Tully didn't know him very well. The first time he met him he thought Morrelli was a bit too slick. Too good looking. Too cocky. Too incompetent. Tully and Gwen had traveled to Boston, to Suffolk County's courthouse. Morrelli's territory. Gwen was only supposed to interview a kid in federal custody and had almost been stabbed inside the interrogation room. Morrelli had been in charge. In Tully's book that was reason enough for him to hold a grudge against the guy.

"So you think burglars are in the habit of bringing teenagers along?"

"Teenager? To me she looks like a pretty young woman."

He smiled up at Tully, obviously unaware that Emma was his daughter. Tully flexed his hands, kept them from balling up into fists. It was the wrong thing for Morrelli to say. "You've already pissed me off, Morrelli. You're lucky you're not kissing concrete right now."

"Did something happen to Maggie?" Morrelli's eyes were

suddenly serious. Maybe he finally sensed Tully's anger was real.

"She's fine, Morrelli. She's out of town for the weekend. That's all."

Morrelli looked past Tully's shoulder.

Tully glanced back and then spun around to find Emma with Harvey pulling her on his leash, coming up the sidewalk.

"Is everything okay, Dad?"

CHAPTER
25

USAMRIID

Colonel Benjamin Platt rubbed both hands over his face, stopping to dig the heels into his eyes then raking his fingers over his short cropped hair. It didn't do much good. He was exhausted. His vision was still a bit blurry from staring at the monitors and computer screens for the last several hours. He sat back in the rolling leather chair and twirled it around to look in through the glass wall.

Thankfully she had fallen asleep about an hour ago. What a nightmare this must be for her. To have a spaceman come into her home and take her mom away in a plastic bubble. Then to be brought here. The Slammer tended to freak out even the most stable people. It was bad enough to be locked in but worse being poked and prodded by doctors in space suits. There had been plenty of studies done on the psychological effect of human contact, human touch and, of course, the psychological effect of its absence. The Slammer proved most of those studies to the extreme.

Still, they couldn't justify taking her to a civilian hospital where a child would be much more comfortable. They couldn't risk exposing hospital personnel who simply would not be trained to deal with something like this. And, of course, they couldn't risk the exposure to the media. Platt knew that was, in part, Janklow's reasoning. His directive had been quite clear.

Platt gulped what was left in his coffee mug despite it being bitter and lukewarm. He couldn't remember when he had eaten last. He rubbed at his eyes again. No matter how hard he tried he could not stop thinking about Ali. Mary Louise triggered something inside him and his exhaustion wasn't allowing him to shut it down. The little girl's big, blue, curious eyes and long tangle of curls reminded him so much of his daughter. What was worse than the memory was the physical ache. He still missed her and it surprised him how much. It had been almost five years. More years had passed since she was gone than the years that she had been in his life.

He was in Afghanistan when it happened. He had left only months before, leaving behind a loving wife, a beautiful daughter and starting a promising new career as an Army doctor. He knew how dangerous it would be but exciting, too, because he was one of the chosen few who would protect the troops against biological weapons. It was considered a heroic mission and after 9/11 it felt like a worthy obligation. It was a chance to put to use all his textbook knowledge, to try experiments in the field what had only been proven in the labs. To save lives.

He had been willing to take the risks for himself, totally unaware that the real danger was back at home. He would have given up all his so-called valuable knowledge, his golden opportunity to have just a few more minutes with his precious Ali, to be there with her. Even if it was just to hold her hand before she was gone forever. But someone else had made that decision for him, had decided what was more important, had denied him that small wish.

A knock at the door startled him. The door opened behind him and Platt spun around to find Sergeant Landis.

"Sir, I have that information you requested."

"You found something?" He said "some*thing*" when he really hoped Landis had found some*one*.

"There is no father listed on the birth certificate," Landis cut to the chase.

"How about grandparents?"

"A grandmother. Lives in Richmond. The grandfather is recently deceased."

He handed Platt a folded piece of paper. Knowing Landis, Platt expected to find more than enough information, probably more than he needed.

"One problem, sir," Landis stood in front of him, unfolding a second piece of paper, "Commander Janklow left a message for you a few minutes ago. He said——" and Landis read from the paper "'—under no uncertain terms is Colonel Platt to call any relatives of any of the contained victims before Monday morning. We need to know what it is we're dealing with first.'"

Landis handed Platt the note but remained standing in front of him as if waiting to be dismissed or perhaps awaiting further instruction.

Platt took the paper and tapped its folded corner against the desk. He glanced back into the little girl's room and his eyes swept back over the monitors and computer screens that continued to blink and click and gather data.

When Janklow assigned him this mission he told him it was in Platt's hands, he expected them to be steady, unflinching hands that would do what was necessary, whatever he—meaning Platt—deemed necessary. But then Janklow insisted McCathy be included. Now this.

Janklow had assigned Platt the mission because he knew Platt was a play-by-the-numbers, follow-all-orders, dot-all-the-i's kind of leader. And yet, Janklow didn't trust him.

"Do you have kids, Sergeant Landis?"

"Excuse me, sir?"

"Kids. Do you and your wife have any?"

"Two boys, sir." Landis was staring at him now, more curious than confused. Platt never asked personal questions.

"What time does your shift end, Sergeant?"

Landis didn't need to look at his wristwatch. "About an hour ago, sir."

"Go on home to your wife and your boys, Sergeant."

"Sir?" Now he looked confused, almost uncertain as to whether he should leave his boss who was acting strangely. "Is there anything else you need me to do?"

"No, you've given me everything I need." Platt waved the first piece of paper Landis had handed him to indicate this was all he needed. The thought of Mary Louise being alone until Monday tied a knot in Platt's gut. She'd already been alone for how many days?

Sergeant Landis left, making room for Dr. Sophie Drummond's arrival.

"Sir, sorry to interrupt." She stayed in the doorway until he nodded. "Agent O'Dell has been asking to talk with you."

"Restless and uncooperative so soon?"

"Very cooperative. Maybe a bit spooked."

"Slammeritis?"

"Perhaps."

"Any word from McCathy?"

"Not yet."

He nodded again and she slipped back out the door.

Not hearing from McCathy set Platt on edge. If McCathy was working by process of elimination then he should have already ruled out the worst. Not knowing churned up acid to eat away at the knots in Platt's stomach. He knew all too well what Agent O'Dell must be feeling.

CHAPTER
26

Artie closed up the second plastic, Ziploc bag. He couldn't help but smile. For the last three weeks he had followed instructions by the letter. He didn't mind. That's what you did when you were an apprentice, a foot soldier, a student. You expected the sorcerer, the general, the teacher to call the shots and you were grateful to serve at the hand of a great one. But at some point Artie believed a great mentor would want him to show off what he'd learned.

Artie had caught on early what the "game" was even though he hadn't been privy to the "game *plan*" or the "*endgame*." He could see the pieces of the puzzle falling into place. The idea was brilliant, truly awe-inspiring and he wanted to be more than just a pawn. He needed to show that he could contribute.

Ever since he was thirteen he had dreamed of the perfect crime, plotting it out in his mind. He loved true-crime novels, devouring them in one sitting, committing the details to memory, highlighting and dog-earing the pages. His mom thought it was "so cool" that her son enjoyed reading, paying no attention to what it was he was reading.

He still carried around several of his favorite paperbacks in his backpack, what he believed to be an assortment of brilliant crimes and the masters behind them. They included the Unabomber, the Anthrax Killer, the Beltway Snipers and the Zodiac. The worn paperbacks had become handbooks, prized manuals. He figured he had learned more from studying them than he could learn from any one person.

He set the two plastic bags side by side before sliding them into their manila envelopes. The two looked like all the others. The only difference was that each of them contained five-hundred dollars instead of a thousand. The stacks of five hundred was just as thick as the thousand-dollar stack. *A brilliant substitute*. Only recently Artie realized he could use fifty ten-dollar bills instead of fifty twenty-dollar bills. The stack would be just as enticing. How could the recipient not be tempted to open the bag, if only to count all those bills?

By splitting the money Artie could send one of his own packages for every "official" one he sent for his mentor. He'd use the same rules of the game. And he had plenty of the virus. A tiny, almost invisible droplet inserted anywhere between the bills was all that was needed. It didn't take much. Sealed in the airtight, dry plastic the virus remained dormant, waiting for moist, warm human contact. All it took was some point of entry—a cut, an eye, up the nose, at the lips, behind a raw cuticle. He wasn't exactly sure how it worked. That hadn't been part of his job. He did know that if it hit its bull's-eye it was as good as a bullet. Better, actually, because it left no trace. The perfect weapon. Virtually invisible.

For his first package, his first "perfect" kill, Artie had followed in his mentor's footsteps, choosing one of his favorite crimes and an address connected to it: Benjamin Tasker Middle School in Prince George's County, Maryland. On Monday, October 7, the Beltway Snipers shot their youngest victim, a thirteen-year-old on his way to school, practically on the front steps. The boy survived, unlike ten of the other thirteen victims. Also unlike the others, Artie found it daring, bold and totally unpredictable to shoot a kid. So Artie wanted to do something just as daring. If you wanted to spread a deadly virus, where better to start than in a school?

Pleased with himself and satisfied with the two bags, Artie slipped them into their envelopes then began the cleanup process. He hated the smell of bleach but he used it to spray and wipe all surfaces. The smell lingered in his nostrils. Though he was diligent about giving himself a shot every time, he never failed to use a skin decontaminate. The military M291 resin kits had six individual decontamination pads. The dry, black resin powder was designed to show up any contamination spots. He was told it was the best universal liquid skin decon that the military had.

Yet, that wasn't quite enough for Artie. After the resin,

he still mixed fresh .05 percent hypochlorite solution with an alkaline pH and washed his hands again, up to the elbows. He had read in one of his paperbacks that the solution had been used by the military before the M291 resin kits, all the way back to WWII. Artie figured it was an extra safeguard, another one of those things his mentor would expect of him—to do his own research and take his own precautions.

In the small bathroom/supply closet he changed from his scrubs back to his street clothes, bagging all of it, including the paper face mask and shoe covers. He'd toss them in the parking lot's Dumpster. No need to clean them. The closet was filled with an endless supply.

He left the lab, feeling excited and… What was the word? A few monkeys still screeched down the hall, but now Artie ignored them. His step was lighter, almost a strut. For the first time in his life he felt… And then the word came to him. He felt *powerful*.

CHAPTER
27

Emma needed to get some sleep. It was late by the time she and her dad got home. He was so mad at Maggie's friend, Nick Morrelli, that Emma could see the vein in his forehead throbbing. That same vein she thought only she could set vibrating. It'd been a long time since she'd seen her dad that upset. And the poor guy, a real hottie, had only been delivering flowers to Maggie, wanting to see her and then suspicious when he saw someone else going into her home.

Emma thought it was all so totally romantic.

She checked down the hallway to make sure all the lights were out then she closed the bedroom door. Harvey stretched out on the floor beside her bed. He looked up at her and she whispered, "It's okay. I'm not going anywhere."

Maggie had once told Emma about how she had found

Harvey under a neighbor's bed, bloodied and injured, having fought hard to protect his master but loosing the fight. Now the dog was very protective of Maggie. When Emma took care of him that protective instinct extended to her, which Emma thought was very cool.

She petted him and crawled back into bed. She made one last attempt to invite him up with her. He stretched out on the floor instead and Emma pulled out the pile of letters from under the covers. Just one more, she promised herself.

September 2, 1982
Dear Liney,

Thanks for the long letter. Razzy and J.B. are jealous. I have that goofy photo strip of the two of us. Remember the one from the photo booth at the mall? I put it up to remind them how jealous they should be.

It's been a tough week. I'm sore from the obstacle course. Think I might have pulled my shoulder. Don't get me wrong, I'm in great physical shape. Guess I have my dad to thank for that. Lifting all those crates probably helped. Though I'd never admit that to him. Sounds like he's still bellyaching to my mom that I should be home. The bastard's finally realizing how much of the workload I did. Wait until inventory. Then he'll really be bitching. Maybe he'll make my precious baby sister do something for a change. Though I doubt it. Wouldn't want to get calluses on those precious musician fingers.

Sorry, I don't mean to get off on that, but reminding my-

self of that hellhole actually helps me get through the tough load here. Thinking about you helps, too, but in a good way. A real good way if you know what I mean. I think about the good stuff and good times. I've been thinking about you tak-ing me to the Art Institute this summer. Of all places. Me in an art gallery. And a Vatican art show at that. You're going to be a famous artist someday, Liney. Just you wait and see. If I say it's gonna happen it will.

We have the night off. Razzy rented one of those video play-ers. He and J.B. picked out a couple of movies. One I can't wait to see. A guy flick called Mad Max. *I can smell the butter and the popcorn. Better go or they'll eat it all. I'll write more later, I promise.*

Yours truly,
Indy

She couldn't resist looking at the next one. It was dated only a day later. She unfolded it gently, almost reverently. There was something so romantic about the idea that he couldn't wait to write…that he needed to write to her every day.

September 3, 1982
Dear Liney,
We have our first case. It's homework but it's a real case. Pretty exciting stuff. I'm not supposed to be discussing it with any-one other than my classmates, but it's not like you're going to

tell anyone, right? In May a guy sent a bomb to Vanderbilt University. Sent it in the mail via the good old post office. Can you believe it? Actually it was forwarded. Even had insufficient postage, so they're wondering if maybe the target might have been the bogus return address. Pretty interesting stuff.

On July 2 another bomb showed up in a faculty lounge at Berkeley. We're thinking it's the same guy though this one was left there, not sent. We're... Listen to me. I'm already considering myself one of them. Anyway, the bombs look like an amateur with a lot of scrap. They were calling him the Junkyard Bomber. Now they've got a new name for him, an acronym, but I probably shouldn't be telling you.

We get to put together the profile from the evidence. They think the same guy might be responsible for a series of bombs going back to '78. Can you believe that? 1978 and they haven't caught the guy yet. I already have a pretty good idea for my profile. Razzy and J.B. are all hot to discuss it, but I'm not going to share my ideas. Why should I, right? Let them figure it out on their own.

So I'm sure everyone is figuring the guy is a loner with a grudge against either Vanderbilt or universities in general. Maybe he got expelled as a student or fired as a professor. But I think there's a lot more to him. You can't argue that he's got to be smart, right? Maybe he uses scraps to throw off investigators. How do you track down pieces of wood or regular shingle nails? It's hard not to admire someone who can put together something like this and not get caught.

I'll let you in on more details tomorrow. I'm totally wiped out tonight.

Until tomorrow... Hey, did I tell you I miss you?

Indy

CHAPTER
28

The Slammer

Unable to sleep, Maggie paced. Her room was sixteen paces wide and fourteen paces deep except where the bathroom jutted out into the room, which was three paces wide and six paces deep.

With no windows she relied on her wristwatch and the TV to give her a sense of time. In another forty minutes she knew she would be peeing in a plastic cup again. And what was worse, she found herself looking forward to the woman in the blue space suit's visit though it included drawing blood or gagging her for a throat culture or peeing into a plastic cup. And each time the woman came into Maggie's room, Maggie asked to talk to Colonel Platt. Each time, the woman nodded and said, "OF COURSE."

On the woman's last visit Maggie had reminded her that

she had been told they would keep her overnight. They had plenty of samples of Maggie's fluids to know whether or not she had been exposed. USAMRIID had some of the most advanced laboratories in the country. Shouldn't they know by now what Mary Louise's mother had been exposed to? She tried not to run through the possibilities.

In fact, to keep her mind off the possibilities, Maggie resorted to the one thing she knew she could rely on, the one thing that would stop her from thinking about the drafty hospital gown, the electrical hum of equipment and the claustrophobia that clawed at her insides every time she heard the air-lock seal of the door. She tried to do what she did best, work out cases in her mind and start putting together the puzzle pieces, though she had few pieces for this case.

She took a deep breath and let it out. Where to begin? In the morning she would get the envelope to Agent Tully somehow, or at least the return address. She had good suspicion that whatever was or had been inside that envelope was what caused Ms. Kellerman's crash. But from everything Maggie had observed in the Kellerman house, both Mary Louise and her mother seemed unlikely victims of the kind of killer... Maggie shook her head. No, that wasn't right. He hadn't killed anyone yet. They seemed unlikely victims of a terrorist who could leave a box of doughnuts at Quantico with a death-threat notice tucked inside. Not just Quantico, but down in the BSU department.

She wondered if Ms. Kellerman was related or connected

to an FBI agent or some other personnel at the academy. That was easy enough to check. Too easy, perhaps. This guy wouldn't go through the trouble of staging such an elaborate "greet and meet" threat with the FBI if he knew they could connect him to the victims. No. Chances were, the terrorist had no connection to Mary Louise and her mother, but that didn't mean he hadn't chosen them specifically for one reason or another.

Maggie tried to remember the contents of the note. It had sounded like bits and pieces thrown together. Or that might be exactly what he wanted them to believe, that they were randomly chosen words, emotionally charged, when, in fact, every word may have been calculated. Something about the phrases he used rang familiar. Perhaps she had simply read too many notes from twisted, evil minds. It was an occupational hazard, letting the words of criminals take up space in a compartment of her brain. Sometimes the words meant nothing. Sometimes they meant everything, valuable clues like secret messages waiting to be decoded. Words like *crash*.

Despite her best efforts she kept seeing Ms. Kellerman and the blood-splattered bedsheets. She could still hear the poor woman's raspy breaths, the wet gurgle in her throat, the rattle in her chest. She could smell the sour vomit. The bedroom reeked of it, but there was something else, something that hinted at raw sewage, like a septic tank had backed up, only the smell had been coming from Ms. Kellerman's bed.

The medical term was "crash and bleed out." Maggie knew

there were certain toxins, biological agents and infectious diseases that, once they invaded the body, caused severe hemorrhage. Ricin and anthrax attached to and attacked lung cells. Infectious viruses weren't particular about what cells they attacked. The invaded cells eventually exploded. The body's immune system would shut down. Organs began to fail, one by one. In effect, the body did actually crash and bleed from the inside out.

Both she and Cunningham had misinterpreted the note. When the author wrote that there would be a "crash," he didn't mean an explosive device. He meant Ms. Kellerman's body.

The phone on the wall rang and Maggie jumped. She spun around to look at it and saw a man standing on the other side of the glass. He held the other receiver to his ear and motioned for her to answer hers. It rang twice more before she crossed the room and picked it up.

"Good morning, Agent O'Dell."

The voice sounded graveled with fatigue, deeper than before, as though he was fighting laryngitis. She almost didn't recognize the voice or him until she met his eyes.

"Colonel Platt, I thought perhaps you had forgotten about me."

"Never. Though I may not have recognized you in your new outfit."

She remembered the thin hospital gown and restrained from clutching at the back to make sure it was closed. She had been pacing without paying much attention. His smile made her face grow warm. Why should she care whether he got a glimpse of her bare backside?

"I would have brought my overnight case if I knew I was spending the night in Hotel USAMRIID."

"My apologies for not having better accommodations for you," he said as his smile faded and the jovial tone became more serious. "We have to wait several more hours, then I'll have them bring you some breakfast."

"But first we'll talk." It wasn't a question or a request.

He paused, his eyes not leaving hers. For a second she thought he might recognize the panic that she had carefully hidden. He pointed to a chair on her side of the glass while he sat down in similar one on his side.

"But first we'll talk," he conceded.

CHAPTER
29

Pensacola, Florida

Rick Ragazzi jerked awake. The noises outside the studio apartment and down below were familiar but that didn't make them less annoying. He checked the glow-in-the-dark alarm clock on his bed stand. Sounded like Cousin Joey was pulling an all-nighter. He heard two different girls giggle, and Rick shook his head. Joey would never grow up. Sometimes Rick found it difficult to not agree with his uncle Vic who insisted his son would never learn obligation and responsibility until he "knocked up some girl."

Amazingly so, "chasing skirts," as Uncle Vic liked to call it, didn't seem to affect Joey's culinary talents. He'd sleep until noon, go work out and be at the restaurant at three ready to take on another dinner crowd. Of course, while Joey was sleeping until noon Rick would be up at the crack of dawn, waiting for deliveries from vendors, paying bills, stocking the shelves, changing out linens, juggling waitstaff schedules and today waiting for the repairman to change the refrigerator's compressor. Somewhere in between he'd be cutting up vegetables, pounding out chicken and deveining shrimp. His poor hands already looked like a knife thrower's clumsy apprentice.

For now he stretched back into the pillows. He had at least a couple more hours before he had to meet the first truck. Saturdays were long days. He'd need the extra sleep, if only Joey and his harem would keep it down. Rick pulled himself up and out of bed just enough to close the window. His knees suddenly went weak and he had to grab onto the windowsill. Something pounded in his head and he felt a chill sweep over him. That's when he noticed he was soaking wet with sweat. He crawled back into bed, pulling the bedcovers up tight around him.

He wiped his forehead. It was hot. Now he realized his pillow was damp. Even his sheets were damp. He had a fever. *This was crazy.* He never got sick. Could have been something he had eaten, though his stomach didn't hurt. He did have a backache and a headache, more like a dull throbbing inside his forehead. Maybe a twenty-four bug of some sort?

He closed his eyes and thought about waves crashing, the emerald-green waters and sugar-white sand of Pensacola Beach. He tried to think of the hot sun beating down on him instead of the heat that seeped out of his pores from some-where inside him. He wanted to dream of cool breezes and riding the waves on a freshly waxed, fast board, curling his toes over the edge, hanging on and enjoying the roller-coaster ride. He was almost there, relaxed and enjoying, until he felt something running down the side of his face and continuing down his neck.

He reached to turn on the bedside lamp. This was crazy. He never got sick and yet he had a fever and now his nose was bleeding.

CHAPTER
30

The Slammer

"I want to know what I've been exposed to," Maggie said without wasting any time.

"We don't know," Platt answered quickly and it reminded Maggie of the woman in the blue space suit. Was this USAMRIID's mantra of the day? All the latest technology and they didn't know. *Right.*

"By now you must have some idea." She gave him another chance.

"No, not yet."

She thought he might be convincing except that he wouldn't meet her eyes. Instead, his eyes glanced to the side at the wall monitors, flashed over her head, swept back to the counter, like they were preoccupied but really were evasive.

"You'd make an awful poker player," she said and this time his eyes flew back to hers. Now that she had his attention she couldn't help thinking they were intense eyes, the kind that when focused could see deep into your soul. "Knowing can't possibly be worse than not knowing."

He rubbed at his jaw but his eyes stayed on her, as if now he was searching for something in her face that would guide him. Did he hope for a glimpse of courage from her or was he waiting for his own?

"I haven't heard anything from the lab."

"But you must have some ideas of your own." She tried to see if he might be hiding something. He was making this harder than she expected. It had to be bad. By now they would have been able to eliminate a few of the obvious things.

"It's pointless to guess," he said. "Why go through that?"

"Because you've left me with nothing better to do."

He nodded, an exaggerated up and down, showing okay, yes, he certainly understood. "You have cable TV."

"Basic. No AMC. No FX. How about a computer with Internet service?"

"I'll see what I can do. In the meantime let's find something better for you to do."

She thought he was patronizing her, but he looked serious.

"I spent four days quarantined in a tent," he said, "just outside Sierra Leone. No cable. Not even basic. Not much to do. Count dead mosquitoes. Wish that you had enough gin or vodka to pass out."

"Guess I should put in a request for breakfast to include some Scotch." She was joking. She could tell he was not. "So what did you do to while away the hours in your tent just outside Sierra Leone?"

"Okay, don't laugh," he said, arching an eyebrow as though to test her. "I tried to replay *The Treasure of the Sierra Madre* in my head." He paused and rubbed his eyes as if needing to take a break before he dived into a lengthy explanation. She didn't give him a chance.

"Hmm... *Treasure of the Sierra Madre,* quite the heady commentary about the dark side of human nature. Not a bad movie," she said, enjoying his surprise. "But not my favorite Humphrey Bogart."

He stared at her, caught off guard, but only for a second or two. "Let me guess, you prefer your Bogie with Bacall."

"No, not necessarily. If memory serves, he won the Oscar for *The African Queen* but I think he deserved it much more for *The Caine Mutiny*."

"Crazy Queeg?" He offered her a lopsided grin then readjusted himself in the cheap, plastic chair, rolled his shoulders, stretched his legs as if satisfied with her answer and preparing to stay for a while. "So if you had to choose, who would it be, Bogart or Cary Grant?"

Without missing a beat, Maggie said, "Jimmy Stewart."

"You're kidding? You'd choose clumsy and gawky over debonair and charming?"

"Jimmy Stewart *is* charming. And I like his sense of humor." She sat back in her own uncomfortable plastic chair and crossed her arms over her chest. "So how 'bout you? Bacall or Grace Kelly?"

"Katharine Hepburn," he answered just as quickly with the raised eyebrow again, only this time it seemed to be telling her he could play this game.

She nodded her approval. "Did you ever watch *The Twilight Zone?*"

"Yes, but my mom didn't like me watching it. She said it'd give me nightmares."

"My mom didn't care what I watched as long as it didn't interrupt her drunken stupors." As soon as Maggie said it, she was sorry. She saw a subtle change in his face and wished she hadn't revealed so much. What was she thinking? Now he was quiet, watching her. He'd say something like, "I'm sorry," which never made sense to Maggie. Why did people say they were sorry when it clearly had nothing to do with them?

"Do you remember the episode with the woman in the hospital and her face is all bandaged?" he asked

He surprised her. It wasn't at all what Maggie had expected.

He continued, "She's waiting to have the bandages removed and she's worried that she'll be horribly scarred and disfigured."

"And the medical staff is all standing around the bed," Maggie joined in. "But the camera focuses only on her. Sometimes you see the backs of the staff, but that's it."

"The bandages come off and they all gasp and turn away in disappointment and horror."

"But she looks normal." Maggie said. "Then you see that everyone else's face is warped and deformed with pig snouts and bulging eyes."

"Sometimes normal is simply what you're used to," he said. Then he waited for her to catch up with him. His way of telling her he understood. Maybe his way of telling her that no matter how dysfunctional her childhood experiences were they didn't make her some sort of freak.

The door behind him opened into his room and a woman in a lab coat interrupted. Maggie couldn't hear her over Platt's receiver and the glass was soundproof. He nodded and the woman left.

To Maggie he said, "Gotta go." He stood to leave.

She wanted to go with him. Did they finally know something? Maybe he saw a glimpse of panic in her face, in her eyes, because he hesitated.

"So Lieutenant Commander Queeg mistakenly directs the *Caine* over its own towline. Start there," he said with another lopsided grin. "I should be back before you get to Queeg's search for the pilfered strawberries."

He waited for her smile. Then he hung up the receiver and left. Suddenly her small, isolated room seemed even quieter than it was before.

CHAPTER
31

Platt's heart pounded with every footstep. He felt the kick of adrenaline in his gut, a mixture of dread and anticipation countered the exhaustion.

The hallways were quiet, some dark. He avoided the elevators. Took the stairs instead. He needed the motion. He caught himself taking two steps at a time. Slow down, he told himself when he really wanted to break out in a run.

Dr. Drummond had told him that, "Dr. McCathy needs you on the fourth floor. He said you have to see this for yourself."

Best-case scenario, McCathy was being his melodramatic self. Worst-case scenario, McCathy found something worthy of his melodrama, something to justify his pent-up anger.

Despite what he had told Agent O'Dell, Platt's limited examination and observations of Ms. Kellerman had led him to draw some conclusions. She had been coughing up blood and had problems breathing, along with red eyes and obvious severe abdominal pain. Her fever had been high enough and had lasted enough days to cause fever blisters inside her mouth.

Her soiled bedding indicated bouts of vomiting and diarrhea that in the last twenty-four hours had rendered her so weak she hadn't been able to get out of bed. She was in shock and remained unresponsive and incoherent. Early tests indicated that her kidneys had begun to shut down. If his preliminary assessment was correct, her other organs would soon follow.

Because of the severity of her symptoms he had narrowed the cause down to three possibilities, three biological weapons that a terrorist might use. None of them would be easy to treat. An anthrax infection, depending on what form, might be controlled with antibiotics. Hopefully they might be able to contain the spores to Ms. Kellerman's house and to those already infected. Ricin would need minimal containment, as well. But if ingested, ricin was a deadly toxin and caused a painful death. The third possibility he didn't like to even think about. If the terrorist had managed to use an infectious disease like typhoid or a virus like Marburg or—heaven forbid, Ebola, then treatment and containment might be impossible. Ms. Kellerman's house would be a hot zone and anyone within reach of her or it could be a walking epidemic.

Platt slowed when he got to the fourth floor. The procedure would be for McCathy to prepare and seal his sample slides while in a space suit inside a Level 4 suite. Once preserved and sealed they would be able to look at the slides without fear of exposure. Platt knew he'd find McCathy now in the Level 3 suite where the electron microscope was kept. The expensive contraption was a metal tower as tall as Platt. It's beam of light allowed them to see microscopic cells and view them like geographic landscapes.

Platt changed in the outer staging area from his jeans and sweatshirt to surgical scrubs, latex gloves, goggles, a paper mask and shoe covers. Then he joined McCathy.

The microbiologist sat at the counter, hunched over the binocular eyepiece of a microscope. When he looked up at Platt his eyes looked wild and enlarged. He wore thick eyeglasses under the goggles. His face and even his paper mask were damp with sweat. His neatly trimmed beard stuck out from behind the mask, giving him a crazy-scientist look that, ordinarily, Platt would have shrugged off as part of McCathy's melodrama. This time it added to the thump already banging inside Platt's chest.

"It's not good," McCathy said. "This is absolutely amazing. In fact, it'd be absolutely beautiful if it wasn't so goddamn deadly."

"What is it?"

"The cells from Ms. Kellerman. They're busting open with worms."

"Worms?" The banging in Platt's chest invaded his head, as well. "Impossible. There must be a mistake."

"Take a look for yourself," McCathy told him, bolting up and sliding his stool aside, offering Platt a look through the microscope's eyepiece.

Platt swallowed hard and moved in. Adjusted the focus. Tried to ignore his sweaty palms inside the latex gloves. He took a deep breath and clanked his goggles against the microscope's eyepiece. What he saw looked like spaghetti or thin curlicue snakes with threads unraveling from their sides. They pushed against the cell wall, breaking away from a clump, or what they called a brick, in the center of the cell.

Platt forced himself to breathe slowly. Without moving, still staring, he said, "What about our own lab contamination?"

"Impossible. Our samples are in freezers, separated from this lab by three walls of biocontainment."

"There are other things this could be." But Platt couldn't think of a single one. The cell had been invaded and was exploding with what looked like worms, snakes tangled in a pile. "This agent, this invader doesn't loop much. And it's too long. Shouldn't there be a shepherd's hook?"

"There's only one thing I know of that looks like that, whether there's a loop, curl or hook," McCathy said. "I saw Marburg years ago. Samples taken from an outbreak along the Congo. Wiped out a whole village in a matter of weeks."

Platt had seen something similar. The quarantine he had told Agent O'Dell about was one enforced from an outbreak of Lassa fever, another single RNA virus. But Lassa didn't make cells explode like this.

"How can we confirm it? I don't just mean running the cells through the electron microscope. I mean inexplicably. We have to be certain, without a doubt," he told McCathy. They couldn't waste any more time.

"We can test Ms. Kellerman's cells against the real thing."

"What do we have to do?"

"We take more of her blood serum and drop it on cells, on samples from our freezers, samples that we know have the real thing. If any of them glow…" McCathy shrugged. "Then you have your confirmation, beyond a doubt."

"What do we have in the freezer?"

"Marburg, Ebola Zaire, Lassa and Ebola Reston."

"How long will that take?"

"I can suit up now." McCathy glanced at his wristwatch. "Take about thirty to forty minutes to prepare the samples from the freezer. Once I drop Ms. Kellerman's cells onto the real deal it's a matter of minutes."

"Okay, let's do it."

"Wait a minute. I work alone in Level 4."

Platt wasn't surprised that McCathy would balk even at a time like this. He kept calm and steady. He didn't raise his voice, didn't allow a hint of anger when he said, "Not this time."

CHAPTER
32

Saint Francis Hospital
Chicago

Dr. Claire Antonelli arrived early for her morning rounds, though she had left the hospital only six hours ago, just enough time to take a nap, change clothes and kiss her sleeping teenage son, who groaned a protest. But then he smiled—still without opening his eyes—and asked if she had eaten anything.

"Who's looking after who?" she had asked.

He smiled again, eyes still closed, and turned over, mumbling something about a slice of pizza he had saved for her.

She'd grabbed the pizza and had eaten it cold during her commute back to the hospital, washing it down with her morning Diet Pepsi.

Now she marched down the sterile hallways, the exhaustion of the week lingering, but she felt vaguely refreshed, like a worn rag that had been wrung out and left to dry, ragged around the edges but ready to get back to work. Still, she was glad she had exchanged her fashionable heels for a comfortable pair of flats.

She had already checked in on her newest patient, a three-pound, seven-ounce little guy in the NICU, the Newborn Intensive Care Unit, currently known only as the Haney baby boy but called "bellow" by the staff because that's all he had done since he had come out into this world. He was asleep finally with all the connecting monitors taped to his tiny body. The monitors continued to register exactly where Claire wanted them to be. He was doing good for coming into the world much too early.

The patient Claire had gotten here early to see would not be as easy to stabilize and make comfortable. Markus Schroder had allowed Claire to admit him into the hospital two days ago, though "allowed" was even pushing it. The truth was, his wife, Vera, had threatened and coerced him. In less than twenty-four hours he grew too weak and incoherent to argue with either his wife or his doctor. And what was most frustrating for Claire was that after a battery of tests she still had no clue what was wrong with the forty-five-year-old man who, up until a week ago, had been, in his own words, "as healthy as a buck half his age."

Getting here early she hoped to talk to Markus alone, before his wife arrived. Vera had only good intentions but she also had the annoying habit of answering for her husband even when he was healthy and lucid. Claire needed some answers and she hoped Markus might be able to provide them.

She stopped at the nursing station and pulled the file, checking to see if any of the lab results were in. Before she could flip through everything a petite nurse in green-flowered scrubs came around the corner.

"The rash is worse," Amanda Corey said.

"What about his fever?"

"Spiked to 106. We have him on an IV but he's still been vomiting." The nurse pointed to a plastic container with a red twist cap. "I saved you some."

Claire examined the container's contents, a black-red liquid with a few floaters, though Claire knew the man didn't have anything left in his stomach. This didn't look good. She was relieved to see Nurse Corey had double-bagged the container and already labeled it for the lab.

"Anything from the lab last night?"

Corey held up a finger and walked to the other side of the counter. "I saw Jasper drop off some stuff about an hour ago." She grabbed a stack of documents from an in-tray behind the counter. "Let's see if your guy's in here." Halfway through she pulled out three sheets and handed them to Claire.

She didn't have to look closely. Claire could see the check marks, all of them in the "negative" column. Ordinarily she would be pleased, relieved. No doctor wanted to know that her patient tested positive for jaundice, gallstones, malaria or liver abscess. But in this case it felt like a lead weight had been dropped on her shoulders. She dragged her fingers through her short, dark hair, though she didn't let Amanda Corey see her total frustration.

"Thanks," she simply said and then turned and walked down the hall, flipping pages and searching for something, anything she may have missed.

Her patient had a dangerous infection that didn't respond to any antibiotics. She couldn't find the source of the infection. Now he was vomiting up pieces of his stomach lining, an educated guess from the looks of the container. Claire was running out of ideas. Hopefully Markus could help her find a clue, because not only was she running out of ideas, she knew she was running out of time.

She found him lying flat on his back, head lopped to the side, watching the door though he didn't seem to be expecting anyone. He barely acknowledged her entry with a slow blink, eyelids drooping, eyes bloodred. His lips were swollen, his yellowish skin almost swallowed by purple swatches, as though his entire body was starting to turn black-and-blue. It was the red eyes first, then the fever and yellow-tinged skin, that made her think of malaria. Although she couldn't place Markus Schroder close to anywhere that would have put him in contact with the disease. The Chicago area might feel like the tropics in the summer, but an outbreak of malaria wouldn't go unnoticed.

Fortunately, Saint Francis was a teaching and research hospital so Claire had access to quick lab results, but she couldn't keep guessing. She was a family practitioner whose private practice brought her to the hospital to deliver babies, suture the occasional minor scrape and diagnose early signs of common ailments. Whatever was playing havoc with Markus Schroder's immune system was outside her everyday realm.

"Good morning, Markus." She came to his bedside and laid a hand on his shoulder. Long ago she had learned her patients appreciated even the slightest touch, some small and gentle contact outside the cold jabs and pats that usually ensued in a doctor/patient relationship.

He reached out a purple-splotched hand to her, but before he could respond, his body jerked forward. The vomit that splattered the white bedding and the front of Claire's white lab coat was speckled black and red with something that reminded her of wet, used coffee grounds. But it was the smell that set off a panic inside Dr. Claire Antonelli. Markus Schroder's vomit smelled like slaughterhouse waste.

The Slammer

Maggie had wanted to tell the woman in the blue space suit to leave her alone. She was too early and Maggie was tired of being poked and prodded. She stayed curled up in bed. She didn't even look over her shoulder at the woman. She'd simply wait until Colonel Platt returned. But this time the woman brought in a laptop computer and without a word she left.

Maggie booted up the computer and was surprised to find she had access to a wireless network that connected with ease. In a matter of minutes she started trying to track down any information on the manila envelope she had taken from the Kellerman house.

The postage was a metered stamp from a post office in D.C. but the return address was actually Oklahoma. Why go to the trouble of pretending it came from Oklahoma when it was obviously sent from D.C.? If this envelope had delivered the deadly concoction that made Ms. Kellerman ill, Maggie believed there had to be some clue in the return address.

Other criminals had used return addresses to make a statement or confuse law enforcement. If Maggie remembered correctly, at least one of the Unabomber's intended victims was not the recipient of the rigged package, but rather the person listed on the return address. Theodore Kaczynski had even gone to the trouble of supplying insufficient postage so the package would be "returned to sender." It was a cunning way for a criminal to remove himself from the victim, make the victim and the crime look random. It became tougher when law enforcement couldn't make a connection between the victim and the suspected killer. The smartest criminal minds, the dangerous ones, used this knowledge to their advantage.

Maggie suspected this guy was in that category. It was certainly clear to her that he wanted attention or he wouldn't have dropped a note right into the FBI's lap. He wanted to thumb his nose at them, show how smart and clever he was. He didn't just want the FBI investigating his shenanigans, he wanted to drop them smack-dab in the middle of it all. He wanted them to experience this right alongside the victims he had hand chosen. And for whatever twisted reason, Maggie believed he had specially chosen Ms. Kellerman and Mary Louise. There was no doubt in her mind that they were not random victims.

Maggie brought up Google maps and keyed in the return

address listed on the package: 4205 Highway 66 West, El Reno, OK 73036. She expected to find a residence belonging to James Lewis who was listed as the sender. What came up on the screen stopped her.

She checked everything she had keyed in. Maybe she had gotten the numbers wrong. There was no mistake. The return address was for the U.S. Federal Correctional Institution for the South Central Region.

"Okay," she told herself. Federal prisoners had access to plenty of things these days but there was no way one would be able to send out a package that wasn't thoroughly inspected.

She Googled "James Lewis" + "federal prison." Several news articles came up. All of them included the Tylenol murderers in Chicago during the fall of 1982. Maggie sat up on the edge of her chair.

Now, this was interesting.

Maggie was only a girl at the time. Her father was still alive and they lived in Green Bay, close enough to Chicago that she remembered her parents had been concerned. It didn't matter. She knew the case. Every FBI agent knew the case. It was one of the most notorious unsolved crimes in history.

She scanned one of the articles to refresh her memory of the details. Seven people died after taking cyanide-laced Extra Strength Tylenol capsules. The murderer had shoplifted bottles from area stores, emptied and refilled capsules with cyanide, replaced them in their bottle and box then returned them to each store. Hard to image how easy it had been before tamperproof packaging.

Maggie found James Lewis's name and continued reading. Lewis was a New York man who was charged and convicted, not of the murders. There was no evidence that he had access to or had tampered with any of the bottles. Instead, Lewis was convicted of attempting to extort one million dollars from Tylenol makers Johnson & Johnson. He served thirteen years of a twenty-year sentence. And he served those thirteen years in the Federal Correctional Institution in El Reno, Oklahoma. However, Lewis was released in 1995 and was living in Cambridge, Massachusetts.

Maggie sat back. Obviously Lewis hadn't sent this. He wouldn't set himself up. But the person who did send it wanted to draw attention to the unsolved case. Or was it simply a piece of trivia he found amusing?

Maggie browsed the other articles about the Tylenol case. How could it be relevant? It was interesting, but it all happened twenty-five years ago.

She checked the date and slid to the edge of her chair again.

It was exactly twenty-five years ago.

The first victim died on September 29, 1982. And that's when Maggie saw it and she knew she was right. He hadn't chosen at random. Just the opposite.

The first victim of the Tylenol murders was a twelve-year-old girl from Elk Grove Village, Illinois, and her name was Mary Kellerman.

CHAPTER
34

Platt felt like it was taking an eternity. He thrived on order. He respected processes that followed logic and reason. But suddenly the basic procedure for entering a Biolevel 4 hot zone had become a painstaking, excruciatingly long process. Everything took too long. Everything seemed to move in slow motion. And yet, he didn't dare skip or hurry any of it. He knew better and all he had to do was to remind himself of the cells he had just looked at through the microscope. That was enough.

His heart still pounded against his rib cage. At least its thundering in his ears had eased up a bit. At times like this his nervous energy pulsed and raced, making him anxious. It was the same excess energy he liked to slam out on the racquetball court or pound out on the running trail. Years of self-discipline taught him how to control it, but here, inside these windowless walls, it was always a bit of a challenge.

He had helped McCathy into his space suit first. Platt would be able to put on his own suit. In the field it was a little trickier. Here it was routine and Platt had plenty of time. McCathy would need to prepare the frozen samples they'd use for the test, something Platt didn't envy. The samples they were going to use were actual blood serum from human victims with filoviruses, samples in glass vials taken from USAMRIID's freezer, their own private collection of hot agents. Platt tried to stay positive, tried to remind himself that not all filoviruses were equal. Though all were highly infectious, not all were fatal.

Ebola Reston had shown up in a private laboratory's monkey house in Reston, Virginia, about twenty years ago. Platt's mentor at USAMRIID had been one of the task force members who had had the job of containment. The virus spread through the monkeys like wildfire, but it didn't have the same effect on humans. The sample they had in their freezer collection was from a worker who had gotten sick but who had survived. Ebola Reston hadn't taken a single human life. Yet under a microscope it looked like snakes or worms with thousands of threads splintering off of it. It could certainly look just as vicious as Ebola Zaire.

Ebola Zaire had earned the nickname "the slate wiper" and for good reason. Its kill rate was ninety percent. The sample they had was from a nurse in northern Zaire just south of the Ebola River. In September 1976 she took care of a Roman Catholic nun who had somehow become infected with the virus. From what Platt knew of the outbreak, entire villages in the Bumba Zone of northern Zaire were wiped out. The virus jumped from one village to another until the government blocked off sections of the country and allowed no one out or in under threat of being shot. That was Ebola Zaire. The only means of containment was to let it die out and, of course, let everyone infected die with it.

In between was Marburg and Lassa fever. Marburg wasn't much better than Ebola Zaire. Its survivors looked very much like victims of radiation. But the difference was that there were actually survivors. The sample they had of Marburg was from one such survivor, a doctor in Nairobi.

Likewise, Lassa fever was not necessarily fatal. If caught early it could be treated with antiviral drugs, though one out of three victims was left permanently deaf. Still, it was a much better compromise. The sample they had in their freezer for Lassa fever was from a man named Masai. Platt had treated the old man before he himself was quarantined in Sierra Leone.

The test McCathy was preparing would be rather simple. Eventually he would need to do the same test with each of the exposed victims' blood: Ms. Kellerman, her daughter, Assistant Director Cunningham and Agent O'Dell. McCathy would start with Ms. Kellerman, placing only a droplet of her blood serum onto each of the samples from the freezer.

Unfrozen, the viruses were as hot as when they were collected. If Ms. Kellerman's blood reacted to any one of the samples, giving off a faint glow, it meant that she tested positive for that virus. The glow meant that the virus recognized what was living inside Ms. Kellerman's blood. Platt was hoping all of the samples would come up negative and that there might be a chance this wasn't a virus at all.

Still in his surgical scrubs he sat down on the bench in the gray area, his elbows on his knees, his jaw resting in his hands. He was exhausted. He knew McCathy had to be exhausted, too. Platt's training and adrenaline would get him through. He had been in war zones, physically exhausted, mentally drained and forced to perform surgical procedures in makeshift operating rooms with blinking generator lights and limited sterile water. Somehow he'd learned to dig deep and find the stamina and the necessary energy to get through the next minute, the next hour, the next day. If he didn't, it could mean someone's life. A war zone wasn't much different than a hot zone.

He stared at the stainless-steel walls lined with spraying nozzles for the decon shower that came afterward. The gray area was neither sterile nor hot. It was neutral territory. Or, as Platt's predecessor had told him, "One last chance to change your mind before crossing over to the hot side."

Platt checked his wristwatch then took it off and started getting into his suit. Regulations prohibited wearing anything inside your space suit that touched your skin other than your scrubs. Yet Platt knew several people who wore amulets or charms. Here in the gray area outside the Level 4 air lock it wasn't unusual to see a variety of rituals or superstitions. Platt had seen scientists make the sign of the cross. He remembered one veterinarian who took out a picture of his wife and children and studied it before gearing up. Others went through a series of breathing exercises or relaxation techniques. McCathy didn't appear to have any rituals or superstitions, unless his muttering "it's goddamn unbelievable" had become a sort of mantra for him.

As for Platt, he wished he still had the family or even a photograph. Sometimes he thought it'd be nice to believe in making the sign of the cross, just like he did so many times growing up. Instead, he had no routines, no superstitions. Although he did always make sure he used the bathroom. Six hours in a suit had taught him that lesson very quickly.

He rolled his shoulders and stretched his neck. He took several deep breaths before attaching his helmet then he pulled the handle on the steel air-lock door to enter the hot zone.

CHAPTER
35

Reston, Virginia

R. J. Tully grabbed his cell phone before the second ring. Just after seven o'clock on a Saturday morning but he wasn't surprised to hear his boss's voice. He was relieved.

"Good morning, Agent Tully."

"Sir, how are you?" Tully wiped bagel crumbs off his chin as if caught. In the process he discovered a dab of Kleenex from where he'd cut himself shaving.

"I'm fine. How's Agent O'Dell?"

The question took Tully off guard. He expected Cunningham to have a better idea of how Maggie was. From what he understood she was just down the hall from him.

"She was okay last night. I haven't talked to her yet this morning."

"Colonel Platt will be heading the task force," Cunningham went on, all business as usual. "He'll be in charge of containment and treatment if that's possible. That means they'll still be guarding the crime scene, but you and Ganza will be in charge of whatever evidence they collect."

"You were inside the house, sir. *Is* there anything there?"

The pause lasted long enough that Tully wondered if he'd lost the connection.

"There must be something," Cunningham finally said. "Whatever's going on I think this one is personal."

"Personal, sir?"

"Why risk delivering that message directly to BSU? I think he wanted to make sure I received it."

Tully didn't necessarily agree. The guy could have simply been thumbing his nose at all of them, letting them know just how close he could get without being noticed, without getting caught. But Tully wasn't in the habit of disagreeing with his boss. From Cunningham's perspective, especially after a night in the Slammer, Tully supposed it wasn't a stretch to think this was a personal attack.

"Were you able to get Sloane on this?" Cunningham asked.

"Yes. In fact, I'm meeting him this morning at Quantico before one of his classes." Then Tully remembered the impression he and Ganza found on the envelope. If it was personal maybe the message meant something to Cunningham. "Sir, do you know anyone named Nathan who might be involved in this?"

"Nathan?"

"We found a surface impression on the envelope that was

in the doughnut box. The message was, call Nathan at seven o'clock."

There was silence and this time Tully knew just to wait it out.

"My daughter's name is Catherine," Cunningham said and Tully heard a hint of alarm. "We call her Cather. Her mother loves Willa Cather. Any chance the impression spelled out Cather instead of Nathan?"

If Cunningham thought this was personal, Tully understood exactly what he was thinking, but he was trying too hard to make the pieces fit the puzzle. Tully remembered the blow-up image of the envelope and the impression. Under magnification it was quite clear.

"No, sir. I'm certain it was Nathan." He heard the exhale, the gasp of relief before Cunningham could disguise it. "Is there anything else Ganza and I should be looking for, sir?" Tully asked. Did Cunningham know something he wasn't sharing?

"Nothing except…" Cunningham started. "It's just a gut feeling. I don't think this is his only crime scene. There are others or there are going to be others."

Tully wrote down a phone number Cunningham gave him, a direct line to his hospital suite at USAMRIID. He promised he'd call him as soon as he knew anything more. Before he closed his cell phone Tully noticed the pink envelope in the corner, a voice message had come in while he was talking to Cunningham. It was Gwen. She said she'd had a mysterious message from Maggie and couldn't get hold of her. What was up? She also reminded him that they were supposed to have dinner that evening.

Tully thought for sure Maggie would have already talked to Gwen. Now he'd really be in trouble for not calling. Nothing would be a good enough excuse. To make matters worse, in her message Gwen had offered to bring over a pizza that evening for their dinner. She had been hinting for weeks about an invitation to his "cave." If he was already in trouble for not calling, perhaps giving in to this little concession would absolve him.

He looked around the living room: shoes left in the middle of the room; mail and dirty glassware scattered on the coffee table; stacks of newspapers and dust competing for surface space. He winced at it all as he started to dial Gwen's number.

At that moment Emma stumbled in, with Harvey leading the way to the back door. Her hair was tangled, her pajamas wrinkled, her eyes were swollen and half-closed as if she hadn't gotten any sleep. And suddenly the dust didn't seem so bad. What was worse for Tully was that his daughter and the woman he was dating would be in the same house, in the same room.

CHAPTER
36

Every time Colonel Benjamin Platt entered a hot-zone suite he was taken aback by how ordinary it looked. On the outside of the thick steel air-lock door it certainly gave the impression of entering something extraordinary, with the bright red biohazard symbol accompanied by DO NOT ENTER WITHOUT WEARING VENTILATION SUIT. The ID code looked like a digital keypad that could be a prelude to a flight deck. Entry required tapping in the correct code and going through a long list of procedures that when done correctly rewarded you with a voice and flashing green light that indicated YOU ARE CLEARED TO ENTER. All of this, including the gasp of air released from the lock, would insinuate something spectacular existed on the other side. And although the stark and sterile room should have been a letdown, Platt always felt a sense of reverence when he entered.

Yellow air hoses snaked out of white walls that were painted like a Jackson Pollock exhibit, thick clumps of epoxy splattered haphazardly. Similar gobs of white bulged around outlets and plugs, sealing any cracks. A strobe light hung from the ceiling, an alarm that automatically was triggered if the air system failed. Metal cabinets lined one wall, a long counter on another, and a third was a viewing glass to the outside world.

Platt grabbed one of the yellow cords and plugged in his suit. Immediately the roar of air filled his helmet and his ears. McCathy had barely looked up at him, not willing to take his attention from the work his double-gloved hands were finishing. He had prepared four glass slides and had four microscopes, side by side, ready to view each individually.

Finally looking up, McCathy waved Platt over next to him. He placed each slide in its respective slot. Then he checked with a glance down the eyepiece of each microscope, giving a twist, sometimes two twists, to focus.

"FROM LEFT TO RIGHT," McCathy yelled over the noise as he stood back. Platt could see the sweat on the older man's face, fogging up the inside of his helmet. McCathy pushed the plastic against his face, leaving a smear but it didn't distract him. He pointed to each of the microscopes. "EBOLA RESTON, LASSA, MARBURG AND EBOLA ZAIRE."

Platt nodded. McCathy had put the viruses in order from best-case scenario to worst-case. As much as Platt hoped it was Ebola Reston he knew that wouldn't explain why Ms. Kellerman's body was crashing.

"I'LL NEED TO HIT THE LIGHTS," McCathy told Platt, holding up a remote-control device. "IT'LL BE BLACK AS NIGHT IN HERE. WE CAN'T RISK BUMPING INTO EACH OTHER."

Platt nodded again. His heart was back to banging in his chest, almost louder than the air pressure in his ears. It wasn't the impending dark that caused the banging, although he knew better scientists than himself who would never attempt the combination of claustrophobia, darkness and a hot zone.

"YOU STAND THERE AND LOOK IN THOSE TWO MICROSCOPES." McCathy pointed at the two directly in front of Platt. "I'LL TAKE THESE TWO. THEN WE WON'T BE RUNNING INTO EACH OTHER."

Platt stared at the microscopes. McCathy would have Ebola Reston and Lassa fever. He had Marburg and Ebola Zaire. Don't let either of them glow. He would welcome total darkness.

"READY?" McCathy asked, holding up the light-switch remote.

Platt placed his hands on the edge of each microscope so he wouldn't fumble in the dark. He nodded again.

The room went pitch-black. There was nothing that emitted light. Not a red dot on a monitor. Not a crack of filtered light. Not a single reflection. He couldn't even see McCathy who stood right beside him.

He found the eyepiece of the first microscope and tried to look through. His faceplate made it difficult. He saw only black. And now his heartbeat pounded so hard he thought the vibration might be obscuring his view. The faceplate was flexible plastic and Platt pressed it down until he could feel the eyepiece of the microscope solidly against his eye sockets. Still, he could see nothing.

"ANYTHING?" McCathy yelled from beside him.

"NOTHING FROM THE FIRST ONE."

"NOTHING HERE."

Platt waited. Sometimes it took a few minutes for the serums to mix and cause a reaction. Still, there was nothing. He reminded himself: Marburg on the left, Ebola Zaire on the right. He pulled back, took a deep breath and positioned himself over the other microscope, repeating the process.

"NOTHING HERE," McCathy yelled about his second sample.

Platt barely positioned his faceplate and he could already see it. It wasn't a faint glow. It was bright. He sucked in air and shoved his eyes hard against the microscope. Below him it looked like a night sky with a glowing constellation.

"Holy crap," he muttered. He jerked his face away and found the other microscope. Nothing there. Back to the other. Still glowing, even brighter now.

"WHAT IS IT?" McCathy yelled.

"I'VE GOT ONE GLOWING."

"I KNEW IT. WHICH ONE?"

Platt had to stop himself. He had to slow his breathing. He needed to think. He needed to remember. Marburg, left. Ebola Zaire, right. The pounding in his heart was no longer a problem. It was as if all sound, everything around him had stopped, had come to a grinding halt. Everything except for his stomach, which slid to his feet.

"IT'S EBOLA ZAIRE."

CHAPTER
37

Saint Francis Hospital
Chicago

Dr. Claire Antonelli stared at the image of Markus Schroder's liver. On the desk in front of her were various other images and test documents. She had gone over all of them more than twice. The man behind her was seeing them for the first time and even he was quiet. In fact, Claire found it unsettling how quiet Dr. Jackson Miles had become.

She glanced back at him. His deep-creased face was a perpetual frown. She remembered him once calling his wrinkles "well-deserved life lines." He had those life lines for as long as Claire had known him, even back when he shepherded her through a tough residency, taking her under his wing when her all-male class made it clear that she was their outcast. Dr. Jackson Miles told her then that if he could become the first black chief of surgery then she could certainly overcome the discrimination she was dealing with.

"The liver's enlarged," she said, obviously only as a prompt.

"But otherwise doesn't look unusual." He didn't take his eyes off the image, studying it as if it was a puzzle. "What about typhoid or malaria?"

"I've had him on antibiotics with no effects. Not even a break in fever."

"E. coli or salmonella?"

"Not according to the blood tests," Claire said and released a sigh. These were questions she had already asked herself. Confirming or dismissing them out loud to her onetime mentor didn't make this any easier. "I thought perhaps a liver abscess or a gallbladder attack but the ultrasound doesn't seem to agree."

"Might not show it."

Claire watched Jackson Miles rub his jaw with a huge hand that always surprised her in surgery when it was able to delicately work through the smallest incisions.

"I've sent off for more extensive blood tests, but I'm not sure I can wait. He's becoming more and more unresponsive. I'm concerned he'll slip into a coma."

"Any chance he was exposed to something?"

"According to his wife even contracting malaria or typhoid is a stretch. At first I considered E. coli or anthrax. There was that farmer last year, remember who contracted anthrax somehow from his own cattle? Vera, Markus's wife, told me they make periodic visits to Indiana. A family business she still owns, though someone else runs it for her.

She said she hangs on to it for sentimental reasons." Claire stopped herself when she realized it sounded like she was rambling. Too much. It was too much information. She didn't need to go over everything out loud. "Markus works in Chicago as an accountant for a law firm."

"Anyone else at the law firm sick?"

"I've already thought of that, as well." Claire ran her fingers through her hair, trying to settle herself. She was operating on little sleep and cold pizza. The adrenaline high from seeing a healthy and happy Baby Haney had worn off. "There's someone out on maternity leave," she told him. "Another with a broken leg. No one with flulike symptoms."

"Do you think the wife would agree to exploratory surgery?"

"What are you thinking?"

"There may be something latched onto the liver or kidneys that's not showing up in the ultrasound."

"You'll do the surgery?" she asked and made sure it didn't sound like a student asking her mentor for a favor.

"Get the wife's approval." He nodded. "We'll both scrub up and take a look-see."

He made it sound so matter-of-fact that Claire could almost believe it'd be that easy. Then he patted her arm with his gentle bear paw of a hand, and smiled down at her.

"We'll do our best," he said, detecting her apprehension, her skepticism. "That's all we can do."

Claire hoped Markus and Vera Schroder would see it that way.

CHAPTER
38

The Slammer

The telephone on the wall startled Maggie again. She had been so engrossed in her Internet computer searches that she hadn't noticed someone come in and take a place by the window.

When she looked up, Platt's eyes were on her, so intense, so penetrating she didn't want to meet them. He knew something and it wasn't good news. She took her time, closing a file, signing off a site and all the while letting the phone ring and letting him stand there.

"Thanks for the computer," she said when she finally answered. "You're about to tell me I'm going to get a lot of use out of it, right?"

He just stared at her and she could see his jaw was clenched too tight, so tight that the muscles twitched.

"You're always trying to preempt me," he said, his expression remaining unchanged.

"Sorry, it's a habit. I'm usually the bearer of bad news. I'm not used to it being the other way around."

"Are you always this cynical?"

"I chase killers for a living."

"Awww…" He smiled, tilting his head back as if that were explanation enough. "You're used to throwing people in the slammer, not being in it yourself."

He pointed to her chair and started to sit in the one on his side, but stood back up and waited for her. She didn't want to sit. She'd rather take bad news standing up, or better yet, pacing. But he looked so exhausted. His freshly washed hair was still damp. Dark bags puffed out under his eyes. A white smear of something—soap perhaps—left on his chin, bright white against the stubble. And he had changed clothes, a William and Mary T-shirt and navy sweatpants. But the same white Nikes.

"So something tells me you didn't just get back from a leisurely jog?" she asked as she took her seat.

"No jog this morning." He followed suit but sat up straight when she thought he looked as though he'd rather slump down and stretch out like he had before.

"I may have found something," she told him only because she wasn't sure she wanted to hear his news yet. "I think this guy might be duplicating certain pieces of unsolved or old crimes."

"What makes you say that?" He looked curious but nothing more.

"I have a mailing envelope I found at the Kellerman house so I've been searching—"

"You removed evidence from a crime scene? A hot zone?" Now he was on the edge of his chair.

"I double-bagged it." When his brow stayed furrowed, she offered, "It was with me, on my person and inside here now, so I'd say it's as safely decontaminated as I am for the moment." She stared him down, didn't flinch. "Don't you want to know what I found?"

"You know I could charge you with obstructing a United States Army medical operation."

"Oh, sure. Go ahead. What are you going to do to me? Throw me in the Slammer?"

They stared each down again, gunslingers, neither willing to be the first to look away. Finally he did. His free hand went up to his face, fingers rubbing deep at tired eyes, and then they wiped down to his jaw, getting at the white smear; all the while he sank back into the hard plastic chair, but he kept the phone pressed to his ear.

"I'll need to process it," he finally said.

"It's yours."

Maybe he expected her to argue. Maybe he was simply tired.

"So what did you find?"

She explained it him, about the return address, about James Lewis and the Tylenol murders from September 1982, about Mary Kellerman and Mary Louise Kellerman, about the towns' names being almost the same and how this killer wanted the anniversary to be commemorated with a crash.

"What was in the envelope?" he asked.

"Nothing except an empty plastic bag with a zip lock. I didn't open it. It *is* evidence." She smiled at him. She was trying to make amends. He didn't seem to notice.

"Well, the Kellermans were definitely exposed to something," Platt said. "But it wasn't cyanide. I almost wish it were that simple."

"It's not a poison or a toxin?"

"No. It's not a poison." A slow shake of the head as if he wished it had been. "Not a toxin."

She waited.

"I know you have a medical background."

"Premed in college," she said. "It was a long time ago." He was making her a colleague so she'd understand his angst. Yet minutes ago he had treated her like an opponent, obstructing justice. Maybe it was simply his exhaustion. She hadn't slept, either. "Please just tell me," she said, the impatience slipping. "I don't need it candy coated but I don't need all the techbabble."

This time he took a deep breath. Sat forward again. His eyes never left hers.

"Ms. Kellerman has been exposed and her body has been invaded by a virus. It's been trying to replicate itself inside her. Inside her cells. Bricks of virus, splintering off, exploding the cell walls then moving through the bloodstream onto the next cell."

Maggie was sure she had stopped breathing at the word *virus*. She didn't need to hear more, but Platt continued.

"It's a parasite like one you hope to never see. A parasite searching for a perfect host." He stopped himself as if trying to find a better way to explain it. As if trying to remember something from long ago. "The biggest problem is that humans aren't a perfect host. They last maybe seven to twenty-one days. The virus almost always destroys them. Then it bleeds out. It spills out of them and looks for a new host to jump to."

"You sound like you've seen it before."

"That village I told you about, outside Sierra Leone. I held something similar in my gloved hands." He said it reverently, quietly, like a whisper or maybe a prayer.

"But you didn't get sick." Maggie hated that she sounded so hopeful when his face did not look it.

"That was Lassa fever. Also a Level 4 hot agent. Same family of viruses. But nothing like this."

She closed her eyes and sank back into the chair. She didn't wait for him this time. She didn't need to.

"It's Ebola, isn't it?" she asked as she kept her eyes closed and leaned her head back.

The phone's receiver stayed pressed against her ear so she could still hear him clearly. So she could hear him over the catch in her breathing, the ache in her chest, the slamming of her heart against her rib cage.

"Yes," he said. "It's Ebola Zaire."

CHAPTER
39

Wallingford, Connecticut

Artie enjoyed this part. He liked road trips even if they didn't take him to exotic places. He liked driving on interstates, being on the open road, lots of time with his thoughts. Some of his best ideas had come to him during his "drop-off" runs. He had even acquired a taste for truck-stop coffee and day-old doughnuts.

Today his mentor was letting him borrow his government-licensed SUV again. Artie had cleaned it, inside and out. He liked things a certain way. Worked hard to make sure everything was done with a plan, a routine and a dose of self-discipline. Probably the reasons he had been chosen.

Like his mentor he considered himself an encyclopedia of criminal behavior. Sort of an aficionado of true crime. He could appreciate the perfection, the thought process, the creative thinking and skills it took to get away with murder. That he cataloged a history of criminal cases and put them into his internal memory bank didn't seem odd at all. It just made him special. It made him perfect for this mission. And not knowing everything was part of the fun, part of the lesson to see how quickly he could put the puzzle pieces together. How else would he perfect his trade?

No, Artie didn't expect to have anything handed to him. He had never had much. Early on he learned to get by on patience, charm and an uncanny ability to remember details. And he was a quick study. Though he guessed even his mentor would be pleasantly surprised to find Artie joining in so quickly. He probably didn't think Artie would be this good.

Artie's instructions were simply to mail the packages as far away and as discreetly as possible. Artie chose carefully. He knew a lot of thought had gone into choosing the recipients and the senders, why not the drop-offs, as well? So Artie played his own game of tag with the FBI by having some fun, giving meaning to each cancellation on each package.

At first he had kept all his drop-offs closer to home. There were, after all, hundreds of mailboxes to choose from. Before this trip the farthest he had driven had been Murphy, North Carolina, several weeks ago. The package had been addressed to Rick Ragazzi in Pensacola, Florida, with the return address from a Victor Ragazzi in Atlanta. So why choose Murphy, North Carolina?

That one was a no-brainer for Artie. He thought he'd

throw the feds an easy one. There weren't that many "true-crime" connections to someplace like Murphy, North Carolina. Certainly the FBI would peg Murphy, especially since it was one of those cases they'd completely botched for years. They'd have to realize that Murphy was chosen because that's where Eric Rudolph had lived before going on the run. Rumor was the townsfolk had even protected him, misguided the feds and withheld information. But would the FBI get the joke? Would they appreciate his satirical twist? His goading? His subtle "catch me if you can"?

All Artie had to do was drop the package in a mailbox at the local post office so that it would have a cancellation from Murphy, North Carolina. As much as he had wanted to, he couldn't risk eating at the one restaurant in town that had infamously and blatantly advertised on their marquee, "Rudolph eats here." Instead, Artie had settled for a McDonald's quarter pounder once he got back on Interstate 95. Not a sacrifice at all. Artie loved McDonald's quarter pounders.

The trip to Murphy had been an eight-hour drive, one way, 460 miles. Wallingford would be twenty-nine miles less. However, Wallingford, as a chosen drop-off, had been tougher for Artie to put together and he knew it wouldn't be as obvious to his FBI adversaries, although it had been another case they'd botched for months.

He congratulated himself on this particular data retrieval in choosing this drop-off site. It was an ingenious and poignant example of random innocents getting caught in the cross fire. What the FBI or the military would call collateral damage. What Artie liked to call a "bonus kill." But would the feds even recognize it?

So why Wallingford, Connecticut? In the fall of 2001 there was a ninetysomething-year-old widow—okay, so he couldn't be expected to retrieve every detail like her exact age—who had been one of the anthrax killer's victims. Ottilie W. Lundgren lived in Oxford, Connecticut. She rarely left her home, and as far as anyone could determine, she hadn't been a direct target of the anthrax killer. Somehow her mail had unfortunately come in contact with anthrax-laced mail that had gone through the Southern Connecticut Processing and Distribution Center in Wallingford.

The FBI didn't find anthrax anywhere in her little house. But anthrax did show up in Seymour, Connecticut, about three miles away. Cross-contamination had been the final explanation. Authorities considered it a random and unfortunate incident. Family members called it "senseless." Artie thought that random and senseless were two things he didn't mind.

Now as Artie steered the SUV around a second reservoir he glanced at the Google map on the passenger seat. He must have gone the wrong direction. He had taken the Center Street exit off of Interstate 91. Certainly there was no post office out here.

He found a place to pull over. He didn't have time to sightsee, though the winding roads were inviting and the turning foliage sorta cool. What interested Artie even more was the fact that not far from here was a deserted rock quarry where bodies had been found in fifty-five-gallon drums. Bodies with missing pieces. Yes, it was difficult being a crime buff, being so close to a crime scene and not able to visit. He imagined it was no different than a Civil War buff being close to Gettysburg and wanting to just take a step onto those hollowed grounds.

Another time, perhaps. Artie turned the SUV around and headed in the other direction, this time easily finding where East Center became Center and then making his way to Main Street where he could see the post office. He turned into the driveway for the drop-off mailboxes. The SUV's tinted windows would obscure any cameras, if there were any. He grabbed the two packages off the floor.

Then he dropped them into the mailbox slot, one addressed to Benjamin Tasker Middle School in Bowie, Maryland, and the other addressed to Caroline Tully in Cleveland, Ohio.

CHAPTER
40

North Platte, Nebraska

Patsy Kowak looked forward to Saturdays. She'd pick up her daughter and the two of them would go into town for their book-club meeting. They usually met at the café. A corner table that fit all seven of them. The owner of the local bookstore, A to Z Books, offered recommendations, and for the last two years their club had read novels Patsy would have never chosen on her own. This week's selection was by a local author, a mystery writer named Patricia Bremmer. Patsy finished it in two days, partly thanks to Ward not talking to her. Maybe if the silence continued she'd get all kinds of things accomplished.

Only a week until the wedding. She had to admit she was excited, not just for her son and for the day, but to get away. As much as she loved her home and this ranch, she did enjoy a change of pace. It had been ages since she and Ward had been anywhere. Okay, so it was only Cleveland with a layover at O'Hare, but even Cleveland sounded exotic right now. And though there would be few family and friends able to make the trip from Nebraska, Conrad had told Patsy that they expected over two hundred people, mostly friends and colleagues. Patsy couldn't imagine even a pharmaceutical vice president and the CEO of an advertising agency having that many friends and colleagues. But Conrad was excited and happy and that's what was important. This woman made her Conrad happy like no other person had been able to.

Patsy ran a brush through her hair. It didn't look bad despite her habit of sometimes trimming chunks that didn't belong. It was a nervous habit, worse when she was under stress. In fact, Ward could always tell if she was having a bad day. Earlier in the week he had asked if her bangs were shorter. A simple yes made him nod and back off.

But now instead of her hair she noticed her hands. They were more red and chapped than usual from brushing down the horses and digging up the last of her vegetable garden. She traded the hairbrush for cuticle scissors and went after the ragged skin, trying to make her fingers more presentable but leaving one bleeding.

She hadn't had a professional manicure for ages but knew it was out of the question. Ward had already lectured her about running up their credit card. It was just another way for him to voice his complaints about the wedding since the only purchases she had made were a new dress and luggage for the trip. She refused to drag out the worn old set they had. It was ancient and didn't even have rollers. No wonder Conrad was convinced all his father thought about was money. Which reminded her. She didn't have any cash and wouldn't have time to stop at the bank.

She opened the bottom drawer to her dresser, uncovered the square box she used for loose change and trinkets. That was also where she had hidden the plastic bag with cash from Conrad. Ward would never go through Patsy's dresser drawers, so she knew it was safe there. She hadn't really intended to use the money. She could stop at the bank after the book-club meeting and replace it later. What harm could there be in using it and replacing it?

She opened the plastic bag, reached in and pulled out one of the twenty-dollar bills.

CHAPTER
41

Quantico, Virginia

Tully had heard him the first time. He didn't need George Sloane to inform him again that Tully and Ganza had "exactly fifteen minutes" before Sloane had to return to his class.

Tully watched the man make a ceremony of sitting down in front of the documents like a priest about to perform some sacred ritual. He played the role of professor very well, even dressed it—black knit turtleneck, tight enough to show off his trim physique, along with well-pressed trousers and matching suit jacket. He wasn't a big man, five-foot-seven. His strut into the room asked for but didn't quite command attention. He was Tully's age but had none of the salt-and-pepper Tully had been discovering at his own temples. Instead, Sloane's thick hair, that he wore long enough to curl over the turtleneck, was almost jet-black, and Tully suspected it was because of Grecian hair formula rather than youthful genes.

"The lighting is horrendous in here," Sloane announced in place of a greeting. "Does Cunningham expect me to work miracles?"

Tully wanted to say, "No, just your regular voodoo will do." Instead, he said what he knew would pacify the man and not waste their precious fifteen minutes. "We're just grateful you can take time out to help us, George. Anything you can offer will be appreciated."

"See if you can find me a better light," Sloane told Ganza, dismissing the director of the lab with a wave of his hand as if Ganza were one of his college students.

Ganza stared at Sloane's back for a second or two then glanced at Tully, who could only offer a shrug. Ganza checked his watch then pulled down the bill of his Red Sox cap and headed for the conference room's supply closet.

"So terrorists are delivering their threats at the bottom of doughnut boxes now?" Sloane said, scooting his chair closer to the table. "Where were you at the time?" he asked Tully. "If I remember correctly, you can't resist a chocolate doughnut."

"Stuck in traffic," Tully said, trying not to show his annoyance and impatience. Sloane had already used up five minutes fidgeting with his preparations.

"Thank God for morning rush hour, huh?"

Ganza hauled a long, metal contraption out of the storage closet that looked like something from a garage sale. He set it on the table beside Sloane.

"What the hell is this?" Sloane sat back as if the thing had accosted him.

Ganza ignored him. He unwrapped the cord, plugging it in and then snapping on the fluorescent lamp. It lit the area enough that even Sloane couldn't complain though he grumbled a bit before scooting his chair back into position.

He picked up the plastic bag with the envelope first, holding it up and examining it, pursing his lips and furrowing his brow. Tully couldn't help thinking of Johnny Carson's Carnac the Magnificent.

"Uppercase," Sloane mumbled under his breath like it was exactly what he had expected. "Every maniac from the Unabomber to the Zodiac killer used uppercase printing. In everyday life few people print entire words and phrases in uppercase, so it's more difficult to match."

"So it's easier to disguise their handwriting," Ganza said from his perch standing over Sloane's left shoulder.

"That's what I just said. If you already know all this why did Cunningham call me in?"

Tully watched from across the room as the two men exchanged glares. Ganza was totally harmless, definitely not the type who engaged in pissing contests. He was a professional, and he was actually a bit of an introvert. Perhaps George Sloane brought out the worst in everyone.

When Sloane seemed satisfied that Ganza would no longer interrupt he sat up even taller in the chair.

"It's not just about disguising his handwriting," Sloane continued. "Uppercase gives an appearance of urgency to the message. He's shouting it. But see here," and Sloane held up the plastic-encased envelope and pointed. "He pushed down harder on the periods after Mr. and F.B.I. He's taken time to carefully print out the message, letter by letter, but those periods almost poke through the paper. He's revealing a bit of emotion there."

"Yeah, what's up with him putting periods after each letter of FBI?" Ganza wanted to know while Tully wanted to wince. Didn't Ganza get it, that he was supposed to be quiet and this would take less time. Be less painful. Tully waited for Sloane's look of simmered annoyance and wasn't disappointed. Ganza, however, seemed oblivious to it.

"He obviously doesn't consider it an acronym," Sloane slowly said and now he enunciated each word as though he were speaking to a foreigner. "To him it's the Federal Bureau of Investigation."

"So maybe it's somebody who's fed up with the feds?" Ganza persisted.

Sloane glared at the lab director instead of offering a response. He put the envelope aside, glanced at his wristwatch and picked up the second plastic bag.

"The note's open," Tully told him, "but it had been folded to fit the envelope. You can see from the creases it was—"

"A pharmaceutical fold," Sloane finished for him. He looked up at Tully with thick eyebrows raised. "Your people still opened it when it was folded like this inside the envelope?"

"The envelope hadn't been sealed." Tully tried not to

make it sound like he was being defensive despite Sloane's accusation and the man's continued glare. Tully hadn't even been the one to open it and yet he was feeling the need to explain. Maybe it was something that came with the professorship—a superior aura that made everyone else feel like an underling student. "There was nothing inside," he finally said without adding what he wanted to say, that Cunningham was the one who opened it. He knew that would sound childish.

As if on cue Sloane pursed his lips again, reminding Tully of a pouting child. He glanced at his watch.

"Come on, George," Tully said, "we already know this has all the markings of a remote-control killer. This guy might be getting ready to send another of his special deliveries. What can you tell us about him? Are we going to find him holed up in some backwoods cabin or in a suburban garage?"

Sloane sat back and crossed his arms over his chest.

"He won't be holed up in a cabin," he said with what sounded like a snort at the end to tell Tully what he thought of his two-cents' worth. "Nor is he someone in the pharmaceutical business. He may have simply done his homework. The anthrax killer in fall of 2001 used that same fold. I'd say he has it right down to the quarter-inch sides."

"You were brought in on that case?" Ganza asked.

"Who do you think told them to start looking stateside at our own labs and scientists and not at some Muslim living in an Afghanistan cave?" Sloane fidgeted in his chair. "Though I shouldn't be surprised you wouldn't know that. No one hands out much praise around here, do they?" He hesitated, looking as if he was considering whether to share more. "Not that it matters," he said, waving the plastic bag. "You FBI guys believe what you want to believe, like your profile for the Beltway Sniper. You guys stuck to that generic description of a young, white male, a loner in a white paneled van. Never had a clue, did you, that it might be two black guys in a muscle car."

"I wasn't in D.C. then," Tully said.

"Oh, right. You were still in Cincinnati."

"Cleveland."

"Sorry, my mistake." But he didn't sound sorry. He brought the note up close and read it out loud with a sort of bellow like a sports announcer:

"'CALL ME GOD.
THERE WILL BE A CRASH TODAY.
At 13949 ELK GROVE
10:00 A.M.
I'D HATE FOR YOU TO MISS IT.
I AM GOD.
P.S. YOUR CHILDREN ARE NOT SAFE ANYWHERE AT ANY TIME.'"

Then Sloane put the plastic bag down on the table and pushed his chair back, letting it screech across the linoleum. Ganza and Tully waited and watched.

"He's smart," Sloane said without looking up at them.

"Not only smart, but well educated. He's precise and detail oriented. He wants you to believe that all of this may be religious based, but I think he uses his references to God much more literally. He simply thinks he's superior to you. Even using the pharmaceutical folds is sort of a ploy, a..." Sloane waved his hand around and Tully thought of a preacher emphasizing points of his sermon. "He's playing you, wanting to throw you off."

Then the professor shrugged and stood up, signaling he couldn't tell them any more. But still, he continued, "His choice of ten o'clock may be significant. The address or the numbers in the address may be significant. There's no way for me to tell you that without more information."

"What's your best guess?" Tully asked and watched Sloane wince.

"Guess? Is that what you call *your* profiles? Because I certainly don't call mine guesses."

Tully held back a sigh of frustration. Sloane looked from Ganza to Tully like he was deciding whether or not to take pity on them.

"My best *guess*—" he dragged out the word until the *s*'s sizzled "—is that he could be an insider. Maybe you start looking at research labs again. The anthrax killer was never caught. He wouldn't be the first guy to come back out for some attention. Some killers can't stand it. Look at the BTK killer. Nobody would have caught that guy had he not gotten greedy for more attention."

"Maybe this means something to you," Tully said, and he

pulled out a photo of the indentation they'd found. He handed it to Sloane. "We lifted this from the envelope."

Sloane took it and held it up to the light, a smile starting at the corner of his lips. If Tully wasn't mistaken it looked like they might have actually impressed the professor.

"Son of a bitch," he said. "You guys found this, huh?"

CHAPTER
42

The Slammer

It was long past breakfast by the time they brought in a tray for Maggie. By now food was the last thing on her mind. She picked at the eggs, ate half the wheat toast, took two sips of orange juice and left the rest. There was a weight on her chest making it uncomfortable to breathe, like something heavy was sitting on top of her, pressing hard against her rib cage. Even swallowing became a conscious effort. She caught herself listening to her own heartbeat. She put two fingers on the pulse point at her throat. Did she expect to feel or hear the virus multiplying inside her? Is that what the extra weight was?

Colonel Platt had asked if there was anyone she wanted to call or perhaps anyone she needed him to call for her. Off the top of her head she couldn't think of a single person.

Maybe Gwen. Certainly not Nick Morrelli. Probably not her stepbrother who she had only just met within the last year. How would that conversation go?

"Hey, bro, guess what? I've been quarantined with a highly infectious virus. Might not be able to do that first Thanksgiving get-together after all."

And she wouldn't call her mother. Somehow her mother would find a way to make this about her with little or no regard about the impact it had on Maggie.

"But Mom," Maggie could hear the exchange in her mind, "I'm the one dying from a deadly virus."

"And how am I supposed to explain that to anyone?" That would be her mother's response but only after first asking if it was contagious.

No, Maggie had no one. No close family members. No significant other. No one on her first-to-call list. And no one for whom she was a first-to-call. When she divorced Greg the exhaustion of that relationship had left her with more relief than regret. They had gotten married in college. He had been a sort of security blanket for her, an attempt at normalcy, a chance to have a real family. That was until he wanted to tear her away from the one thing, the only thing that had ever given her a true sense of being—her identity, her career at the FBI.

She left that relationship, bruised but relieved. But she also left believing she'd never find anyone who would accept what she did for a living or, more importantly, that it would always be her first priority. Adam Bonzado and Nick Morrelli included. Of course, through no fault of their own. Maggie hadn't quite let anyone into her life long enough or deep enough to give them a real chance. She knew that she was to blame, not them. Maybe she had taken that lesson from her mentor, from A.D. Cunningham, a bit too far. It wasn't something she wanted to share with Colonel Platt. So when he offered to call someone, she simply shook her head.

Colonel Platt had gone on to tell her a number of things. Some of them now a blur. He explained that the virus had not shown up in her blood...*yet*. He added that last word like a lead anchor. He told her about an incubation period. He wasn't gentle with her. He gave it to her straight just like she'd asked.

Be careful what you ask for, she reminded herself.

She knew a little about these viruses. She knew that even if she didn't show any signs now, it didn't mean that it wasn't already in her system, lying dormant, silently waiting.

When Colonel Platt left, Maggie sat staring at the wall of glass, watching the monitors on the other side, listening to their hums and beeps. It all seemed unreal, something totally out of *The Twilight Zone,* indeed. She wasn't sure how long she had sat like that when finally she pulled herself together.

She kept hearing Platt's explanation. He had afforded her too many details, probably thinking that her medical background provided her some sort of safety net of understanding. Knowledge did not necessarily always equal power or control. Instead, it sometimes had the opposite effect. Especially in this case where the more she understood about the virus, how absolutely powerful and unstoppable it was, the more vulnerable she began to feel.

Platt had left her with just enough details to keep her heart racing. And his questions ran on a loop through her brain:

"Did you touch Ms. Kellerman? Did you come in contact with any of her blood? Her bedsheets? Did you touch Mary Louise? Did she take your hand? Did her vomit get on your face? Your eyes? Your mouth?"

Maggie knew some of the little girl's vomit had splattered her jacket, but she didn't think it had gotten on her face. But Cunningham? Maggie remembered him wiping his face. He was holding Mary Louise when she threw up. Cunningham had taken the little girl to the bathroom to help her wash up, ordering Maggie to stay put.

And what about Mary Louise, that beautiful little girl, crawling onto her mother's bloody bedsheets, living amongst the ruins for how many days?

That's when Maggie remembered the line from the note: YOUR CHILDREN ARE NOT SAFE ANYWHERE AT ANY TIME.

The words fit his purpose just as Mary Louise and her mother did by sharing the same name and partial address as one of the victims in the Tylenol case. But Maggie knew these particular words were not his. She suspected they had been copied, too. He had pulled that line from somewhere else but where?

She went back to the computer. She sat down but hesitated. She ran her fingers through her hair and realized her hands were shaking. She sat and waited for them to settle, for the sudden nausea to pass, for the pounding in her head to quiet. None of it did. She needed to ignore the swelling panic, push it aside. She had done it before. She could do it again, at least long enough to retreat, to escape, to work.

She went back to Google, and with fingers still a bit unsteady she typed in the phrase, exactly as she remembered it: YOUR CHILDREN ARE NOT SAFE ANYWHERE AT ANY TIME.

Immediately her answer came up in a dozen different sites. She couldn't believe it. There on her computer screen, staring right back at her were the exact same words. They had also been used as a postscript on another note. Why hadn't she recognized it earlier?

There were other phrases, other duplicates: "I AM GOD" and "CALL ME GOD." Instead of "MR. F.B.I. MAN" was a close substitute: "FOR YOU MR. POLICE."

And just as she suspected, the phrases had all been lifted from notes and messages of another killer, actually a pair of killers. They were phrases used by the Beltway Snipers, John Muhammad and Lee Malvo in October 2002.

CHAPTER
43

USAMRIID

Platt would have preferred to put off talking to Janklow until Monday. The commander had put him in charge of this mission and yet he appeared to be watching over Platt's shoulder every step of the way. How else could he explain yet another message, another order this soon? Platt had barely checked in on his four patients and already the commander was summoning him to his office. He suspected McCathy probably alerted Janklow the minute he saw worms through the microscope, probably even before he had called Platt.

The commander's office door was left open, his secretary gone, reminding Platt that it was Saturday. He found Janklow in his office, standing at the window, looking out. Only then did Platt see that it was raining. The window framed a dreary gray day punctuated by gold and red splotches of swirling color. When had the leaves started to turn? In the last twenty-four hours he had lost all sense of time, of season.

"Colonel Platt." Janklow glanced at him then back out the window, as if not quite ready.

"Yes, sir," Platt said then simply waited.

He had been running on adrenaline for the last several hours. Janklow had the benefit of a night's sleep. Platt had been through this sort of thing with other superior officers. He expected Janklow to remind him that he had entrusted him with this very important mission and he was counting on him not just to take care of it but to take responsibility for it, as well. In other words make sure Platt understood that if and when something went wrong or leaked to the media, Platt alone would be the one to take the fall.

He kept his hands at his sides when instinct told him to dig the exhaustion out of his eyes. He wiped at his jaw to make sure there wasn't any leftover milk. He had convinced Mary Louise Kellerman to eat her breakfast only after making a special event of it, an event that included him joining her for Froot Loops.

Despite the glass wall separating them the little girl insisted they count out and eat all the yellow ones first. It had actually been a welcome reprieve—though a bit of a surreal one. One minute he was in a hot zone staring at twisted loops and ropes of virus, one of the deadliest viruses on earth, and the next minute he was eating Froot Loops with a five-year-old. He couldn't help thinking of Alice in Wonderland sitting down to tea with the Mad Hatter.

"So it's much worse," Janklow said suddenly without turning or looking at Platt. A good thing. His voice startled Platt back to attention. Strange as it might be, he'd give anything to be back with Mary Louise, playing the Mad Hatter and eating cereal with milk than here explaining any of this to Janklow.

"Yes, sir," he said. He figured Janklow was expecting a summary of Platt's strategy, so he started with the basics. "We still have the Kellerman home contained and under guard."

"Plainclothes guard?"

"Yes, sir. Construction crew with public-utility vehicles. CDC can handle contacting anyone who may have come in contact with the Kellermans. We can start administering the vaccine immediately. I ordered—"

"You haven't already contacted the CDC, have you?" Janklow spun all the way around to look at Platt.

"No, not yet."

The commander nodded and placed his hands behind his back. Platt recognized the gesture as guarded satisfaction. Janklow walked to his desk in the middle of the room, hands still clasped at his lower back, chin tucked down on his chest. Platt knew to wait. Janklow would instruct him to continue when he was ready again.

"Right now these four people you have here in the Slammer are the only ones we know of who have been exposed. Is that correct?" Janklow asked.

"Yes, sir."

"A mother, a child and two government employees, correct?"

"FBI Assistant Director Cunningham and one of his special agents."

"I understand the mother is in the final stages?"

Platt hated to admit it but said, "Yes, it looks that way. Her kidneys have begun to fail. We have her on—"

Janklow held up a hand to stop him. Platt hated the gesture but hesitated as ordered. "She won't make it," Janklow said as matter-of-factly as though they were talking about the stock market. "Isn't that correct?"

Platt had spent the night doing everything possible. As a doctor he wasn't ready to admit failure.

"Most likely that's correct," he agreed. "However, I have seen cases—"

The hand went up again. This time Platt had to stifle a frustrated sigh.

Janklow paced from his desk to the window, hands clasped, chin still resting on his chest, perhaps his own version of Rodin's *The Thinker*. From what Platt knew of Janklow's career, this was bigger than anything he had faced and probably the most pivotal battle he'd ever face. The man didn't look panicked or tortured by the challenge. Instead, Platt thought he looked calm, too calm, like a man calculating whether to buy, sell or hold his investments.

"McCathy tells me that this virus jumps easily from host to host," Janklow said, continuing his leisurely pace without looking at Platt, almost as if he were presenting a lecture on the topic. "That it's been known to destroy entire villages in Africa."

So Platt's suspicions were correct. McCathy and Janklow had spent time chatting about all this. So much for chain of command.

"McCathy says it would take as little as a microscopic piece, preserved, sealed and delivered, perhaps even through the mail, to start an epidemic. Something like this," Janklow said, "could start a mass panic."

Platt didn't disagree and waited for what he expected to be instructions on media containment. He didn't, however, expect what Commander Janklow said next.

"What if they all disappeared?"

At first he wasn't sure he had heard the commander right.

"Excuse me?"

"There's only four now. Two are most likely doomed," Janklow said, stopping now in front of Platt. "You said so yourself that the mother won't make it. The daughter certainly couldn't have spent that many days in the same house and not have the virus."

Platt tried to conceal his surprise. Janklow mistook it for confusion, because he continued, "We make them comfortable, give them supportive care. Let the virus burn itself out."

"What about the vaccine?"

"It's never been proven to be a deterrent let alone a cure. Why risk it not working?"

"How can we afford not to take that risk, sir?"

"You're thinking like a doctor, Colonel Platt. When you

must think like a soldier. Must I remind you your mission is to contain and isolate? You let this virus burn itself out so there's no possibility of it lying dormant, hidden by the guise of a vaccine that may or may not work." He avoided looking at Platt when he added, "No one even knows they're here."

"We're talking about the FBI," Platt said, swallowing hard over a lump that seemed to appear inside his throat. He still couldn't believe what Janklow was suggesting. Platt was tired. The adrenaline rush had left his body drained and his mind foggy. Perhaps he misunderstood what the commander was proposing.

"The FBI," Janklow snorted like it made no difference. His chin was back on his chest in his best thinking spot. "FBI— they're government employees, same as us. Sometimes sacrifices have to be made…" He glanced back at Platt. "For the greater good. In war zones…and hot zones."

Then he marched to the window and took up his stance, exactly where and how Platt had found him.

Platt waited, hoping if he was patient enough Janklow would retract what he had just suggested. What he was suggesting was that they let the virus run its course inside Ms. Kellerman and her daughter as well as A.D. Cunningham and Agent O'Dell.

In other words, Commander Janklow was proposing they allow them all to crash and bleed out.

CHAPTER
44

Chicago
Saint Francis Hospital

It had been years since Dr. Claire Antonelli had scrubbed up alongside chief of surgery Dr. Jackson Miles. Ever since she started her own private practice her hospital visits were limited to visiting recovering patients and delivering a baby now and then. She wasn't a surgeon. She recognized her limitations and appreciated her strengths. An exploratory laparotomy was not one of her strengths.

Vera Schroder had not been pleased. Her husband had never had surgery in his life, had never spent a night in the hospital until now.

"Markus takes very good care of himself," she had told Claire, offering it as further reason that all of this had to be some horrible mistake.

"He has an infection somewhere in his body," Claire had tried to calmly explain to Vera while right next to them Markus stared out with red eyes and unblinking but droopy eyelids. In just two days his face had taken on an expressionless mask, the facial muscles drooped as if the tissue was disconnecting. There was little indication that he was listening to them. Claire worried that he had already started slipping away.

To make matters worse, Vera answered all the questions, not waiting for her husband. She touched his hand and swept his thin hair from his forehead, not expecting him to respond to the questions or to her touch. Claire had noticed early on that even when Markus had been alert and lucid this was the relationship between the two—Vera did the talking, the gesturing, the patting and caressing while Markus simply stood or sat by.

"There may be an inflammation or an abscess," Claire had persisted. "Perhaps even a perforation in the intestine that isn't showing up on our tests."

"You think it's cancer, don't you?" Vera had asked in a whisper.

Claire had never believed in being anything less than straightforward with her patients. She didn't want to alarm Vera Schroder, but she wouldn't sugarcoat it, either. She told her they weren't ruling out anything. They simply needed a better picture of what might be going on inside Markus. Finally Vera had no comeback. She wanted her husband back home. She wanted things back to normal.

Now Claire watched Dr. Miles make the abdominal incision and she hoped they would find an answer, *the* answer, something that could explain why a perfectly healthy forty-five-year-old man had suddenly turned into a vomiting and feverish zombie.

"We'll do a checklist," Dr. Miles said without looking up, his large fingers gentle and confident. "We'll start with the gallbladder, appendix, pancreas, liver."

His voice was deep, calm, smooth and reassuring. Claire was reminded of the image she had of him when she was a resident, the image that they all had of him. He was a larger-than-life father figure and even his voice was like that of God's. If Dr. Jackson Miles couldn't find what was wrong with Markus Schroder, then no one could.

"Pancreas looks normal," he continued. "There doesn't appear to be anything taking a ride on it."

Claire dabbed sponge laps at the blood while Miles's surgical nurse, a young Asian man named Urie, readjusted the suction. Blood continued to ooze up. More dabs from Claire. Urie applied clotting gel. Another small, wiry nurse reached up on tiptoe and swiped the sweat from Miles's brow. He added a hemo clip to the incision. Then he added another.

The incision filled up with blood again.

Usually during surgery the blood vessels the surgeon cuts through will clot up. Additional bleeding can be clamped off or gelled to stop. Periodically the wound and incision need to be suctioned. But that wasn't the case here. Something was very wrong.

Miles waited for Claire to dab again, but her sponges became soaked with blood faster than she could change them out. Same for Urie. As soon as he would apply more clotting gel, the blood would overtake the application. The other nurse added her hands, dabbing and collecting blood-soaked sponges. Even the anesthesiologist looked ready to jump in.

Miles's eyes met Claire's, avoiding the rest of the surgical team. There was a flicker of uncertainty that she had never seen before. Claire found herself thinking, *It's like seeing God worried*. Recognizing the alarm in Miles's face made her stomach take a brief plunge.

Urie suctioned off more blood while Miles tried to pinch off the blood vessels with another clamp. Claire continued to soak sponge laps. Nothing seemed to work. Markus Schroder's abdomen continue to fill up with blood. Claire couldn't help thinking it was like scooping sand out of a hole in the beach. As soon as you pulled up a handful the sand walls caved in, filling the hole as quickly as you could dig.

"This isn't good," Miles finally said. "Let me cut a piece of tissue then let's get out of here."

He did the biopsy quickly, which was amazing to Claire, who could no longer differentiate anything through all the blood. Miles handed the sample off to the nurse. Then he and Claire began closing up, suturing quickly as Urie suctioned and dabbed.

Finally finished, the entire team of six stood back and exchanged looks. No one said anything. Claire could feel the sweat trickle down her back as she watched a stream slide down Miles's face. At one point his black eyes held Claire's and there was as much question and concern as there was alarm.

Urie was the one who broke the silence. "That dude's got some serious problems."

CHAPTER
45

The Slammer

When the telephone rang this time, Maggie wanted to wave it away. She kept her head bent, her eyes focused on the computer screen. As long as she lived inside that computer screen she didn't have to remember the room was only sixteen paces wide and fourteen paces deep. She didn't have to remember that the virus might be silently duplicating itself inside her body. Diving into her work had always helped her push aside her emotions, helped her to compartmentalize the stress, the chaos, the throbbing inside her chest. It would work. It could work, if that stupid phone would stop ringing.

After a half-dozen rings she finally looked up, more annoyed than resolved.

When she saw the woman on the other side of the glass

Maggie slid back her chair and stared. Finally she realized she was holding her breath, afraid she was hallucinating. If she attempted to breathe, if she moved, would the image disappear?

She stood up. Took a quick swipe at her eyes, pretending they were tired and not moist with emotion.

This was ridiculous.

Twenty-four hours in this place and she was already letting it get the best of her. She left the sanctuary of the computer and snatched up the telephone receiver off the wall.

"Hey, kiddo," Gwen Patterson said with a smile that couldn't hide her concern.

The petite strawberry-blonde wore a black power suit, her makeup impeccable, never mind that it was Saturday. To the Army scientists that peopled USAMRIID she probably looked like a Wall Street power broker. To Maggie she looked like a lifeline and she found it difficult swallowing, the carefully compartmentalized emotion was now stuck in her throat. She could barely get out a simple response.

"How in the world did you get in here?"

"Are you joking? I'm the psychologist of choice to half the Army colonels in the District."

Maggie laughed…hard. It felt good. But she knew Gwen wasn't exactly joking. She did have a client list that included members of congress, senators and even colonels.

"God, it's good to see you," Maggie said with a sigh that ended up more a gasp for air. She didn't care that it sounded needy, not with Gwen, only with Gwen.

"Have you been able to get any sleep?" Gwen put her hand up against the glass as though she could recognize that Maggie needed at least the gesture of a touch. "What about food?"

Maggie smiled.

"Seriously, have you eaten? Is there anything you need?"

Maggie shook her head thinking, *ever the mother hen*. Gwen Patterson was fifteen years Maggie's senior and sometimes it showed up in their friendship.

Finally Gwen waved her hand for Maggie to sit down. Gwen sat in the plastic chair on her side of the glass at the same time that Maggie dropped into her own. Again, Maggie wiped at her eyes. Damn it. She would not cry. Funny how four walls behind a steel air-lock door had a way of shoving all your emotions to the edge and then pricking at them over and over again.

"You got my message. You talked to Tully," Maggie said.

"He should have called me last night."

"Don't be too hard on him," Maggie told her friend. "Cunningham and I missed this one. We should have seen it."

"Okay, so tell me everything," Gwen said, sitting back and crossing her legs as if they were back at Old Ebbitt Grill, their favorite hangout, getting ready for one of their chats. "And don't leave anything out."

CHAPTER
46

USAMRIID

Colonel Benjamin Platt couldn't be sure how long he had been sitting in his own office with the door shut and the lights off. He sat staring out his window, a much smaller version of the commander's, and he watched the wet gray daylight dissolve into blue twilight. Earlier he had leaned his head back and closed his eyes, waiting and hoping to silence the steady hum inside his brain. He needed to rest his eyes, rest his body and his mind for just a few minutes.

The exhaustion played games with him. Pieces of memories kept flicking images on the backside of his eyelids. Ali cuddling the white Westie puppy. Ali in her favorite white summer dress. She looked like a little angel. And just as quickly the image flashed to Ali with mud all over her, a huge grin on her dirt-smudged face and her hands presenting him with the ugliest frog he'd ever seen. "Daddy, look what Digger and I found."

The sudden tightness in his chest made his eyes fly open. He jerked forward, sitting upright in his chair. His hands clutched the edge of his desk, white-knuckled and fisted like he needed to hang on or else he'd fall.

He'd joined the Army as a means to help pay for medical school. But he believed, he truly believed in every mission. Patriotism was not just a trigger word for him. He respected authority. He understood honor. He appreciated discipline. And he had never disobeyed a direct order. He hadn't even considered it...not before today.

He got up now and started pacing, his nervous energy sidelining the exhaustion. In one pass by his desk he flipped on a lamp and continued by. He had to stop and think what day it was. How many hours had passed since he and McCathy removed the Kellermans from their home?

Twenty-four hours? Thirty-six hours?

It felt like a week. And then he tried to clear his mind. He needed to focus.

What had Janklow said...exactly? What words had he used?

Janklow had said, "What if?" Platt was certain those were the commander's exact words.

"What if" did not sound like an order.

When it came right down to it, Platt knew he would be the one held accountable for this mission whether he followed Janklow's suggestions or recommendations. If all of this ended up in a court-martial it would be Platt's neck and career, not Janklow's. The age-old defense "I was only following orders" hadn't saved any soldiers lately.

Platt needed to make a decision. If he was careful he could override Janklow before the commander even realized it. And if he was smart Platt would to find a way to make it impossible for Janklow to reveal what his original orders—or suggested orders—had been.

Platt tried to remember everything he knew about the vaccine. He knew the report, although it had been almost a year since he had read it. The vaccine had only been tested on macaque monkeys. The most important thing was that it depended on how quickly after exposure the monkeys received the vaccine. Thirty minutes after exposure the vaccine protected ninety percent of the monkeys. Twenty-four hours after exposure there was a fifty-percent survival rate.

The FDA hadn't approved the vaccine's use, not yet, except in the case of lab accidents with scientists. Fortunately, accidents with Ebola were rare. Unfortunately, because of that, there wasn't enough data about the vaccine's use on humans. Even if Platt decided to use it now, especially on civilians, it would require something called an emergency "compassionate use" permit from the FDA.

He glanced at his watch—a knee-jerk reaction.

He was already looking at thirty-six-plus hours after exposure for two of his patients. Several days for the other two. He couldn't afford to wait out the time that the FDA would take just to consider his request for emergency use.

Platt stopped his pacing and stood in front of the window, but he paid little attention to the darkness outside, swallowing the last bits and pieces of twilight.

Access to the vaccine wouldn't be a problem. He had it right here, a couple stories above him. And they had plenty of it available because USAMRIID had been one of the research facilities involved in its development.

He sat back down, the exhaustion weighting him down. He planted his elbows on the desk. He rubbed at his temples and moved his fingers to his eyes. The humming was still there inside his head.

He glanced at his watch again. And then he decided. "What if?" was not a direct order. Janklow had worded it precisely the way he wanted to word it. He wanted to put Platt in the position of making the decision.

His decision.

It was clear to him what he needed to do. And what was also clear was that he would not include, consult or inform McCathy.

CHAPTER
47

The Slammer

Maggie hated the panic that now crept into her friend's eyes. She had known Gwen Patterson too long for Gwen to use her professional-psychiatrist tricks on her.

"It's a good sign," Gwen said, keeping her voice level, her mood optimistic, apparently unaware that her eyes were betraying her. "Colonel Platt said it isn't showing up in your blood."

"Yet," Maggie added. "He said it hasn't shown up yet."

"From what I know about these viruses they work quickly."

"Or they can remain dormant inside a host."

"You're strong and healthy. You said you haven't felt sick."

"The first symptoms can be subtle, almost like having the flu."

"You said the little girl didn't even throw up on you."

"My sleeve. I think there was some vomit on my sleeve." Maggie tried to smile as she pulled at the ribbing on her blue hospital gown. "I had to exchange my clothes for the Slammer's latest fashion trend."

"That's not enough." Gwen's voice hitched. She saw that Maggie noticed. She readjusted herself on the plastic chair. Recrossed her legs, smoothed her skirt, switched the telephone receiver from right ear to left ear as if repositioning herself might make her stronger. "On your sleeve, that's not enough. It's passed through blood."

"Any body fluids," Maggie corrected.

"Okay, any body fluids. But it's not airborne."

"In lab tests it's displayed a capability—"

"Stop," Gwen shouted, so suddenly it made Maggie jump.

The panic in Gwen's eyes threatened to dissolve into tears. Maggie wasn't sure why she had resorted to sounding like a textbook. She was saying out loud all the frightening things she had learned, tossing them at Gwen because Gwen was her buffer, her crutch. But it was a mistake. It wasn't fair. She wasn't used to seeing Gwen like this. She was biting her bottom lip, her free hand a fist in her lap. She had always been Maggie's mentor, her rock, her advocate. She was the stable, logical, optimistic one of the pair, but it wasn't right to foist this on her, not now.

Gwen sat back, took a deep breath. Maggie waited, only now realizing that her chest ached. Gwen's panic was contagious. It crushed against her lungs.

"You'll be okay," Gwen said as if reading Maggie's mind.

Maggie shifted in her chair, suddenly chilled. She tucked the gown around her. The panic had transferred to Maggie, because now Gwen seemed calm, genuinely so this time. Had she slipped and caught herself, realizing she needed to be strong for both of them?

Her eyes held Maggie's. "Is there anyone you want me to call?"

"I've already called you."

"What about your mother?"

"She'd be a nervous wreck."

"She's still your mother."

"Yes, she's my mother, but she's never been motherly. I can't handle taking care of her right now. And believe me, that's what it would be. Me taking care of her."

Gwen nodded then she smiled, her bottom lip almost completely void of lipstick. "You're going to be okay. It might be different if the little girl sprayed you in your eyes or your mouth. But that didn't happen."

"That did happen," Maggie said, the memory twisting a knot in her stomach. "It happened to Cunningham."

CHAPTER
48

Reston, Virginia

Emma tossed a kernel of popcorn to Harvey. One for her, one for Harvey. The two of them sat on the living-room floor, surrounded by the newest editions of Emma's favorite magazines.

In *Bride* was the article "Pretty in Pink," saluting Breast Cancer Awareness Month. She still couldn't believe her mother was wearing a pink wedding dress.

Okay, so it was kinda cool, but it was hard to imagine anything other than a white wedding dress. In fact, if it wasn't for this article and a couple of others, Emma would have thought her mother—who was the ultimate slave to fashion—had made up the whole "pink wedding dress" thing. Even so, get real, who's that politically correct that they'd use their wedding as some social statement?

No, Emma guessed that being in the advertising business her mother probably saw the whole "pink thing" as a way to avoid white. Her mother was very big into subliminal messages. *You are what people think you are.* That was a favorite line her mother used. It totally worked for her. Besides, she'd already done the white-dress thing with Emma's dad. No sense in reminding people, and at the same time, why not pretend that she cared about breast cancer?

Emma was very certain that when it came her turn, she would definitely choose white. Not like it was something she needed to worry about right this minute. How could she have time for boys when her dad kept nagging her about college applications and scholarship stuff and keeping her grades up. All Emma really cared about were the gorgeous sling-back shoes that matched her bridesmaid's dress. Even if pink wasn't quite her color she knew she looked hot in those shoes.

She glanced at the other magazines spread around her, all of them flipped open to must-read articles. In *Cosmo* was "The Four Things He Doesn't Dare Tell You." *Entertainment Weekly* had something about *Project Runway.* The TV show *The Office* was on the cover. J Lo was all aglow in *People*. Exciting stuff and yet Emma chose to stick with the packet of love letters.

September 16, 1982
Dear Liney,
It was so good to see you. I wish you were still here. I can't believe how much I miss you.

   J.B. is still going on and on about the grape jelly beans you bought him. He's just jealous. He knows he'll never be like me and get someone like you. You know, it's funny I can't even remember knowing, let alone mentioning to you that grape was his favorite flavor, but you're amazing.

So are you wearing the T-shirt I gave you? I knew you'd love it. It about killed me to not give it to you this summer. I bought it the day we went to the Art Institute. Do you remember how I didn't even want to go? Vatican art? Who cares? Remember? But you made that whole day such an adventure I wanted to repay the favor. I'm big on that, you know. I always repay favors. And it was easy to sneak off and buy it when you were standing there mesmerized. Actually, it was when you were looking at the one by that Caravaggio dude, Deposition from the Cross. See, I remember. I've been telling you, I'm a details guy.

Also, I wanted to apologize again for leaving you right when the pizza got there. Even if it was just an hour. My sister's such a moron. I can't believe she had to pick Saturday night to call me. She's been trying to guilt me into coming home. Like I told you, that's not my home anymore. I know you said it wasn't a big deal and I know you're not mad or anything. Sometimes I wish my family would just disappear, you know?

Emma heard a car door slam and started folding and tucking the letters safely away. She rolled her discarded sweatshirt around the packet and grabbed the *People* magazine just as her dad came in the front door.

CHAPTER
49

USAMRIID

Platt took over the small conference room next door to his office. He made a pot of coffee and ate an apple he found in his desk drawer. He started retrieving, sorting and compiling information. In no time he had the contents of file folders spilled across the tabletop. On his laptop computer he accessed documents, browsed and read and printed out pages that went into a separate stack. And on a legal pad he scrawled a series of lists and notes.

On one page he jotted bits and pieces about Ebola Zaire.

The symptoms:

First stage (within 1-2 days of infection):
fever, severe headache, sore throat, muscle aches, weakness, nosebleed.

Next stage (within a week, as little as 3 days):
vomiting, abdominal pain, jaundice, diarrhea, con-
junctivitis (red eyes).

Final stage (7-21 days):
tissue destruction, organ failure, massive hemorrhaging,
shock, respiratory arrest, death.

On a separate pile was everything he could find about
the vaccine, including a copy of the original report that first
appeared in the *Journal Public Library of Science Pathogens,*
January 2007. The research team that developed the
vaccine had been from Canada's National Microbiology
Laboratory in Winnipeg and USAMRIID, right here at Fort
Detrick.

On another page he scribbled pieces about the vaccine:

Most effective when giving injections in a series (com-
parable to rabies shots)
Administered after infection within 30 minutes—90%
survival rate.
24 hours after infection—50% survival rate.

Administered before infection—potential for the vaccine to protect but unproven to date.

Tests to date all performed on macaque monkeys.

Human trials limited. Not enough data to establish
survival rates.

Not approved by the FDA.

Would require an emergency "compassionate use"
permit.

Platt underlined "compassionate use." He wouldn't have
time to make an argument to the FDA, but as part of a
military research facility he would try to find an exception.
He'd do whatever it took. Janklow had said that there were
sacrifices that often had to be made in war zones and in hot
zones. The same was true about exceptions.

He remembered Afghanistan and a makeshift medical
facility in the back of a truck. Every time they came under
fire the protocol was to move, get the hell out, but in the
middle of an amputation no way could you rumble to safety.
So you sat in the line of fire, trying to keep the soldier on
the gurney from bleeding to death and hoping all of you
didn't get blown apart.

No one ever questioned breaking protocol. You did what
you had to do under special circumstances. Protect and
serve. You certainly didn't leave a soldier behind to bleed to
death and you didn't stand back and watch while four people
under your care crashed.

In a short time, Platt was finished. He packed up what
he needed, left the mess in the conference room to clean
up later, locking the door behind him. Then he headed back

up to the labs, the confidence back in his stride. As the head of the facility he required no other signature but his own. He didn't need Janklow. He didn't needed McCathy. All he needed now was the vaccine.

CHAPTER
50

Reston, Virginia

Tully rummaged through the kitchen cabinets. He had spent the afternoon fast-forwarding through security tapes from Quantico. He had looked at three-days' worth and found no one entering who didn't belong and nothing remotely close to a doughnut box being carried in. He was exhausted. He wanted simple and easy like paper plates. They had to have paper plates.

Emma leaned over the service counter, watching him, not helping, of course, just watching. Then out of the blue she asked, "How did you and Mom meet?"

"Excuse me?" The question startled him so much he bumped his head on an open cabinet door.

"Mom. Where'd you meet her?"

"I think it was at a party or something." He made it sound

like no big deal instead of adding that Caroline had been wearing a baby-blue sweater and pearls. He remembered thinking she was the classiest act he had ever met. "She was with a buddy of mine."

"You stole her away?"

He found paper plates, an unopened package. "Not exactly," he told Emma. "I guess she thought I was charming or something."

He pulled out a shaker of hot peppers and grated parmesan cheese and suddenly remembered that Caroline hated getting any hot peppers on her side of the pizza. Then he realized he didn't know whether or not Gwen liked hot peppers or grated parmesan. He still put them out on the counter.

"When did you stop?" Emma asked.

"When did I stop what?"

"Being charming."

He quit rummaging and glanced back at her. "You'll have to ask your mother." Then he turned to give her his full attention. "Why the sudden interest in all that? I thought you were happy your mother was getting married?"

"I guess I'm glad she's happy. It's just…I don't know. He's so different from you."

"Evidently your mother wanted different."

"I guess. But he's such a dork."

This made Tully smile. "So I'm not a dork?"

"For sure not. You're like…I don't know, like Indiana Jones."

"Indiana Jones?" It seemed an odd reference for his teenage daughter, but then he remembered there was a new movie in the series. Strange to have his daughter referencing someone, even if it was a movie character, that he actually knew.

"Indiana Jones. Rugged but cool, not so smooth sometimes but funny...all in a good way."

"Well, Conrad makes your mother happy. That's the important thing, right?"

"Yeah, I suppose." She came around the counter now and started helping him, getting napkins out and silverware. "And Dr. Patterson...I guess she makes you happy?"

Tully watched her tuck a strand of hair back behind her ear as she busied herself with pulling drinking glasses out of the cabinet.

"Yes, she does."

"What about Maggie?"

"What about Maggie?"

Emma shrugged. She avoided looking at him. There was another swipe at her hair. "I don't think she's interested in that Nick guy."

"Why do you say that?"

"Like get real. He didn't even know she wasn't coming home. She obviously hadn't called him."

"Good point." Tully nodded, keeping that in mind and reassuring himself. He hadn't told Morrelli where Maggie was or why he was taking her dog. He had figured the same thing as Emma—if Maggie wanted the guy to know, she would have told him herself.

"You like her, don't you?"

"Maggie? Of course I like her. Sweet pea, Maggie's my partner, my coworker."

"Mom worked with Conrad for a while before they started, like, dating or anything."

"That was different." He wasn't sure where all this was coming from. "They didn't work for the same company. Your mom is the CEO of an advertising agency. He's what? The vice president of a pharmaceutical company."

He opened the refrigerator to check for sodas, when he really wanted to sit Emma down and ask what was going on. He knew better than to make a big deal of her questions or else she'd never ask questions again. "Maggie and I are friends," he said and moved on to check the ice maker. "You're gonna really like Gwen. I promise."

She shrugged like it didn't matter. Flipped her hair back to reinforce that it didn't matter.

As if on cue the doorbell rang and Harvey came running into the kitchen, circling Emma, making sure she was okay. Emma smiled but Tully knew it was because of Harvey and not anything he had said. He went to answer the door and took a deep breath when he knew Emma couldn't see him. Everything would work out. Of course the two women he cared about would like each other.

CHAPTER
51

Razzy's
Pensacola, Florida

Rick Ragazzi couldn't believe his luck. Just when the refrigerator repair job was finished—okay, $778—he got the call from his best waiter, telling him he couldn't make it in tonight. Something about a Jet Ski accident and being in the emergency room at Baptist Hospital. Rick had heard sirens in the background.

Saturday night was the absolute worst to find a substitute, especially an hour before the shift began, which meant Rick had to fill in. And he was feeling like crap, full-blown flu symptoms—fever, headache, muscle ache and a nosebleed that stopped only long enough for him to take orders. As soon as he retreated to the kitchen, it started all over again.

Joey was giving him a hard time about it, calling him a

cokehead because he knew it was safe. Rick was no closer to being a cokehead than Joey was to being an altar boy. It was funny until the fourth or fifth time and then his cousin grew concerned. He grabbed Rick's arm at one point during the evening and took him aside.

"What's going on, dude? Are you okay? You don't look so good."

"Just a bug," Rick told him.

Then he realized he was probably inflicting his bad luck on every one of his customers. He'd need to be more careful, though he had already accidentally gotten a finger in someone's soup. A little boy at table five kept sticking his French fries into Rick's ear every time he leaned over to serve the rest of the boy's family. Who knows what else? He didn't feel good. It was difficult to pay attention. Toward the end of the evening it was difficult to care.

Joey pulled Rick aside again when the dessert crowd came. He made him drink a syrupy concoction that tasted like black licorice and coffee.

"My dad swears by this stuff," Joey told him. "He claims it'll cure anything from a hangover to anthrax. I can testify to the hangover. Fortunately, I have no idea about the anthrax."

"What are you talking about? Uncle Vic's never been drunk or sick a day in his life."

"Yeah, right," Joey said. "My mom says he was quite the party hound before his FBI days."

Rick couldn't help thinking that Joey actually sounded, if not proud, then somewhat pleased.

"We just know him as Mr. FBI man," Joey told him. "Mr. Macho Shithead, Mr. My-Way-or-the-Highway."

"You sound disappointed."

"Nah. I'm not disappointed. I just wish he'd remember sometimes that he wasn't always perfect."

Rick watched Joey get back to his soufflé. And more than ever Rick realized that he'd never be able to tell his cousin about the thousand dollars his dad had sent.

CHAPTER
52

Reston, Virginia

"For centerpieces they're having pink and white calla lilies," Emma was telling Gwen as Tully sat miserably across from them hoping for something, anything that would get his daughter to stop talking about his ex-wife's upcoming nuptials. He'd even considered kicking her under the table. And Gwen was being polite, listening and nodding like Tully imagined she did with her patients, especially the severely narcissistic ones. But then who could be more narcissistic than a teenager?

It had taken Tully two slices of pizza—one piece of his favorite, supreme, and another of Emma's favorite, pepperoni—for him to realize Gwen somehow knew what their favorites were. His, he could understand. They'd gone out for pizza, but had he ever mentioned Emma's favorite? Was it coincidence that she had chosen pepperoni? After all, lots of people liked pepperoni pizza.

He watched Gwen smile at Emma. God, this woman had a great smile. It crinkled her nose a bit and showed off the tiny freckles. But there was something tight in the smile tonight. She said she had just come from seeing Maggie.

"How is she?" he'd asked.

"I'll tell you later," she had answered too quickly, obviously not wanting to discuss any of it before dinner and in front of Emma.

Now Gwen asked Emma about the sling-back shoes that the bridesmaids were wearing. Tully couldn't help thinking she was a glutton for punishment, but somehow she managed to look interested.

That's when Tully decided it was no coincidence that Gwen had brought both his and Emma's favorite pizzas. She's a psychologist, for God's sake, of course, it was no coincidence. All of Emma's questions earlier about him and her mom had stirred up a sense of nostalgia. Gwen bringing his favorite pizza reminded him that Caroline used to buy him his favorite flavored jelly beans. At the time he was never sure whether or not it was because she cared about him or she simply wanted to make her old boyfriend jealous. With Caroline there always seemed to be an ulterior motive to everything she did.

"They have over two hundred people invited," Emma announced like it was a competition.

Tully thought Caroline hadn't changed much. It sounded

as if she was using even her wedding as a way to impress her friends and colleagues. He had wondered more than once or twice during their marriage if she regretted her choice of husband, especially when Tully settled into the FBI field office in Cleveland. After all, he wasn't the D.C. hotshot making the evening news and busting up cases like the Unabomber or the Beltway Snipers or finding Eric Rudolph in the woods.

Even now with all of Caroline's own successes—she still seemed to be looking for something or someone else to make her bigger and better. That wasn't fair, Tully realized. Maybe she really loved this boy VP. And he realized that despite the feeling of nostalgia there was no longer that sense of loss that he had felt in the early days after the divorce. He couldn't remember when it disappeared. Didn't know that it had disappeared so completely until this very moment. It was gone and that was the important thing.

Emma had finally taken a breath long enough to let Gwen talk. When Tully tuned back into the conversation he couldn't believe his ears. The two of them had gone from pink wedding dresses and sling-back shoes to Gwen telling Emma about a New York university that specialized in fashion design. And Emma was actually listening.

God, he loved this woman. Then his stomach did a pleasant flip. Evidently it was an evening for revelations, because he hadn't realized before how much he did care about...perhaps even loved, Gwen Patterson.

Tully sat back, watching the two of them. Neither one

appeared to remember he was in the same room, let alone at the same table. Harvey came over and laid his chin on Tully's knee. He patted the big dog's head, the two of them bonding after being ousted by their women. Except that Harvey really just wanted Tully's pizza crust.

Emma's cell phone interrupted and she grabbed for it, but stopped. "It's Andrea. We've got that project for lit."

Tully immediately knew it was really Emma's safety net. She and Andrea had probably planned for the interruption or rather what Emma might consider an escape. But she was waiting for Tully to say it was okay. And she looked...apologetic, maybe even a bit regretful. His daughter had surprised herself and was enjoying Gwen Patterson.

"Go ahead." He waved her away from the table.

"This won't take long," Emma told Gwen.

Tully waited until his daughter disappeared into her bedroom.

"She likes you." He knew he sounded like he was about twelve.

"Does it matter?"

That wasn't at all what he expected her to say. Of course, it mattered but he stopped himself. That obviously wasn't what she wanted to hear.

"Is it wrong for me to want the two most important women in my life to like each other?"

"And if we didn't?"

It was a good question. A legitimate question. One he hadn't bothered to ask himself.

"I'm sorry," she said before he had a chance to respond. She set her elbows on the table and placed her chin in her hands, looking suddenly exhausted. "They're saying Maggie and Cunningham were exposed to a virus."

"So it's not anthrax or ricin?" He thought that should be a relief. Gwen looked anything but relieved.

"It's Ebola."

"Jesus! How is that possible? Where would he have gotten his hands on it? Ebola doesn't just happen here in the States."

Gwen shrugged. "There was an incident right here in Reston. Back in the eighties. The government kept it quiet. A private lab had gotten a shipment of monkeys. The monkeys started getting sick. Then they started dying. But that was 1989. Almost twenty years ago."

Tully raised an eyebrow, wondering how she knew all this.

"I checked it out after I left Maggie," Gwen said. "The virus was Ebola, but it didn't jump to humans. Ebola Reston. That's what they called it. They name the different strains by the region where it was first found."

"Maggie and Cunningham. Is it Ebola Reston?"

"Ebola Zaire."

"That's a bad one?"

"It's called the 'slate wiper.'"

Tully winced. Gwen noticed and looked away. It was too late. He saw the fear in her eyes. He shoved around some pizza crumbs on his paper plate.

"That might help narrow down who this guy is. Unless

he's traveled to Africa in the last six months he'd have to get the virus from a research lab, maybe a government facility or a university. He couldn't just special order it."

Tully drummed the tabletop. This was worse than he thought. The guy was much more dangerous. He didn't just have opportunity and motive. He had access.

"The anthrax killings in 2001," Tully said and waited for Gwen's eyes, for her attention. "Do you remember them?"

"Not in detail. I remember the letters looked quite ordinary and they were sent through the mail. One ended up in Tom Brokaw's office. A couple of others were sent to congressmen. Right? It happened after 9/11. I remember being too numb to pay much attention."

"Twenty-two incidents. Five dead. No one was charged or convicted." This time Gwen raised her eyebrow. "George Sloane," Tully explained. "The documents guy. He brought it up this morning. So I did some research." He stopped drumming, scratched at his jaw and realized it was clenched.

"One of the few suspects was a scientist," he continued. "A scientist who previously worked for USAMRIID. They accused him of sneaking out samples of anthrax from the lab at Fort Detrick." Tully didn't like what he was thinking. "I imagine USAMRIID has samples of Ebola, too."

Chicago

Dr. Claire Antonelli hated that she had let Vera Schroder down. The woman's face had become a mirror image of her husband's, an expressionless zombie, void of emotion. But for Vera it was shock, not pain, that caused the conversion.

She escorted Vera from the surgery waiting room to a suite on the same floor that was reserved for families. She wanted Vera to rest until they could tell her more, though Claire didn't have a clue as to what she could tell her. They had stabilized Markus for now, but after what Claire had just seen, she didn't expect him to make it through the night. And the worst of it was that they were no closer to finding out what was wrong with him.

Claire stopped herself long enough to call her son. She asked what he had planned for his Saturday night. He could have said anything at that moment and it wouldn't have mattered. She simply wanted to hear his voice, know that he was okay, remind herself how very lucky she was.

He asked if he could go over to a friend's and watch college football. They were ordering footlongs from Chicago Dog. No beer, he promised. An empty promise, but she knew she didn't have to worry about him. They agreed on a time he'd be home. He wanted to know when she'd be home. How did her day go? Did she want him to get an extra footlong for her?

Yes, very lucky, indeed.

Then Claire joined Dr. Miles back in his small office down the hall from the surgery suites. He was sitting quietly behind his desk, his hands folded together. He didn't say anything when Claire first entered. There was just a nod. She took the chair on the other side of the desk and they sat for what seemed a long time to Claire.

He leaned back and his chair groaned. He scratched at his five o'clock shadow then folded his arms over his chest. Still, he didn't say anything.

Claire glanced at her wristwatch and Miles noticed. Everything she thought of to say seemed too obvious or unnecessary. It had been several hours since they'd closed up Markus Schroder's abdomen and sent a piece of his tissue downstairs to the lab. All that was left now was to wait.

The phone on Dr. Miles's desk rang and both doctors jumped. Miles's bear paw grabbed it immediately.

"This is Dr. Miles."

Claire watched, looking for any clues in Miles's eyes. They

darted from the door to her face and down to his desk as he listened. They wouldn't stay still long enough for her to detect calm or panic or confusion. His shoulders hunched forward and the lines in his forehead deepened.

"What kind of confirmation?" he asked and this time his eyes stayed on Claire's. The man she had always counted on for strength suddenly looked afraid.

He listened for several more minutes then said, "Okay," and hung up the phone.

"They need to send a sample to the CDC for confirmation," he told Claire.

"Is it MRSA?" she asked.

Staph infections were not uncommon in health-care facilities. But MRSA (pronounced "merca") was the worst of the bunch. It was highly resistant to antibiotics. Recently a case had been found in a Virginia school. An entire district had to be closed while administrators and health-care workers scrubbed down facilities.

"It's worse," Miles told her.

"What do you mean? Worse than MRSA?"

"They believe it's a virus."

Claire stared at him, waiting for more of an explanation. If they were sending it to the CDC they must be thinking it was highly infectious.

"This isn't something we've seen before," Miles said.

"Hemorrhaging, purplish blotches, fever—" Claire stopped. "Plague? Smallpox?"

"I don't think we should speculate." He stood up, his way

of putting an end to the discussion. "Besides, we don't have time for that. They told me to shut down this floor and the surgery center."

"A quarantine?"

He nodded. "Nobody leaves."

CHAPTER
54

Sunday, September 30, 2007
The Slammer

Maggie stood in the small but private shower, letting the hot water dismantle the chill that had seeped deep inside her, down to her bones. Then she put on a fresh hospital gown—there was a stack of them in the bathroom. She tried not to count them, tried not to think how long they expected to keep her here.

Hair still damp, she lay down on the bed and managed to dose off between the stiff bedsheets. She wasn't sure how long she slept. She had convinced herself to close her eyes. Just for a minute or two. Staring at the computer screen all day had given her a headache. That was all it was. Eyestrain. Sleep deprivation. Stress. Not a parasitic virus duplicating itself throughout her bloodstream.

She wouldn't let herself think about it. She couldn't, and yet, visions invaded her sleep. It was like an old jerky, film projector with colorful purple and pink amoebas that joggled from side to side, bumping each other and splitting into two. Another bump, another split. Dozens turning into hundreds.

Her eyelids fluttered open several times before she noticed him. He stood on the other side of the glass wall, watching her, watching over her. That's what it felt like. Warm brown eyes—serious, soulful eyes—keeping watch, and for a second or two in that half-asleep, dreamlike state she could almost convince herself that he could protect her.

He smiled when he saw that she was awake, but he didn't move, didn't shift, didn't wave her over. He just stood there, arms folded over his chest, his smile the only movement. His smile and his eyes.

She sat up on the edge of the bed, disappointed to hear that throbbing in the back of her head was still there, joined by a quickened heartbeat that the amoebas had caused. Rest had not relieved her.

They picked up the phone at the same time, already a synchronized deliberation between them.

"I didn't expect to see you again so soon."

"Are you kidding? You're my favorite patient."

For an Army colonel he certainly could be charming. The dimples only added to the effect.

"How are you feeling?" Face serious again, eyes still soft, genuine, caring. Meaning no more jokes.

"I have a headache." It wasn't something she would

normally complain about, but she knew he needed to know, to make a checklist.

"Tell me where exactly."

She sat down. He followed her. She closed her eyes and listened to the throbbing. "Back of the head," she said, eyes still closed. "At the base of the skull. Right above the neck. The pain's a throb more than an ache."

She opened her eyes, met his. Only she couldn't assess what he was thinking. She automatically reminded herself that he was good at hiding alarm. He was a doctor and soldier, a combination sure to disguise and dissuade emotion. Only something about his eyes gave him away, told her that it wasn't all that easy, that it was a constant challenge.

"Your blood is still not showing any indication of the virus. You're not breaking with any of the symptoms. Usually the headache is behind the eyes, circling inside the head, like someone knocking against the inside of your forehead. Chances are what you're experiencing is stress and fatigue. You haven't eaten much, either. I'll have them send up whatever sounds good. Get something into your immune system. We need to keep you strong. And I'll have Dr. Drummond bring you some Advil gelcaps."

Dr. Drummond. She found herself realizing she had never been given a name for the woman in the blue space suit. Only now, after almost two days, she wondered why she had never asked.

Being a professional cynic, Maggie examined Platt,

looking for cracks in his facade, indications that he might be keeping something from her.

"You don't believe me," he said, startling her. She didn't realize her skepticism was so obvious.

"I've read the virus can lie dormant within a host." Maggie said it quickly. Go ahead and hit him with your best shot. No apologies. It was her life they were batting around, after all.

He hesitated. Did she know too much? Was he sorry he had been so straightforward with her before?

"The virus lives somewhere in Africa and yes, we believe it must lie dormant in a perfect host though we're not sure what that perfect host is. There's speculation that it could be bats. Scientists have practically swept every foot of places like Kitum Cave at the base of Mount Elgon in Kenya and Uganda, looking for any signs of where Ebola lives when it's not jumping to primates and humans. But here's the thing…" He waited until he was certain he had her full attention or maybe he wanted to make certain that she believed him. "Ebola doesn't lie dormant in primates and humans. It devastates them and it does it quickly."

"But there's an incubation period. Anywhere from two to twenty-one days. Does that mean I could have been exposed and not know it for twenty-one days?"

"Victims usually break with symptoms within one to three days. The incubation period refers to the time it takes for the virus to run its course from symptoms to illness to organ failure to—"

"Crash and bleed," she finished for him.

"Yes," he said. Then continued, "Understand I'm not saying that it's impossible to be exposed, to show no symptoms and then break with the virus on day twenty-one. I'm telling you what is statistically probable. What is known evidence and what I've seen myself. This virus usually can't just sit in humans. It's instinct is to replicate itself and to do it quickly."

She nodded. Her eyes wandered before she could stop them. His face told her he knew he wasn't convincing her. His straight talk brought no comfort. She was beginning to think the throbbing might actually have moved to behind her eyes. Her focus blurred a bit. She didn't care that he was staring at her.

He sat forward, tugged at the crew neck of his sweatshirt as if he was suddenly too warm. He took a deep breath, blew it out, kept it from rattling through the phone's receiver.

"Even if you break with symptoms it doesn't mean it's fatal."

"Ebola Zaire? The 'slate wiper'?" She raised an eyebrow to let him know she really had done her homework. He wasn't gaining any points here.

She wasn't sure why she was throwing around so much cynicism, first at Gwen, now Platt. Her own survival instinct kicking in perhaps. Fear had the tendency to make her look over her shoulder and search every shadow rather than sit back and wait for a lifeline to be tossed to her. And inside this airtight, air-locked, air-sealed room she could do nothing but search through the shadows.

Platt let out another sigh. But it was exhaustion. Not frustration. He rubbed at his jaw and swept a hand over his face. Maggie took notice of his long fingers, manicured nails, veins and tendons taut, a strong hand but gentle as he massaged his temple. He mistook her examination for contemplation. He must have thought he finally had her attention. Those intense eyes held hers for a long minute before he said, "You need to trust me."

He let that statement sit. When she didn't respond, didn't object, he added, "There's a vaccine. It hasn't been approved yet by the FDA. It's proven to be safe and effective in primates. We've had only a few opportunities to use it in human cases, lab-research settings where a scientist accidentally got exposed and infected."

This time Maggie sat up. She hadn't read anything about a vaccine. Treatment, in all of the literature she had accessed, talked only about "supportive care" and making the patient comfortable for the inevitable.

"It's most effective," Platt continued, "if it's given in a series of injections. Sort of like rabies. It helps the immune system fight off the invading virus. But it also depends how soon the injections are administered after the exposure. I'm not going to lie to you. There's only a fifty-fifty chance if the immune system has already been compromised or if symptoms have already started. But that's not the situation in your case."

Maggie didn't need to ask. She knew that was the case for Ms. Kellerman. Was it for Mary Louise, too? Cunningham?

"I want to use the vaccine on you. I don't have the FDA's approval to use it on civilians, so I can't unless you sign a release that—"

"I'll sign whatever you need," she interrupted. She didn't need to think about it.

He looked surprised that compliance would be that easy. But he didn't question her, didn't ask if she needed time to think about it. She knew there wasn't time for any more questions.

"Dr. Drummond will be in shortly to administer the first injection." He stood, finished. "I'll also have someone bring you something to eat. You have to eat. Any requests?"

"I do have a request," Maggie said. "But it's not food." He nodded and waited. "I want to see Assistant Director Cunningham."

"That's not possible."

"Why? Is he not here at this facility?"

"No, he's here. Why would you think he's not here?"

"I don't have to talk to him. I just…I want to see him." It looked like Platt wasn't going to budge. "I need to see him. See that he's okay."

He shifted his weight from one foot to the other and Maggie could see his jaw start to clench. She knew the argument—patient confidentiality. There was a privacy issue. He couldn't divulge anything about any of their cases. They were probably classified. They wouldn't even let Maggie tell anyone where she was. That's what she believed the colonel was struggling with in trying to decide. Whether or not to break the rules and let two of his patients see each other.

"I can't let you see him." Platt said. "Because he's not okay."

CHAPTER
55

Chicago

Dr. Claire Antonelli leaned her forehead against the window looking into the NICU. The babies, including Baby Boy Haney, didn't look any different, still pink and wiggling just as they had been twenty-four hours ago. But now, because of her, the entire ward had been included in the quarantine.

Claire had spent the night as part of a team drawing blood samples from everyone who may have been exposed to Markus Schroder. The CDC's early report had left the few administers and doctors who knew about the case in shock. Dr. Miles was pushing for a press conference to warn all those who may have been to the hospital in the last several days. The administration wanted to wait. The CDC wanted to wait. No one wanted to create a panic. But Claire could feel one already brewing in silent glances, shrugs that replaced answers, a nervous tension that already shortened tempers. It wouldn't take long. Employees would be telling spouses that they wouldn't be home after their shift ended. Families would start demanding explanations for why they couldn't visit loved ones. Parents would insist on seeing their newborns. No, Claire knew it wouldn't take long for the panic to begin.

The CDC representative, Roger Bix, had arrived at four in the morning, wearing an Atlanta Braves jacket and pointed-toe cowboy boots. He looked more like a sports agent than a CDC infectious-disease specialist. And he was young—too young, Claire thought. Young and cocky, giving orders before he even introduced himself. Not a good combination.

She had taken a break and come to the NICU, not to be reminded that these precious babies may have been exposed to a deadly virus, but because she wanted to be reminded of goodness and innocence. Dr. Miles had asked her to think where Markus Schroder may have contracted the virus. The CDC wouldn't confirm until Monday what exactly the virus was, but Miles had already told Claire they were almost certain it was Ebola.

Days ago, when she was hunting for a clue, she had been over and over with Vera where Markus might have contracted something unusual. But the only trips the two made were to Terre Haute, Indiana, to check on a business that had been in Vera's family for years. There was nothing remotely close to a safari in Africa or a tour of a research facility. Nothing that could have put Markus in contact with something like Ebola.

Now Vera sat quietly by Markus's bedside, Markus unconscious and Vera taking on his earlier expressionless mask. She barely responded to outside stimuli, let alone any more questions.

But Vera, Claire was quick to note and to bring to Miles's attention, didn't seem to have the virus. Or at least she had no symptoms. They'd find out soon enough from her blood sample—the most difficult sample Claire had drawn all night. Vera had refused at first. Had told Claire that she didn't want her touching her or her husband. Then she'd relinquished, sticking out her arm and whispering to Claire—fear momentarily cutting through her mask—that she didn't want to go through what Markus was going through.

"You okay?" Dr. Miles asked from behind her. She hadn't heard him come up the hall. Hadn't even noticed his reflection in the glass.

"Tired. But not bad." She rubbed her neck as she glanced back at him. "How about you?"

"I'm good."

He gestured for her to walk with him. This ward was quiet, interrupted by the occasional baby cry, unlike the simmering chaos back in the surgery center and critical-care unit.

"Anyone who's followed procedure," he began, "should be safe. If they've gloved up, disposed of Schroder's body fluids properly, kept basic protocol, there shouldn't be a problem."

"Mr. Bix confirmed that the virus most likely is not spread through airborne particles, but only direct contact with body fluids."

"That should be a relief, but we both know there are a few who take shortcuts."

"I know, but there won't be any denying it this time if they did take a shortcut. I've got the unit secretary calling every single person who was in and out of Schroder's room since he's checked in, even if it was to change a lightbulb."

Claire realized he was leading them in a circle around the NICU, a privacy buffer of sleeping babies.

"Surgery's a different story." He glanced down at her but kept walking. "We've both seen what this virus can do. There was a helluva lot of blood. We all had our hands soaked in it. Hopefully no ruptures in our gloves, no leaks, no swipes at an itch." At this he smiled. "What a way to test procedure, right?"

"You said body fluids?" Claire tried to retrieve her other examinations of Markus. Did she wear gloves every single time? Then she remembered the black vomit. The alarm must have registered on her face and Dr. Miles noticed.

"Look, Claire, the hospital is letting the CDC call the shots. That's their business." He lowered his voice. "Out of all of us, you spent the most time with Schroder. The emergency ward's setting up an area for employees' families to come get tested. Get your son in here as soon as you can."

CHAPTER
56

USAMRIID

Tully thought Maggie looked thinner. She insisted it was his imagination.

"It's only been two days," she told him.

He held up a square white box for her to see through the viewing window.

"Courtesy of Ganza." Tully tucked the phone receiver so he could use both hands and lift the lid. "He assured me you would appreciate the humor."

"Doughnuts." It worked enough for a smile. "Chocolate ones are your favorite."

"These are all yours."

"I can't believe they let you in here with those."

"Guess they trust that an FBI guy certainly isn't gonna bring in tainted doughnuts. Dr. Drummond even said she'd bring them in for you. She did have to test one."

"Really? Under a microscope?"

"In the mouth. So you're one shy of a dozen."

Despite the awkward setup they went into their regular briefings. Tully knew Maggie was itching to dive into work and avoid the personal stuff. Something they had shared since day one.

Maggie told him about the envelope inside the Kellermans' house and how she was able to connect the Kellermans' name, along with the return address, to a cold case—the Tylenol multiple murders in Chicago in 1982. Then she explained how she had discovered that phrases from the doughnut-box note had been lifted from the Beltway Snipers case.

"Funny, George Sloane just mentioned the Beltway Snipers and how we feebies screwed that one up."

"Sloane's in on this?"

"Cunningham requested he take a look at the note."

"He should have recognized the phrases if he worked the Beltway Snipers case."

"Didn't sound like he was on it. He just wanted to get his digs in. He did work the anthrax case and recognized the similar pharmaceutical fold. That would make three cases this guy used—the Tylenol poisonings, the anthrax murders and the Beltway Snipers. Is he just being clever? Showing off? Or is he telling us who he is and where he'll strike next?"

"I think a little of both. It certainly makes him sound like a textbook profile of the clinical narcissist."

"He wants recognition, needs validation for his brilliance."

"He's obviously planned all this for some time," Maggie added. "He's probably rehearsed it over and over in his mind. Calculating, deliberating every move like a chess player. Now he's shuffling out pieces of his puzzle for us to put together."

"Finding the Kellermans in Elk Grove just so he could duplicate one of the victims' names in the Tylenol murder…" Tully shook his head. "The guy has too much time on his hands. Is it possible he's unemployed?"

She shook her head.

"Maybe he has access to inside information?" Perhaps even a database, but this Tully kept to himself. He wasn't ready to share with Maggie his theory about the Ebola coming from USAMRIID. He didn't have any evidence. It seemed cruel to suggest the idea, especially when she was locked up here. She looked exhausted, shadows under swollen eyes. Dressed in the hospital gown and white socks made her seem smaller, even more vulnerable.

He'd wait.

But what if he was right? What if the guy was someone right here? Getting his jollies, watching his victims slowly crash and bleed in front of him. That, too, might fit the profile. Tully hoped he was wrong.

"Has he sent other envelopes?" Maggie asked, startling Tully back to attention.

"Others? Like the one you found? You think that's the way he sent the virus? No doughnut box? No pizza box? A mailing envelope?"

"Colonel Platt will be able to tell us for sure, but yes, there was a plastic Ziploc bag inside."

"He could do that? Mail Ebola? Anthrax I understand. It's like a powder. But Ebola? What would you need for that? Do you have any idea how that's possible?"

She hesitated but Tully knew she did know. He had noticed the laptop computer. The swollen eyes weren't because she couldn't sleep, she *wouldn't* sleep. She'd already been using work and research as her sanity safety net.

"It would have to be actual cells, infected cells from blood or tissue. But it could be a small amount, even microscopic. It wouldn't take much. The virus can't survive without a host for more than several days. But it can if it's been preserved, frozen or sealed like in an airtight plastic bag."

"So anyone who opened up the bag would take one whiff—"

"No, I don't think so. From what I understand, it's not airborne. Not like anthrax. The Ebola virus needs a point of entry."

"It has to enter into the bloodstream?"

"Yes, or enter the body through other body fluids, mucus, semen, saliva."

"Or vomit sprayed in your face, your eyes, nose."

Maggie blinked and Tully wished he hadn't said it. Before he could respond, she added quickly, "Or through a cut. Just a break in the skin, a cuticle or a razor nick."

"That's all it would take?"

She nodded.

"Cunningham thinks this is personal," Tully said. He wasn't, however, convinced that it was some personal vendetta. "Is it possible he worked on the Tylenol case?"

Maggie shrugged.

"They wouldn't let me see him. He gave me a phone number. There's no answer."

Quiet. They stared at each other, neither willing to voice their suspicions.

"Maybe I should start taking a look at guys Cunningham helped put away."

"Or the ones who never got caught."

Tully remembered the impression left on the surface of the envelope. "He may have made one mistake. Does 'call Nathan R. 7:00 p.m.' mean anything to you?"

"What was the context?"

"He wrote a note to himself on top of the envelope he used. It pressed into the surface. No block printing. Regular handwriting. Sloane says the guy probably didn't even know he left an impression."

Tully thought Maggie recognized the phrase. There was something, but then she shook her head.

"Should I start looking for someone named Nathan?"

"I don't know," Maggie said. "I honestly don't know."

Tully thought her voice sounded exhausted. But then she sat up to the edge of her chair as if pushing for another surge of adrenaline.

"I do know this guy may crave attention, but he doesn't want to get caught," she said. "It's not like the BTK killer, coming to the surface twenty years later just because he misses the attention. This guy has been simmering for years, possibly stewing over grievances real or imagined. He's been planning, strategizing every step. Somewhere in his life he feels he's been wronged or not given credit that was due to him.

"Maybe he holds a grudge against law enforcement and that's why he wanted to render us powerless. He's disciplined. He's smart. He takes risks but he's not reckless. I think he holds a full-time job but he's a good liar. He looks and acts cool and calm, is able to function on a normal day-to-day basis, but the whole time there's a rage simmering inside him. You have to remember though he's not like a serial killer who enjoys the kill. This guy's satisfaction is retribution. He wants to even a score. He wants his victims to get sick, to linger, to know they're dying. In his mind it's his own perverted sense of justice. His own way of dealing out a death sentence."

Tully sat back and let out a breath. She still amazed him when she did this, spouted out a profile that nine out of ten times was dead on. This wasn't like George Sloane. Tully wasn't quite sure what the difference was. Sloane seemed ruled by statistics and ego. Maggie followed her gut instincts. He'd trust Maggie's gut over Sloane's ego any day of the week.

Tully mock gestured a wipe at his forehead, along with a sarcastic "whew," garnering another smile from Maggie.

"I asked George Sloane if we should be searching cabins in the woods," he told her.

"This guy's hiding in plain sight, Tully. And I know he's sent other envelopes."

CHAPTER
57

Platt watched from the viewing room, leaning against the wall so that he was close enough for Mary Louise to see him through the glass. She was coloring, sitting cross-legged on the rug with crayons scattered around her. Her eyes had lit up at the box of ninety-six. When he gave them to her she said she'd never seen so many.

"I won't break any of them," she promised.

Now every once in a while she'd glance over her shoulder at him and hold up the coloring book to show her progress. He'd smile and nod his approval. And she'd go back to work, her lower lip sticking out in concentration, trying to color within the lines, choosing her crayons with too much thought.

He wanted to tell her she didn't have to stay inside the lines. But someone had already told her otherwise. Earlier he had watched her playing one of the board games he had left. She had two tokens set to play and moved them separately; taking turns with an imaginary friend. This was a little girl who had learned how to play alone long before she came to the Slammer. Platt should have been pleased that she was so content. Instead, it bothered him, plucked at heartstrings he didn't know were still there.

Janklow had ordered that no family members be notified before Monday. Platt glanced at his wristwatch. As far as he was concerned Monday would begin at a minute past midnight. He kept the phone number for Mary Louise's grandmother tucked inside his pocket.

The little girl still had only mild symptoms. Her blood showed what could be bricks of virus. No worms. No progression of anything that looked like worms. And unlike her mother, Mary Louise's blood didn't light up when tested with actual Ebola.

Not yet anyway.

Platt knew the statistics by heart. Ten to fifteen percent infected with Ebola Zaire recovered. No one understood why or how. It was a small percentage, but Platt hoped Mary Louise would be included in that small percentage. The vaccine would improve those odds.

With her mother incapacitated and without her grandmother here, there was no one to sign the waivers. So Platt had given Mary Louise the first injection himself. It would all fall on his shoulders anyway. He was willing to take the heat for this, too.

He had told Mary Louise that the needle would sting, but

just for a second or two like a "big ole mosquito." She crinkled her nose at that and laughed, then asked, "Will it itch?"

In his mind he kept calculating the hours and minutes. By now he couldn't shut it off if he tried. Time ticking away and yet he couldn't remember what day of the week it was.

Sunday. It was Sunday.

Mary Louise searched for a different crayon. She seemed perfectly content. Totally unaware of the firestorm brewing all around her.

Sunday. It meant nothing to Mary Louise. Families attended church services. Read the Sunday paper. *Read the comic strips out loud, Daddy.* Frisbee in the backyard. A movie at the theater. That's what families did on Sunday. They spent the day together. Didn't they? *How would he know?* It'd been too long ago.

His Sunday routine—when he took a Sunday off—was quiet, with him and Digger on the screened-in back porch overlooking the woods. His parents took care of Digger when Platt worked long hours, never once suggesting he find a different home for the dog, knowing the two were insep-arable, dog and man bonded by the absence of a little girl they both adored.

Dr. Drummond came into Mary Louise's suite and the little girl stood to greet her. Platt waved goodbye and she waved back. He hated to leave. It was silly but he wished that if he could just keep watch over her maybe nothing more would happen.

He left the Slammer and took the stairs.

Down in the Level 4 suites he changed once again into scrubs and prepared to get into a space suit for the third time in as many days. He had decided to keep his circle of staff small, pulling in those who had worked on some of his toughest assignments. Earlier he had handed off to Sergeant Hernandez the mailing envelope that Agent O'Dell had taken from the Kellerman home. He knew it was a tall order for the budding scientist even before he saw the surprise in her eyes. She had assisted him plenty of times in the lab and he knew she was more than capable. He also knew that she would test and retest her results before she presented them to him and that would be a bonus.

She was still working when he came in, her gloved hands too busy to wave an acknowledgment. He stood quietly beside her, making sure she noticed his presence despite the hiss of her space suit. He didn't crowd her or rush her.

Hernandez must have pinned back or tied up her unruly curls but he could still see them swirling around inside her helmet. A few now stuck to her damp forehead. She glanced up and Platt caught a glimpse of her green eyes through the plastic. Her eyes were intense, a little wild. She'd found something.

"WHAT IS IT?" he asked, no longer able to wait.

"THE PLASTIC BAG INSIDE THE MAILING ENVELOPE…" She sounded breathless. "I FOUND SOMETHING. TISSUE, BLOOD CELLS."

"ENOUGH TO TEST?"

"YES."

"EBOLA?"

"YES, DEFINITELY. THE CELLS ARE BLOWN UP WITH WORMS." She stopped her hands. "THERE'S SOMETHING ELSE, SIR." She looked up at him and met his eyes. "THEY'RE NOT HUMAN CELLS."

"MONKEY?"

"AS FAR AS I CAN TELL IT'S MACAQUE. I'M TESTING AGAINST OUR OWN MACAQUE SAMPLES. THEY'RE VERY CLOSE."

Suddenly Platt got a sick feeling in the bottom of his gut. He'd asked McCathy about a possible contamination. Could they have contaminated Ms. Kellerman's tissue sample from inside their own labs? McCathy had shrugged off the idea. Too many walls of biocontainment. No way one of their recorded tissue samples got mixed up with Ms. Kellerman's or any of the other three patients'. They ran a tight ship, no doubt about it.

But how was someone able to send Ebola to Ms. Kellerman in the first place? Where had the microscopic tissue from a macaque monkey come from, tissue hot with Ebola? Was it possible it had gone missing from their own freezers? In their research experiments they used macaque monkeys. So did other research facilities, but few other facilities had Ebola. Could someone from within USAMRIID have stolen it? Could one of their own have done this?

"GOOD WORK," he told Hernandez. "GO AHEAD AND FINISH UP HERE." He gestured that he was leaving.

He needed to do an inventory. He'd check their Ebola

samples, every last one of them. But would he be able to tell if any was missing? All it took was a small amount. A microscopic amount. Years ago a scientist, an ex-employee of USAMRIID, had been accused of smuggling out anthrax, the anthrax that had caused five deaths. It ended up there was little evidence to support that accusation but just the speculation had raised questions about their procedures and security measures.

Now Platt realized that Janklow must be thinking the same thing. He had to wonder whether the virus could have come from within their own laboratories. Was he concerned about new accusations? Did the commander want this to all go away quietly, secretly, because he worried about USAMRIID's reputation? Or was it his own reputation he was worried about? And just what was the commander willing to do to keep it under wraps?

CHAPTER
58

Reston, Virginia

With her father gone, Emma had spent the entire afternoon reading the letters from Indy to Liney. He wrote to
her almost every day of September, filling her in about his
life at Quantico, the cases he was working, his friends
Razzy and J.B. Some of them rambled, others were brief
but sweet. Actually, she thought it was sweet that he
couldn't go a day without talking to her even if it was in
a letter.

At first Emma didn't understand why they didn't just call
each other, that was, until she found out they didn't have cell
phones back then. Long-distance calls were expensive. What
an ancient civilization.

September 26, 1982

Dear Liney,

I'm in Chicago for a few days. It's killing me that I'm here and you're in Ohio for your art conference thing. I can't be-lieve we'll miss each other, but it's probably best. I'm here on a case, you know. Classified. So I can't tell you about it. I'm not even letting my folks know I'm here. Though I'll let you in on a secret. I plan to drive down to their house Sunday morning while they're all at church. I want to leave them a little something. Maybe get them off my back.

Oh, and Liney, just a heads-up. It's not in the news yet, but stay away from Extra Strength Tylenol capsules. Don't ask me why or how I know, just don't take any at all, okay? I'm seri-ous. Don't tell anybody that I warned you but it's gonna be huge. I shouldn't even be telling you.

Love,
Indy

Emma flipped through the previous letters. Wow, she thought. This was the first time he'd signed a letter, "Love, Indy." She wondered what the difference was. He didn't even make a big deal out of it, just signed it. Maybe he was just missing her badly.

Emma went on to the next letter but she stopped when she saw the date, December 24, 1982. She flipped through the remaining envelopes. Had she sorted them incorrectly?

There were only three left. There had to be some missing. Her mom wasn't the most organized person in the world. How else could she explain Indy telling her he loved her and then not writing for three months?

She opened the December 24 envelope and discovered only a Christmas card. No letter. Inside, the card was signed, "Merry Christmas, Indy." No note. No postscript. Not even a "Love, Indy."

CHAPTER
59

Artie had never been here on a Sunday. The place was deserted. It was perfect. He loved it. At first he was just going to drop off the car and put away his road trip's stash. But the place was so deserted he felt comfortable enough to bring his fast food in with him.

At the last minute he wimped out and decided to eat in the lab next door instead of in the small quarantined lab. Too much bleach smell, he told himself. Of course, his decision had nothing to do with the dead monkey in the corner freezer. His key-card pass worked on all the doors down here, so access wasn't a problem.

At the end of the hall the live monkeys were quiet for a change. Artie ate his double cheeseburger, extra ketchup, extra pickles—they cheated you on the pickles if you didn't insist on extras—and fries. He snarfed it down and once he was finished he moved to the lab next door. From his backpack he pulled out the small notebook he carried everywhere he went. Alongside the notebook he started laying out his most recent stash of paraphernalia.

His road trips provided a treasure trove. He kept his findings in one of the small storage lockers, so anything from hair to fingernail clippings were readily accessible for the next package. For now Artie placed them on the counter to admire. He had each piece bagged and labeled like the crime-scene evidence it would someday become. He was particularly proud of a tooth he had found in a corner bathroom stall at a rest area off Interstate 95. He had hair samples from four different states. In each of his packages he included something, letting crime-scene techs believe they had a piece of evidence, believing their suspect had gotten sloppy when in fact he was outwitting the best and most seasoned investigators.

He opened his notebook to the list of package recipients. While driving to Wallingford, Connecticut, something had occurred to him almost out of the blue. He thought he may have made a connection, figured out another piece of his mentor's puzzle. Now he was anxious to see if he was right.

He skimmed the list:

Vera Schroder, Terra Haute, Indiana
Mary Louise Kellerman, Elk Grove, Virginia
Rick Ragazzi, Pensacola, Florida
Conrad Kovak, Cleveland, Ohio
Caroline Tully, Cleveland, Ohio

Then he pulled out his true-crime paperbacks and the articles he had downloaded from the Internet. He had already connected Mary Louise Kellerman of Elk Grove, Virginia, to Mary Kellerman of Elk Grove Village, Illinois. Using James Lewis's return address confirmed the connection to the Tylenol murder case. *Slam dunk*. That was an easy one.

The other packages were different. All of the others, at least as far as Artie could check out, had return addresses from people the recipient knew. Rick Ragazzi's was from a Victor Ragazzi. Easy one. Had to be a family member. Caroline Tully's was from an R. J. Tully. Same with Patsy Kowak. Although Conrad spelled his name Kovak, it had to be a relative.

That one had been a particular stroke of genius. The intended victim was actually listed as the sender, Conrad Kovak, instead of the recipient. Artie's instructions called for insufficient postage, enough so that the postal carrier wouldn't deliver it to Patsy Kowak but would return it to Conrad.

Artie loved that extra touch. And he'd recognized it, too. The Unabomber had sent at least one package with insufficient postage. The person Theodore Kaczynski had really wanted to blow up was the one he'd listed as the sender. He knew law-enforcement officials would stew over the packages' recipients, trying to figure out who their enemies were, why they would be targeted. It gave the phrase "return to sender" a whole new meaning.

Artie smiled. Yes, it was brilliant, absolutely brilliant.

The only other exception that Artie hadn't been able to figure out was Vera Schroder. It was the only package to have no return address. Artie thought the answer might have something to do with the recipient's address, Terre Haute, Indiana. On his long, quiet road trip something about Terre Haute had nagged at him. He'd seen that city listed somewhere recently, but he couldn't remember where.

He started at the beginning of his notebook, flipping through the cases and the information he had highlighted. The first case in his notebook was the Tylenol murders. The case remained unsolved. From September 29 through October 1, seven people died after taking Extra Strength Tylenol, 500-mg capsules laced with cyanide. One family lost three members. The very first person to die was twelve-year-old Mary Kellerman, who had taken one capsule when she woke up the morning of September 29 with a sore throat and runny nose.

Artie knew the names of all seven victims by heart. He knew the six stores in the Chicago area—with the exception of one unnamed retailer—that the tainted capsules had been traced back to. It was suspected that the killer had shoplifted boxes of Tylenol capsules, taken them home, added the cyanide and then brought them back to the stores and replaced them on the shelves. Most likely the killer had to have done this within the week or days prior to September 29.

What Artie was more interested in were those cases that

followed, the ones that were never confirmed nor refuted as connected to the Chicago tampering. During the months that followed, the FDA had 270 reports of product tampering. Anything from poisoned chocolate milk to insecticide-laced orange juice to Halloween candy with needles stuck inside. However, only thirty-six of those were confirmed.

He flipped through more pages. The tampering cases that involved more Tylenol, but outside the Chicago area, included a woman in Pittsburgh, an elderly man in Detroit and two family members—yes, here it was—in Terre Haute, Indiana. A local business owner and his wife were found dead in their home by their daughter. Extra Strength Tylenol capsules, laced with cyanide, were found inside the couple's house.

Their daughter's married name was Schroder, Vera Schroder. That was the connection. It was exactly what Artie was looking for. What he wasn't prepared for was to recognize the couple's last name.

Son of a bitch, it was the same last name as his mentor's.

CHAPTER
60

Razzy's
Pensacola, Florida

Rick Ragazzi washed down a couple more gelcapsules while he read the bottle's label. He had all the symptoms of the flu, symptoms the medicine claimed to relieve yet he felt absolutely no relief after twenty-four hours of taking the recommended dosage. He wished he could just silence the jackhammer inside his head. Even Joey's famous syrupy concoction did nothing.

He popped an extra capsule into his mouth and emptied the glass of orange juice just as he noticed another group of diners come through the restaurant door. Ordinarily he'd be pleased. Sunday evening and they were packed, even had a twenty-minute waiting list earlier in the evening. But his best waiter was still out. Something about stitches and a concussion. Rick wished he could blame a Jet Ski accident for his headache.

"Sorry, sugar," Rita said from behind him. "I had to place them at one of your tables. The new kid's a bit slow. How about you get their orders and I'll shuttle all the food?"

"Sounds good." It had become his easy response when he'd rather say he was out of here.

"You don't look so good," Rita told him. "Maybe you should be home in bed."

I wish, Rick thought, but said instead, "I'm fine."

He knew an owner shouldn't show weakness or vulnerability to his employees and always lead by example. He had read that somewhere. Wasn't it bad enough he let Rita call him sugar? But then she called everyone sugar in that lovely Southern accent that sounded so sincere each and every time and made you feel special.

Rita had handed out menus when she seated the three newcomers. Rick zigzagged his way through the tables as he tapped his pocket to make sure his notebook and pen were there. He insisted his waitstaff commit orders to memory. And yes, he knew that he should he be leading by example, but with the jackhammer headache he'd already gotten four orders screwed up. Better he slip a notch as an instructor than they eat any more of their profits in his mistakes.

All three menus were still open, tall accordions hiding their faces.

"Good evening. May I get you started with something

from our bar? We have our special beach rumbas for half price this evening."

"What the hell is a beach rumba?" one of the men asked as he slapped down his menu.

"Uncle Vic," Rick said. "What are you doing down here in Pensacola?" He hoped his smile looked genuine and excited instead of mimicking his inner voice that was shouting, "Oh, crap!"

CHAPTER
61

USAMRIID

Platt sat behind his desk with the chair turned away and toward the window. The rain had started again. A gentle pitter-patter. Drops slid down the glass. Darkness had returned. In his mind he kept calculating the hours and minutes. He still couldn't shut it off, a ticktock that kept rhythm with the rain.

He hadn't been able to prove or disprove any of his theories, his speculations, his suspicions by checking their samples of Ebola. McCathy had been the last one to slide his security card and activate the code. How much had he used to test against Ms. Kellerman's blood and the other victims'? Was it possible for a small amount to go missing without notice?

Exhaustion played wicked tricks on the psyche and Platt

kept that in the forefront of his thoughts as he sorted through his suspicions. What if the Ebola that was sent to Ms. Kellerman had come from their labs? What if Janklow knew? Even in the beginning when Platt thought the note and the setup might all be a hoax, Janklow seemed convinced it was the real deal. And why assign McCathy? Why so adamant about it including McCathy, a microbiologist who specialized in bioweapons, when Platt already had enough experience to handle the possibility of bioweapons?

Had Janklow known what they would find in Ms. Kellerman's house even before they arrived? Had he already been expecting Platt to be his scapegoat and McCathy to corroborate?

He was tired. He was being paranoid.

He rubbed at his eyes. Sat back. Tried to clear his mind.

But he couldn't shake Janklow's words, *"What if they all disappeared?"*

Platt checked his wristwatch. It was late. But hopefully not too late.

He fingered a piece of paper, folding and unfolding the already creased three-by-three that had ten numbers scrawled on it, the personal cell-phone number for Roger Bix, the CDC's chief of Outbreak Response and Surveillance Team.

Platt knew Bix from conferences, a few formal dinners and a few less formal rounds in the hotel bars. Fortunately the two had only shared war stories and never had to work on a case together. If nothing else, Bix might be able to confirm or deny whether there was any Ebola missing from another lab. Platt knew he could do this without admitting or confessing.

It took only two rings despite the late hour.

"This is Bix."

Platt sat up straight.

"Roger, it's Benjamin Platt."

Before he could respond, Roger Bix said, "So how much of the vaccine are you able to scrape together?"

"Excuse me?"

"The vaccine."

Platt was stunned. Had Janklow gone ahead and called the CDC? What the hell was going on?

"Look, Ben," Bix continued, misreading Platt's hesitation. "I appreciate the dilemma you all are facing." His normal, slow Southern drawl held a tinge of panic. "But like I explained to Commander Janklow, we can't afford to wait too long. I have a full-blown case of Ebola Zaire right here outside of Chicago. They opened up this poor son of a bitch in surgery. Who knows how many people have been exposed. I'm not just talking about hospital personnel. We've got visitors, patients, even newborns down in the maternity ward."

Platt shoved the cell phone closer to his ear. He couldn't hear above his heart pounding in his head. He sucked in air. Moved the phone away from his mouth. Let the breath out. There was another case. Another exposure.

"He was here at the hospital. Schroder, Markus Schroder.

Here for three or four days. An accountant, for Christ's sake. How the hell does an accountant come in contact with Ebola?" But Bix wasn't waiting for an answer. He wasn't finished. "This is a fricking nightmare and it's only gonna get worse. I've got Homeland Security up my ass trying to keep it quiet. Everybody's worried about the fricking media starting a panic. I tell you, Ben, I don't get that vaccine soon and we won't have to worry about the media starting a panic."

"Let me get to work on this, Roger. I'll get back to you as soon as I have the vaccine ready to go."

"Make it soon, Ben. We both know how quickly this virus moves."

The click that followed sounded like a trigger hitting on an empty chamber, abrupt and hollow.

Platt felt paralyzed.

There was another case. As far away as Chicago. Had he sent other packages with microscopic bits of Ebola, preserved and sealed in Ziploc plastic bags waiting to be opened? This was bigger than any of them had imagined. No way Janklow could make it all disappear.

Then Platt remembered something. Something Janklow said McCathy had told him about the virus. That it would take as little as a microscopic piece, preserved, sealed and delivered, perhaps even through the mail, to start an epidemic. That was before Maggie handed over the mailing package. Before they knew how the virus was delivered to the Kellerman house. Did McCathy know that's how it was delivered? Or was it a lucky guess?

CHAPTER
62

Artie tried to think of someone to share the news with. Someone who would appreciate the brilliance of his puzzle-solving skills. He'd been able to answer a question that cold-case sleuths and law-enforcement officials across the States hadn't been able to figure out for twenty-five years. It was as big as unveiling Ted Kaczynski as the Unabomber.

Almost as if his wish was being granted, he heard a door close. Not a slam. Just a soft tap.

It was probably nothing. Could have been his imagination. No one was around down here on the weekends.

He started flipping through his pages again, jotting down notes in the margins of his notebook.

Footsteps down the hall. He was certain.

Crap!

He stood frozen in place, eyes darting around him. The light switch. He needed to flip the fucking light switch.

Too late.

The footsteps were closing in. Right outside the door now.

He twisted around, looking for something to use as a weapon, and grabbed the closest thing he could find. A syringe. He pulled off the plastic needle guard just as he heard a key card slide into the door's security lock.

"What the hell are you doing here tonight?"

Artie let out a sigh of relief that almost included, *speak of the devil*. "You scared the crap out of me," he said instead.

"Don't you realize you can see the light on underneath this door from the hallway?"

"Nobody's around," Artie defended himself. "It was your idea that I use the lab on the weekend."

"I thought you were supposed to make the delivery yesterday."

"I did," Artie said, slipping the syringe into his pocket and trying to nonchalantly stack his paperbacks onto the incriminating pages of his notebook and the articles beneath it. "I went to Connecticut yesterday. Mailed them from there."

"Them?"

Damn! This probably wasn't the time to reveal his contribution.

"I meant the package. I mailed it yesterday."

"So what are you doing here tonight?" His eyes darted around the countertops.

"I was just dropping off some stuff. You know, the DNA samples that I collect."

Artie watched him look around the room and settle on the paperback of the Unabomber. He picked it up.

"How many times do I have to tell you not to carry these around in your backpack?"

He tossed it onto Artie's pile and the books and articles shifted. Artie watched his eyes and held his breath, but he knew he was seeing exactly what Artie didn't want him to see. He pulled one of the Tylenol articles out of the stack.

"What are you doing?"

"Just researching?"

He didn't buy it. Artie needed to think fast. Then suddenly he relaxed. What was he worried about? They were the same. Artie knew that. Not just teacher and student. Kindred spirits.

"I figured it out," Artie told him.

He didn't respond. Just cocked an eyebrow and waited for Artie to explain.

"You're brilliant," Artie said, and he meant it. "The Tylenol murders. That was you. They always wondered if someone had done seven random murders just to cover up the one they really wanted to get away with."

Still no response. Artie took that as a good sign.

He continued, "And by planting seven bottles in the Chicago area everyone believed your real target, which was in Terre Haute, had to be, like, some kind of fluke."

There was no smile, but Artie reminded himself that he wasn't really a smiler. That he no longer looked angry was good. He was rubbing a hand over his jaw, but waiting and listening.

"That's what you're doing now, too. Right? Mailing out a bunch of random packages with the virus so it looks like the work of some homegrown terrorist. All the while you have one target in mind. Right?" He glanced at his notebook, still opened to the list. "So who is it? Who's the real target?"

"You think you're pretty smart," he told Artie. "But there're all real targets. I'm taking care of every son of a bitch who's screwed me over the years."

Then he did something Artie should have known was a ruse. He smiled. "How did you figure out the Tylenol thing? I mean with Indiana? Something in here?"

He pointed to the stack and Artie grinned. He bent over and started to sort through the mess. He didn't even see the microscope come crashing down onto his head.

Artie fit perfectly right on top of the dead monkey. He was unconscious when the freezer lid slammed shut and the padlock clicked back into place.

CHAPTER
63

The Slammer

Maggie dreamed of burnt flesh wrapped in plastic. She could even smell it. Her viewpoint was that of a child's, eyes at waist level to the crowd of adults that she pushed and shoved her way through. The feel of linen fabric and metal buttons brushed her cheeks as she squeezed through two men in navy-blue suits and black shiny shoes.

Finally she reached her destination, a coffin at the front of the room. It towered above her, a polished mahogany casket set up high on a gold altar. There were flowers surrounding it, but their faint scent couldn't mask the odor of ashes. Ashes and burnt flesh.

"You are dust and unto dust you shall return." She could hear a voice whisper. *"Ashes to ashes."* But she couldn't see anyone.

She already knew what she'd see when she looked over the

smooth edge of the coffin, past the satin bedding. The dream was a familiar one, a replay of the actual event. She was twelve years old all over again, going through her father's funeral, step by step, all over again.

By now her mind accepted the images, not skipping a single frame, lingering over details. She'd see her father dressed in a brown suit, his hands wrapped like a mummy and tucked down by his sides. She'd hear the crinkle of plastic under his clothes. She'd examine the burnt skin on his face, blistered and black despite the mortician's best efforts to paint over it. The smell was so real each time that she would awaken nauseated, sometimes gagging and holding her stomach. She couldn't stop it no matter how many times she tried, going as far as pinching herself in her dream, not feeling the sting and knowing that once the images began they would play through the entire reel.

She climbed the altar, twelve-year-old knees scraping against the polished wood and sweaty fingers gripping and pulling herself up to look over the edge. But this time it wasn't her father lying inside. Instead, she saw Cunningham, eyes closed, hands folded over one another. He looked so peaceful, so content.

And then she saw movement.

At first just a flicker of cloth, a pucker beneath a shirt button. Then another and another until his entire body seemed to be boiling, maggots popping out of the seams, down through his sleeves, crawling on his hands, over his face, out of his mouth.

Maggie jolted awake. She swatted at her arms. Wiped at her face. Batted down her hair. She jumped out of the bed and threw back the bedcovers. She gasped to catch her breath. Her chest heaved and her heart pounded. She was on the verge of hyperventilating, trying to calm herself, wrapping her arms tight around her body. Her skin was slick with sweat. She swallowed blood and realized she had bitten her lip.

A dream, she told herself. *Just a stupid dream.*

Still, she stumbled to the glass viewing wall. The monitors on the other side blinked green and red. Silent lines danced across computer screens, but there was no one there. She picked up the phone receiver, listened to the dial tone and stared at the contraption. There were no numbers, no keypad. *Of course not.* It was simply an intercom between the two rooms. She slapped the glass with the palm of her hand, resisting the urge to ball up a fist and pound.

She looked back at the other phone. *Who could she call?* She stayed paralyzed, leaning against the cool glass.

Other than Gwen there was no one.

Her choice, she reminded herself.

No. Somewhere along the road it had stopped being a choice.

She made her way to the small bathroom and peeled off the damp gown, exchanging it for another from the pile. She glanced at herself in the mirror. Her hair was tangled. Her skin pale and damp. Her eyes swollen. She looked like crap. She ran her fingers through her hair. Splashed cool water on her face, cupping handful after handful, waiting, hoping for it to revive her.

When she returned he was standing on the other side of the glass, watching for her. Concern in those intense brown eyes. It was as if he knew.

His eyes never left hers as she crossed the room. She picked up the receiver.

"Are you okay?"

"I'm fine," she lied.

"I don't think so." He tapped his own lip to remind her of her bloodied one. Then he pointed to the bed where the covers were twisted in a pile, half on the floor.

"Just a bad dream," she told him, wiping at her lip.

"Fever?"

"I don't think so."

He waited, examining her, a doctor confined to using only his eyes.

"I need to see Assistant Director Cunningham." Before he protested she added, "I just need to see him. He doesn't even need to know I'm there."

"Okay."

He surprised her. She'd expected an argument.

"You can see him. And then I'm taking you home," he said.

At first she didn't think she heard him correctly.

"Excuse me?"

"I'm letting you out of the Slammer."

She closed her eyes, leaned against the glass, hoped this wasn't just another episode in her cruel dream.

"Understand there are conditions," he said, his voice gentle in her ear.

She opened her eyes but stayed against the glass. It felt as if she was leaning into him, so close despite the thick wall of glass.

"We'll still have to vaccinate you every day," he continued. "The first sign, even the smallest symptom, and I'll want you back in here. And you'll need to be careful. No swapping body fluids…" He paused, and when she looked up at him he was smiling. "Not even a kiss."

"You're really cramping my style."

"I figured as much."

"Why?" she asked. "Why now?"

"Because it's been over forty-eight hours. Your blood is showing no signs of the virus. You haven't had any symptoms." Then he hesitated as if he was still deciding whether to share more. He stood closer to the glass. "And because I think you'll be safer away from here."

CHAPTER
64

Reston, Virginia

Tully found Emma watching TV and eating leftover pizza on the sofa.

He opened his mouth to ask but she beat him to it. "On the counter. Only one slice of supreme left but there's pepperoni."

His daughter knew him too well. He grabbed a paper plate, filled it, sprinkled it down with hot peppers and plopped down beside her.

"It's awfully late, sweet pea."

"No school tomorrow. Fall break."

"Right. I forgot."

"What about you? Were you with Gwen?"

"No, at work." He had spent the entire evening at Quantico, searching databases and looking for some connection to Cunningham and this killer. "What are we watching?"

"Nothing. Just filling dead air."

They sat, quietly watching for a few minutes.

"I guess she's pretty okay," Emma said.

Tully thought she was referring to the actress on the TV show.

"She dresses a lot classier than Mom."

He was exhausted. It took him a minute to realize the "she" was Gwen.

"Sometimes I think Mom still wants to be twentysomething instead of fortysomething."

"I'm glad you think Gwen's pretty okay," he said.

"You and Mom were together a long time, weren't you?"

More questions. Maybe the wedding had brought it on. Didn't all kids have a fantasy that their divorced parents would someday reunite?

"We dated for quite a while before we got married." He didn't add that he didn't want to marry Caroline until he was certain she wanted him, not either of his buddies. He didn't like remembering that emotional battle. Sometimes the pawn. Sometimes the knight. Caroline had that effect on men. That ability to make them feel special one minute, worthless the next, and the whole time still competing for her attention.

"Long-distance, right?" Emma continued, bringing Tully back. "You were training at Quantico and she was in Chicago studying art?"

"Right."

"How did you guys end up in Cleveland?"

"I grew up in Cleveland. You know that. Can I have a swallow of your Diet Coke?"

She handed it to him without a single eye-roll or a heavy sigh. Instead, her mind seemed focused on one subject.

"Where does Indiana come in?"

"Indiana?"

"Yeah. Didn't they call you Indy when you went through training?"

Another reminder he didn't like. Even after all these years.

"No, Indy was one of my roommates at Quantico. Actually, he was dating your mother first. That's how I met her."

She looked confused. "But what was your nickname?" Before he could respond, she answered her own question. "Oh, wait. You were J.B. Reggie was J.B. Jelly beans."

Tully winced. "I hated the name Reggie. Being called J.B. actually gave me the idea to just use my real initials."

"Your real initials?"

"Reginald James."

"That's not so bad," she said then went quiet.

When he looked over, her face was crinkled in thought and she had her thumbnail inserted between her teeth. The biting and gnawing had stopped years ago but sometimes she still put it in her teeth out of nervous habit.

"Your mom told you about Indy?" Tully asked.

She shook her head.

"I found some letters she had stashed in that old desk down in the spare bedroom. I thought they were letters from you to Mom."

"I can't believe she kept them after all this time." But in a way he wasn't surprised. A few years ago Tully would have been hurt to learn Caroline had kept Indy's letters. Now it didn't sting, just a tug, nothing more.

"I'm sorry, Dad." Emma sounded a bit shaken—not as if she was worried she'd be in trouble, so much as she couldn't believe she had made such a mistake. "I really did think they were from you."

"It's okay, sweet pea. Those letters were from a long time ago."

"Actually not that long ago."

"Excuse me?"

"Well, most of the letters are from 1982, but then there're three others. The most recent one was from July."

"This year?"

"Yeah," she said. "Congratulating her on getting married, again. But he didn't sound like he meant it."

"Why do you say that?"

"Because he says something like, 'Congratulations for choosing the wrong man, again.' That's kinda rude." She rolled her eyes. "I should have known you'd never say anything like that."

CHAPTER
65

USAMRIID

She should have prepared herself.

"He's getting a treatment," Platt told her as he led her through the cinder-block hallways.

Maggie had dressed back in her street clothes. It was amazing how something that simple could feel so good. She had to leave behind the purple-flowered jacket. It had been confiscated early on because of Mary Louise's vomit. A splatter on her sleeve. The one thing that separated Maggie's fate from Cunningham's.

Funny how life was, Maggie thought. As an FBI agent she had come face-to-face with killers, been sliced on, shot at and left for dead in a freezer. But she never would have guessed that life or death could depend on her proximity to a little girl's vomit.

"How is Mary Louise?" she asked Platt as they continued through the maze of hallways. She didn't expect any details. He'd already made it clear none of the others' conditions were something he would discuss.

"She's good," he said, glancing back at her. "So far."

They came to the end of a hallway and he punched in a code then slid a key card through the designated slot. This time the hiss of the air-lock door didn't make Maggie's stomach plunge. Platt stopped with his hand on the door handle and looked back at Maggie again. She caught his apprehension.

"You're not used to seeing him like this," Platt warned her.

Maggie figured Platt was an Army colonel. It was part of his job to make things sound more dramatic, to take everything at its most serious level. He had to overcompensate especially in life-or-death matters.

She followed him into the viewing room and immediately noticed that all the monitors and equipment were humming, flashing, beeping a steady rhythm. She stayed away from the glass wall that separated this room from the small hospital room. She tried not to draw the attention of the two spacemen working inside the room. They were hanging IVs, double bags, one clear liquid, another possibly blood or plasma. Maggie couldn't tell, either way, there were enough tubes to warrant something serious. And there was the equipment. Though she couldn't hear the hiss or whirl or beeps, she saw one of the spacemen pushing buttons on machines and monitors and could see their correspondence to some of the computer screens in the dark outside room where she and Platt stood.

At first Maggie concentrated on the spacemen and their smooth, deliberate movements. They worked together seamlessly, not at all encumbered by the suits but almost as if in slow motion. It was like watching the Discovery Channel, only with the sound muted.

One of the spacemen went to the other side of the room and then Maggie saw the man in the bed.

She didn't recognize him at first. His salt-and-pepper hair looked thin, his face pasty white. His eyes were closed. Tubes ran from his arms and nose to the equipment beside the bed. He looked smaller than his six-foot athletic frame. Smaller and so vulnerable. She stared at him, watching for something that would connect this helpless figure to her energetic boss.

"Mary Louise hasn't broken with any of the symptoms." Platt startled her. She had forgotten he was standing right beside her. "The virus may have been lying dormant inside her. It's difficult to understand, sometimes almost impossible to explain. It's a parasite, jumping from host to host, completely destroying one while only traveling in others. It may never show up in her. Just like you."

They stood there silently for what seemed a long time. Maggie swore she could hear her own breathing, a vibrating force inside a wind tunnel that sounded like staggered gasps. She had to be imagining it. Maybe it was simply one of the machines.

"But Cunningham isn't so lucky?" she finally said, glancing at Platt. He was looking straight ahead. "He already has symptoms?" And this came in a whisper she hardly recognized as her own. Maybe she was having problems breathing.

"Yes," he said.

"You've already seen it? In his blood?"

Hesitation. A long enough pause that she had to look over at him, again. This time he let her have his eyes and she saw it there before he said, "Yes."

CHAPTER
66

Monday, October 1, 2007

Platt drove Maggie home, a sixty-minute trip in the wee small hours of the morning. *Under the cover of darkness.* It felt like a covert mission, more drama than necessary. Yet he kept an eye on the rearview mirror, his heart tripping into overdrive whenever car lights followed one too many of his turns. Each time it ended up being nothing. The cars eventually turned another direction or passed. He was being paranoid.

Earlier he had authorized a shipment of vaccine to be air-lifted directly to Bix in Chicago. The CDC had faxed Platt the official request. As the head of this mission Platt had the authority to respond. In the process he discovered that Janklow had already approved a much smaller shipment but with orders that it be released only to the director of

Homeland Security. Not the CDC. Red tape? Personal grudge? Platt didn't care to know. His best guess was that Janklow was maintaining political correctness despite the clock ticking on a potential epidemic.

Platt was also quick to notice that nowhere in Janklow's orders for the release of vaccine to Homeland Security was there an acknowledgment of the four victims already at USAMRIID. It would have been the perfect opportunity now that both Homeland Security and the CDC were involved. But Janklow was still covering up his own backyard. As for McCathy, Platt wasn't sure if or how he was involved. There would be time to confront both of them but only after he made sure the four victims under his watch were safe and secure.

Platt couldn't ethically release Assistant Director Cunningham, Ms. Kellerman or Mary Louise. Each needed the specialized medical care of USAMRIID along with the daily dosage of the vaccine. Agent O'Dell, however, needed only the vaccine at this time. If she ended up being the lone survivor, what would Janklow do with her? Platt would rather make that decision than leave it to Janklow.

Platt glanced at Maggie's silhouette, highlighted only by the green dashboard lights. She was different here alongside him without the barrier of glass. She had been quiet after seeing Cunningham. Yet she didn't look as vulnerable back in her street clothes. As a temporary replacement to the purple jacket she'd had to leave behind, Platt had offered her his William and Mary sweatshirt to ward off the night chill.

She had hesitated at first, giving the gesture more meaning than necessary. He wondered if Maggie O'Dell simply wasn't used to someone looking out for her.

"It doesn't mean we're going steady or anything," he had joked, expecting one of her witty comebacks.

She'd simply said, "Thank you," and slipped it on.

After they were on the road and safely away from USAMRIID, she said, "You're worried the Ebola this guy is sending may have come from your own labs?"

He glanced at her, again, not sure why he was surprised that she would cut immediately to the chase. She had done so throughout their conversations.

"It's crossed my mind."

Platt wasn't sure how much of his suspicions he should share. He might already be on the verge of getting court-martialed despite all his efforts to do the right thing.

"He's someone with a bruised ego," she said. "He may have worked on some high-profile cases and never been acknowledged. Someone intent on retribution, on doling out a perverted sense of justice. Does that sound like anyone you know?"

"Maybe," Platt said, though he thought immediately of Michael McCathy.

Instead of pressing the matter, she said, "The outbreak in Chicago, do they know how it started?"

"A Chicago accountant named Markus Schroder was there for tests. They had no idea what was wrong with him. Ended up doing exploratory surgery."

"Any idea if he received a package in the mail?"

"I asked Bix. He's the CDC guy. He's going to check."

"Markus Schroder," she said and stared off into the dark countryside.

"You think the name means something? Like with the Kellermans?"

"Possibly. Chicago can't be a coincidence. It was Chicago where the Tylenol murders took place. There has to be some connection. I can tell you this much. If Markus Schroder received a similar package he wasn't a random victim."

"You always look for logic even within the madness?"

He could feel her eyes on him now, studying him to see if he was serious. He kept his eyes on the road ahead.

"It'd be convenient to believe people who commit these types of crimes are simply mad. That there's a neuron or two misfiring inside their brains."

"If they're not mad, not crazy, what then?"

She hesitated but only briefly before she calmly and quietly said, "They're evil."

CHAPTER
67

Saint Francis Hospital
Chicago

Dr. Claire Antonelli couldn't argue with Roger Bix. She knew he was right. Her son needed to be included in the quarantine. She didn't want to admit that he may have been exposed to the virus, thanks to her. Neither of them displayed symptoms. She had to believe they were okay, though it scared the hell out of her. Her son, however, pretended to see it all as an adventure.

"We just read about Ebola in World History. Maybe I can get extra credit," he had joked.

The nurses in the surgical center had prepared a room for him. There was something ironic yet comforting about having him so close in the middle of all the chaos. She was on her way to see if he'd gotten settled, when Roger Bix sidetracked her again. Bix was making a habit of treating her as what he called his "point person." On several occasions Bix and Dr. Miles had gone head-to-head on procedure and policy. Claire was simply too exhausted to argue...with anyone. This morning the media had shown up. WGN-TV, Channel 9 had cameras out front. If Bix was looking for a spokesperson he would need to keep looking.

Now Bix walked alongside her when she didn't bother to stop or slow down by his presence. "We have the vaccine," he told her. This, however, stopped her.

"That was fast."

"Special air delivery."

"How much?"

"Enough to get us started. It's a series of shots. That's what we need to focus on. What we need to tell everyone."

So not enough, Claire wanted to say. That's what he was really telling her. The idea of distributing false hope left a sudden lump in her stomach.

He must have seen her skepticism because he countered with, "It'll be enough. We'll start getting blood test results this morning. Not everyone who came in contact with this guy will be breaking with Ebola. The initial shots will simply be a precaution."

"Of course," Claire said, watching Bix's eyes travel over her shoulder, across the lobby, everywhere except to her eyes.

"I need you to ask Mrs. Schroder if Markus received an unusual package in the week or so before he got sick."

"A package? What kind of package?"

"Anything with a Ziploc plastic bag inside."

Claire stared at him, but it was obvious this was as much as Roger Bix was ready to tell her. He started, instead, giving her a rundown of where and how they'd start administering the vaccine, when nurse Amanda Corey hurried up the hallway toward them.

"Sorry to interrupt," she said, out of breath and flushed. "I figured you'd both want to know as soon as possible. Markus Schroder is dead."

CHAPTER
68

Quantico

Tully had files open all over his desk. He'd spent most of yesterday looking for something, anything that might connect Cunningham to this killer. Their boss had been involved with all the national biggies: the Unabomber, the Beltway Snipers, Eric Rudolph, Timothy McVeigh, the anthrax killer. The list went on and on. It was overwhelming. There was no easy way to search. So Tully shifted through the original files, trying to find repeat names, especially anyone from USAMRIID.

He was starting through another box, when Ganza's lanky frame leaned in his doorway.

"Did you hear about Chicago?"

"Bears or the Sox?" Tully asked before he saw the scared look in Ganza's eyes.

"CDC has a case of Ebola in a suburban hospital."

"You're kidding."

"I wish."

Ganza filled him in on what little he knew. When he finished he pointed to the mess on Tully's desk.

"Trying to find a link," Tully said, "to Cunningham. But going through the cases he's worked on is like looking for a proverbial needle in a haystack."

"Have you heard from him?"

Tully shook his head. "Not since Saturday. He gave me a phone number but no one picks up."

Both men stared at their feet in silence. Finally Ganza muttered something about calling a colleague at the CDC.

"I'll let you know what I find out." And he was gone, leaving Tully to his mess.

It was difficult to think about Cunningham. Tully knew agents who had been killed in the line of duty. It was something all agents kept in the back of their minds. But somehow this was different. Cunningham was one of those invincible guys. You knew bullets didn't bounce off of him but at the time you really wouldn't be surprised if they did. He was their leader, the one who held them up. And it seemed cruel and unfair to have an invisible weapon from an invisible killer take him down. No amount of training prepared you for something like this.

It reminded him of his own training. Emma had brought back a lot of memories with her questions. When he, Razzy and Indy were together they believed they'd change the world, conquer evil. All that good stuff. It was the 1980s. The Soviet Union was crumbling along with the wall. No more Cold War. Reagan made it okay to be proud again. The three of them were young, strong and idealistic and very different from one another. One common goal pulled them together and ironically, one silly and flirtatious, but absolutely beautiful girl pulled them apart.

Tully looked at Emma's framed photo on the corner of his desk. Actually he could barely see her face behind the stack of files. He considered all the cases he had worked over the last twenty-five years. There were biggies on his own résumé: the Unabomber, Jeffery Dahmer, Albert Stucky, Timothy McVeigh, 9/11. But in the end, hands down, Emma was what made everything in his life worthwhile. Emma and now possibly Gwen Patterson.

He was thinking about Gwen when his phone started ringing.

"R. J. Tully," he answered.

"Why are you sending me cash? And in a plastic bag, for Christ's sake."

It was his ex-wife. The onetime silly and flirtatious but beautiful girl was mad as hell.

CHAPTER
69

North Platte, Nebraska

Patsy Kowak couldn't believe it. She fingered the envelope left for her in the middle of the kitchen table, its contents half sticking out: two first-class airline tickets to Cleveland, Ohio. She had found them waiting for her this morning when she sat down to have her coffee.

"I booked us a room at the Hyatt Regency," Ward said from behind her. She hadn't heard him come into the room. "That's where you said you wanted to stay, right?"

"I said it. I didn't think you heard it."

"I listen to you." He poured himself a cup of coffee and sat down across from her. He never took time out to sit and drink coffee. His usually went into a thermos to-go mug and out the door with him.

"These tickets are for Wednesday," Patsy said, tapping

them against the tabletop as if she still didn't believe they were real.

"Yeah, well, we have a layover in Atlanta. It'll take us most of the day to get there. I thought we could have all day Thursday to ourselves, to sit back and enjoy. Relax."

She raised her eyebrow at him. "You sure you know how?"

"What? Relax? I think I can figure it out. Lee and Betty offered to look after things."

She held up the first-class tickets. "Whatever got into you? Last time we talked you didn't even want to go."

"I realized how much it means to you."

"But not to you?" She was disappointed in his answer. He noticed. Thirty-two years of marriage, how could he not notice.

"I don't agree with Conrad's choices," he said, avoiding her eyes and staring into his coffee as though it held the correct answer. "I might not agree but he's still my son."

She reached across the table and put her hand over his callused one. He wasn't much for shows of affection and quickly found a way to change the subject.

"Go get yourself one of those manicures," he said, taking her hand in his and pretending it was only to examine it. "You work hard around here. Treat yourself."

Her hands were an embarrassment, dry and red skin, raw gouges where she'd cut the cuticles too deeply. Yes, she'd treat herself.

She knew Ward would come around. Her husband was a good man. A good father. Patsy was so pleased, she had almost forgotten about getting out of bed earlier with a headache and a backache. All she had to do was stand up for an instant reminder. Her head throbbed with a thousand little hammers beating behind her brow. She cupped the palm of her hand over her forehead. A bit of a fever, too. She couldn't come down with the flu now. In two days she'd be traveling to her son's wedding. She refused to get sick.

She glanced at the wall clock, picked up the phone and dialed from memory.

"Conrad Kovak's office." The woman's voice was abrupt in a way that discouraged callers from even responding. Patsy wondered if she should say something to Conrad.

"Is Conrad in?"

"Mr. Kovak will be in meetings all morning."

"This is his mother."

Patsy waited. With Conrad's previous assistant, it made a difference. If Conrad really wasn't in a meeting Renae would put the call through when she learned it was Patsy. With this assistant it obviously made no difference.

After a long pause the woman asked, "Do you want to leave a message?"

"Yes, I suppose so," Patsy said, getting ready to tell her to have Conrad call later, but there was a click and buzz and suddenly another voice telling her to leave a message after the tone. The assistant had sent her on to voice messaging, something Renae would never have done.

"Conrad, it's Mom. Just wanted to let you know we'll be leaving for Cleveland on Wednesday. Your dad bought first-class tickets for us. And he did it all on his own. I didn't even tell him about the money you sent. Call me later, sweetie."

Patsy hung up the phone. Now she needed to take something so she didn't end up with the flu.

CHAPTER
70

Newburgh Heights, Virginia

Maggie left Benjamin Platt asleep in her spare bedroom. Satisfied with a couple hours of sleep and anxious to get back to her regular life, Maggie had put on a long-sleeve T-shirt, shorts and running shoes. She grabbed her cell phone and keys and set out for her morning run. She felt as if she needed to make up for lost time. That's what she told herself when she launched into mile number two, but the tightness in her calves and the ache in her chest made her reduce her run to a brisk walk. Her lungs breathed in the crisp air, greedy like they'd been deprived for weeks.

She'd forgotten how wonderful a blue sky looked, scrubbed clean after the rain. A flock of geese honked overhead. The beagle up the street had already started baying, anticipating her approach. He'd be disappointed to discover Harvey not with her. Gold and orange mums competed in neighboring yards with purple ash trees and fiery-red bushes. Someone was serving bacon for breakfast.

It sounded like such a bad cliché but it was as if all of her senses had suddenly started firing again after a long stretch of paralysis. Even her daily routine seemed fresh. She had convinced herself to think positively. The virus hadn't shown up yet in her blood. Maybe she could stop it.

But she couldn't stop thinking about Cunningham. Her mind played over the details like a loop in her brain. Several things nagged at her but she couldn't figure out why. She had awakened with the answer to one of the puzzle pieces, the answer so crystal clear she couldn't believe she hadn't seen it earlier. But she wasn't sure it mattered. So what if this killer was an expert in crime trivia? Maybe the puzzle piece meant something. Maybe not. He could just be showing off.

She glanced at her watch and pulled out her cell phone.

He picked up quicker than she expected. "This is Agent Tully."

"It's Maggie."

"My caller ID says they gave you back your cell phone."

"Yes, and I'm back home."

Silence. It lasted so long she thought she had lost the connection.

"They let you out?"

The way he said it made her smile. Was he really worried she had escaped without anyone knowing?

"Colonel Platt drove me home early this morning." She

thought she heard a sigh of relief. "Listen, I think I solved another one of the puzzle pieces. 'Call Nathan.' You said it was a blind impression left on the envelope?"

"That's right."

"I think it was in 1993. I'm not sure about that date. But the FBI offered a million-dollar reward for any information regarding someone named Nathan R. in connection to the Unabomber."

"Okay, that's starting to sound familiar."

"There was an impression found on a letter the Unabomber sent to the *New York Times*. They thought he had slipped, that maybe he had written a note to himself on a piece of paper on top of the letter and it pressed through without him knowing. If I'm remembering correctly it read, 'Call Nathan R. 7:00 p.m.'"

Maggie noticed a car up the street slow down, stop where there was no stop sign and continue up the street. This wasn't a neighborhood with idle traffic. She decided to turn around and head back toward her house.

"I'm looking it up on the computer," Tully said.

"It ended up being a mistake. I think it was an editor or someone else at the *Times*. He wrote himself a note on top of the letter before he realized the significance of the letter. It was his note that pressed through onto the Unabomber's letter."

"So it meant nothing," Tully said. "And it means nothing in this Ebola case. Except that this guy is jerking us around."

"It could be that law-enforcement officers in general are

his target and the victims are just convenient pieces to his puzzle."

"Could be." The tone in his voice said otherwise.

"What is it?" She knew there was something.

"My ex-wife got a package in the mail this morning. Block-style lettering. A plastic Ziploc bag inside. The return address was mine."

"Jesus, Tully. Please tell me she didn't open the plastic bag."

"No, she didn't. I don't know if this is something or just a cruel coincidence."

"It's not a coincidence. What's inside the bag?"

"She said it looks like a stack of ten-dollar bills."

Maggie winced. Could it be that easy? That simple to get someone to open a bag of Ebola without hesitating. She saw the car again. She was still about two blocks from her house.

"This thing with 'Call Nathan R.' Tully, George Sloane should have recognized it."

"Yeah, the Beltway Sniper phrase, too. He was in a hurry that day. Impatient. He didn't like that he had to work with me and not Cunningham."

"I think we need to talk to Sloane again. Show him the note one more time. See if we can get a copy faxed to us of the mailing envelope the killer sent to the Kellermans."

"Sure. If you think it'll help."

"Do you have any information on Chicago?"

"Ganza's calling someone at the CDC."

"I'll call Sloane. See if he can meet with us. And Tully,

one thing you really need to consider. Cunningham may have been right about this being personal. It just may be you, not him."

"I've already thought about that."

She could hear the car coming up behind her.

"Gotta go. I'll talk to you later."

Before she snapped her phone closed she heard the engine slow.

"Hey, lady. It's about time you get home."

Maggie turned to find Nick Morrelli in the driver's seat of a dark blue sedan.

CHAPTER
71

Newburgh Heights, Virginia

Benjamin Platt felt perfectly comfortable sitting on Maggie's patio in only his T-shirt, jeans and bare feet. She'd left a fresh pot of coffee though he knew from her food requests in the Slammer that she wasn't a coffee drinker. He had poured himself a cup and gravitated to the patio.

Her backyard was beautiful. A lush and private sanctuary. He wasn't surprised. It actually reminded him of the wooded area behind his own house and the screened-in porch that overlooked it. However, he didn't know much about landscaping. It looked like Maggie did. The six-foot wood fence stretched all the way to the creek behind the property. Huge pine trees bordered the other sides of the fence line, blocking views of her neighbors' yards and homes. Every corner looked professionally landscaped with decorative trees, an

English garden with fading blooms and a rock garden surrounded by rosebushes.

From the chew toys in a wicker basket at the corner of the
patio he guessed she shared the backyard with a dog. A big
dog. And from the bouquet of fresh flowers—with a card
sticking out of the middle signed, Love Nick—Platt guessed
she had someone else with whom she shared portions of her
life. Also not a surprise. She was a beautiful, intelligent
woman. Even Platt, with his workaholic blinders, had
noticed.

And he had noticed long before she offered him her spare
bedroom. Platt realized her offer was one she didn't make
often. Boxes of files lined one wall of the bedroom and
stacks of books took up most of the space on top of the
dresser. Yet he had slept hard even if it had been for only
several hours. No dreams. No visions of little girls, Ali or
Mary Louise. No sounds of medevac helicopters or IEDs
being set off. For once he simply slept. It was a rare treat.

Platt rubbed at the stubble on his jaw. He checked his
watch. Sipped his coffee. He needed to get back to
USAMRIID. He needed to confront Janklow. He needed to
know if Michael McCathy had something to do with these
Ebola cases. The more he thought about it the more he
believed it was possible. Last night he had checked McCathy's
file. Besides being a weapons inspector in Iraq, McCathy had
also been one of the team that scoured the world in the hunt
for viruses, not in order to cure them, but to acquire them.
It wasn't a secret that once upon a time, back in the 1970s

and early 1980s the United States stockpiled biological agents to possibly use them in their defense program. To use them as weapons. It was probably one of the reasons McCathy had later been chosen to travel to Iraq as a weapons inspector. Of course, he could identify weapons of mass destruction when long ago he had acquired them for his home team.

Platt made himself sip when he caught himself gulping. He leaned his head back, closed his eyes and listened to the quiet. It might be the only quiet he would have for quite some time.

CHAPTER
72

"What are you doing here, Nick?"

"I've been in D.C. since Friday for a conference. I just wanted to see you before I left for Boston."

When she didn't respond he continued, "I left messages." There was that smile. "And flowers."

"I've been gone," she said without offering any more of an explanation. He couldn't just show up in her neighborhood, trolling the streets, even if he did look good in a navy suit that brought out the blue in his eyes.

"I'm working a case. And I have somewhere I need to be," she said.

She started walking again, ignoring the slamming car door. He trotted up beside her.

"Are we ever just going to sit down and talk?"

"What do you think we need to talk about, Nick?"

"Well, I've been trying for months to talk to you about what I'm feeling."

"What you're feeling? Not necessarily what I'm feeling."

"No, of course not. I mean, of course I want to know what you're feeling. Can we just go have lunch and talk about it?"

Any other time his persistence may have seemed sweet, endearing. But taking into account everything she had just gone through in the past several days, this...this naive courtship seemed frivolous, hollow, maybe even disingenuous. Though it wasn't his fault. Nick Morrelli didn't know any different.

She stopped in front of her house at the edge of her yard. Platt's Land Rover was still in her circle drive.

"You say you have feelings for me, Nick, but you don't even know me."

"Sure I do. I know you like Italian sausage on your pizza. You graduated from the University of Virginia. You're tough and beautiful and smart. What I don't know I want to know. That should count for something."

She ran her fingers through her hair, frustrated and not sure why. If this didn't matter, if he didn't matter, then why was she frustrated that he didn't understand?

"Have you ever been alone, Nick?"

"Sure. I'm alone now. I've been alone since Jill and I split."

"No, I mean ..." She wasn't sure she could explain what she had felt in the Slammer. "I mean really alone. You have your family, your mom, your sister, Christine, your nephew,

Timmy. And you've never been without someone for long. What was your longest stretch between girlfriends?"

"Why would that matter? Very few of them did matter. Yeah, I've had a lot of girlfriends. Is that what bothers you? That I've had a lot of girlfriends?"

"No, of course not." She shifted from one foot to the other. She didn't want to have this conversation and she certainly didn't want to have it in her front yard. "This isn't about you. It's about me."

He started to say something and she stopped him, putting up her hands in surrender.

"I'm not ready to be with anyone, Nick. Not right now."

"Is everything okay?" Platt asked.

She turned to find Benjamin Platt in her doorway, his eyes on Nick, his stance ready to move into action if he needed to.

"Everything's fine," she told him.

When she looked back at Nick he was staring at Platt, taking in the Land Rover for the first time. Maggie watched the charm and confidence slide off his face. Confusion gave way to hurt.

"I understand," he said, his eyes avoiding hers.

He was wounded, embarrassed.

"It's not what you're thinking," she told him though once again she reminded herself that she didn't owe him any explanation.

"I'll leave you alone. That's what you meant, right? About being alone? You just want *me* to leave you alone."

"That's not at all what I said."

But he was already walking away from her, headed back to his car, so easily convinced he was right. He hadn't listened to a word she had said.

She told herself that if it mattered, if he mattered, she'd go after him. It should come natural, be instinctive. She was used to following her gut instinct. It had never steered her wrong yet. She followed it now as she turned around and went back into her house.

CHAPTER
73

"Sorry," Platt said.

"It's not your fault."

"If I wasn't here he wouldn't have gotten the wrong impression."

"He got the impression he wanted to get."

Platt couldn't read her. He wasn't sure if she was upset, angry, sad? He had been concerned that Janklow had sent someone to retrieve her only to realize, and realize too late, that he had stumbled upon a lovers' quarrel.

Paranoid. He was way too paranoid.

"I have to get back to USAMRIID," he told her. "But I need to give you a shot before I leave."

She nodded and sat down by the kitchen counter, shoving the bouquet of flowers to the side. She looked tired, drained and not just from the confrontation outside.

"Did you have anything to eat this morning?"

"I usually eat after I run."

She'd been out running. He stopped himself from scolding her. Instead, he took the liberty of opening her refrigerator. It was well stocked. He grabbed a carton of eggs, milk, a package of cheddar cheese and a green pepper.

"Skillet?" he asked.

She pointed to a drawer under the oven.

"I don't have time to eat," she said without moving from her place at the counter. "I have to get to work. I need to shower. I have an appointment I need to make."

"I can't give you the vaccine on an empty stomach. So go make your appointment. Get your shower. I'll have omelets ready by the time you're done."

"I thought all Army doctors had wives to cook for them?"

"Army doctors aren't home enough to keep wives."

"Is that what happened?"

He stared at her, wondering how she did that. She had a way of throwing him completely off guard when he least expected it.

"How did you know I was divorced?"

"Old trick. You just told me. I also know you have a dog."

"Excuse me?"

"Something white, but not a Lab because the hair on the sweatshirt you loaned me isn't as coarse."

"How do you know it's not a cat?"

"You're definitely not a cat guy."

"Hmm…pretty good trick." He pulled out a cutting board and knife and started chopping the pepper. "His name's

Digger. He's a West Highland terrier. He's good company. He was my daughter's dog."

"Your wife wouldn't let your daughter have Digger at her house?"

"My daughter died five years ago."

"Oh, God, Ben."

He could feel her eyes on him now. He didn't look up. He continued to work, breaking eggs, sloshing a dab of milk.

"It's okay," he said. He had the phrase down pat.

"That one I didn't know."

"She died of complications from the flu. I was in Afghanistan. It was right after the war began. My wife thought Ali would get better. Said she knew the Army wouldn't let me come home just because Ali had the flu, so she didn't tell me. She didn't tell me until it was too late."

He realized he had stopped working with his hands. They were gripping the edge of the counter as if he needed to hold on to something. He didn't want to know if Maggie noticed. He reached for the mixture of eggs and milk and then tried to think of something, anything, to get back on track.

"Since we're sharing," he finally said. "How long have you been divorced?"

It was her turn to be surprised.

"No trick," he smiled. "It's in your file."

"Ah, of course. It's been about four years."

She didn't sound sure. Platt figured that was a good sign.

"Was that the ex-husband?"

"No."

She didn't offer more of an explanation. He didn't push.

"It's interesting," she said without prompting, "how much you realize…how much *I* realized…"

He waited and listened. He already knew she didn't share easily.

"You asked me," she said, "if you could call someone for me. And I realized there was no one."

"But someone did visit you."

"A friend. A very special friend."

He wanted to ask about the guy outside. Why he didn't seem to know about her weekend in the Slammer. Why she hadn't called him. Instead, he said, "Most people would consider themselves lucky to have at least one very special friend like that."

"There's someone at USAMRIID you suspect." She said it without question, a statement of fact. "Is that why you thought it was too dangerous for me to stay?"

He looked up at her this time and held her eyes.

"My commanding officer wants to make all of this disappear."

"Including the four victims." There was a spark of panic in her eyes. "Can he do that?"

"No, he can't. The victims' family members were being contacted early this morning. I started dispensing the vaccine yesterday without his official consent. The outbreak in Chicago means there could be others. What happened in Elk Grove can't disappear now."

"Is it possible he's covering for someone at the facility?"

"That I don't know."

"But you think it's possible this killer may have access to USAMRIID?"

"We have quite a few big egos and most of them with access to Level 4 agents. Whether any of them are capable of sending Ebola through the mail, I just don't know. But I'm going to try and find out."

CHAPTER
74

Tully knew Maggie was right. This was personal. How else could they explain Caroline getting a package with a plastic Ziploc bag inside? A package with Tully's return address. She had faxed him the label and at first glance the block-style lettering looked identical to the note found in the doughnut box. It had to be the same guy.

Now Tully realized that he himself may have been one of the targets. The box of doughnuts. He had been late getting to work Friday morning, otherwise he might have been the first one to dig in, to find the note, to respond to the threat at the Kellerman house. To be where Cunningham was right now.

After Tully got off the phone with Maggie he called Emma. A knee-jerk reaction. She was home alone today. No school. Fall break. He wanted to call and tell her not to leave the house. Don't answer the door. No, that wasn't right. Don't open any packages. Especially ones with money inside.

Her voice-messaging service kept picking up. She was on the phone probably talking to friends. Damn! And he'd been too cheap to add call-waiting to their cell-phone plan.

He'd have to stop by the house. What time did the mail usually come? There was a sense of urgency pumping through his veins. A sense of dread. Who else did the killer intend to hurt? He grabbed his jacket and car keys. As he rushed to the elevators he punched in Gwen's number. Four rings and her voice-messaging service picked up. Didn't anyone answer their phones anymore?

"Gwen, it's Tully. Don't open any packages you get in the mail. I'll explain later. Just don't open any."

In the parking lot he called Maggie back.

"This is Maggie O'Dell."

"If I'm the target, how does Chicago fit in?" He tried to hide the panic in his voice.

"Does the name Markus Schroder mean anything to you?"

"Not a thing. At least not off the top of my head." He was sweating, though the day was chilly. He wrestled out of his jacket, balled it up and tossed it into the backseat.

"You may be one on his list of targets. Like a hit list. People who've done him wrong over the years. That doesn't mean you'd know everyone on the list."

"Good point." He was already gunning the engine, zigzagging out of the parking lot. He needed to calm down. "But why Caroline? She's my ex-wife. Why does he think he'd hurt me by hurting her?"

"Maybe he thinks you still care about her," Maggie suggested. "Listen, Tully…" She waited as if to get his attention. "Have you ever worked with anyone at USAMRIID? Ever had a confrontation or a run-in with one of their scientists?"

Tully remembered his earlier suspicions. That the Ebola may have come from one of the Army's labs. Now Maggie must be thinking the same thing.

"I don't think so," he said slowly. He couldn't think straight. He just wanted to make sure Gwen and Emma were okay. "Let me think about that."

CHAPTER
75

Maggie left at the same time Platt did. Both of them on a mission to find the killer.

After breakfast he'd given her the shot, his fingers gentle, his eyes comforting. With him so close and without the glass between them Maggie found herself thinking about his conditions of release from the Slammer. No swapping body fluids, not even a kiss. She was surprised to find her mind wondering what might happen without those restrictions.

Now on her way to Quantico, Maggie pulled into a gas-and-shop parking lot. She flipped through the personal phone directory she kept in her briefcase. She punched in the number, expecting to leave a voice message and surprised when he picked up.

"Yeah?"

"Professor Sloane? It's Agent Maggie O'Dell."

"Agent O'Dell? What can I do for you?"

"I understand you talked to Agent Tully and Keith Ganza on Saturday about the note we found."

There was a pause, then a gruff, "Yes, that's right."

"I found some things on my own that I'd like to run by you and see if they make a difference in your assessment."

"What things?"

He sounded defensive. From what Maggie remembered of her brief encounters with the professor, being defensive was nothing unusual.

"You had mentioned that there were some similarities to the anthrax case. I think I may have made some connections to a couple of other cases."

"Good for you." There was the George Sloane she knew. "I can't be racing up to Quantico every time you people have something you want to run by me."

"Of course, I understand. It's just that you mentioned the anthrax case. I believe I've made a connection to the Tylenol murders in 1982, the Beltway Snipers in 2002 and the Unabomber."

"All of that? Well, you hardly need me, Agent O'Dell. Sounds like you have it all figured out."

She ignored his sarcasm. "Except I'm not sure of the significance of any of it other than to show off."

"To show off?" He sounded angry now rather than defensive. "You think he's gone through all this trouble just to show off what he knows about a few famous criminals? And tell me, Agent O'Dell, when you find this *show-off*, will he be wearing a double-breasted suit and living with his two elderly sisters?"

Sloane was referring to the Mad Bomber in New York during the 1950s and Dr. James Brussel's on-target profile.

"You either need my help, Agent O'Dell, or you already have it all figured out." He was back to his mocking self. "You can't have your cake and eat it, too."

She was growing impatient with him. He was playing with her. The cake reference was from the Unabomber's manifesto. She was on the verge of saying to hell with talking to him but she knew Cunningham had respect for the man's work. The note and the mailing envelopes were all the evidence they had right now.

"Look, Professor Sloane, I'm just hoping you might be able to help us connect more dots here. Perhaps I could stop in at the university later. I understand it's fall break this week."

"Christ," she heard him mumble. She wondered if he was surprised she had already checked out his schedule. "If it's that important. I suppose I can make time. Meet me in forty minutes. My office is in the basement of the Old Medical School Building."

He hung up before she could tell him whether or not that worked. She checked her wristwatch. It would take her at least forty minutes to get to the university.

She leaned back in her car seat. She had a backache. Probably from her morning run. Not true about her headache. It had started before the run. When she'd called Gwen earlier, her friend had told her she shouldn't go back to work so soon.

"Kiddo, stay home and relax for a couple of days. Or at least work from home."

Maggie had tried to explain that the best thing for her right now was routine. She didn't need more time alone to think. She'd had plenty of that in the Slammer.

She punched in another phone number. It went over immediately to voice mail.

"Hey, Tully, it's Maggie. Sloane agreed to meet at his office in forty minutes. It's almost noon. I'm heading over to UVA now. I'll see you over there."

She sat back up. They didn't have much to go on. She kept trying to think what Cunningham would advise. *Sometimes the ordinary becomes the invisible.* What wasn't she seeing here?

That's when she felt something drip down her chin. On the steering wheel was a drop of blood.

She glanced at herself in the rearview mirror. Just the sight of blood dripping from her nose stirred up a panic. She grabbed for a tissue. *This wasn't happening.* And just as quickly she tried to calm herself. *It didn't mean anything. It was just a nosebleed.*

She held the tissue to her nose and leaned her head back against the car's headrest. She closed her eyes and steadied her breathing.

Oh, God, a nosebleed.

CHAPTER
76

Platt stood in front of Commander Janklow's desk, unflinching and prepared for an attack.

"You were out of line, Colonel Platt," Janklow told him. "I didn't authorize you to release the vaccine to anyone."

"I had no direct orders that forbid it, sir. And as the head of this mission—"

"Cut the crap, Platt."

Janklow surprised him. His voice was impatient, bordering on not just anger but something else. There was an edge to it.

Platt waited, not sure how to respond. Not sure how far to push. This morning the man looked shredded, though his uniform was pressed as usual and his office tidy. His stance slouched a bit at the shoulders. His face creased in places Platt had never noticed before. His eyes were bloodshot. And when he showed his hands, Platt could see a slight tremor in the fingers.

"At some point in your career, Dr. Platt—if you still have a career available—you will need to choose between being a soldier, a doctor or a politician. The three contradict each other on many levels. They cannot coexist for long. Today you're choosing to be a doctor. That's fine. You probably think that's noble. I'm here to tell you, it's not noble. It's foolish."

He turned away from Platt to stare out his window, and for a minute Platt thought he was dismissing him. Platt decided he had to push.

"Sir, I think I know why you did it."

Janklow turned slowly, eyebrows raised but his face still angry.

"What is it, Dr. Platt, that you *think* I did?"

"I considered it myself. That the Ebola may have come from our own labs. You want to protect USAMRIID. After the anthrax debacle I can understand—"

"You have no idea what you're talking about."

"Sir, I just know—"

"Did you find any Ebola samples missing?"

"No, sir, I did not, but it would be difficult—"

The hand went up to stop him. Palm facing out. A definite tremor.

"There are no Ebola samples missing from USAMRIID."

Platt kept his shoulders back, his stance tall, his face impassive.

"Let me ask you this, Dr. Platt…" Janklow's voice leveled to normal. "Do you have any idea how much the vaccine for Ebola brings on the black market?"

Platt stared at him and he could see it wasn't a question Janklow expected an answer to.

"I better find out that you have no clue," Janklow warned. "Because although there are no Ebola tissue samples missing from this facility there is vaccine missing."

CHAPTER
77

Reston, Virginia

Tully found Emma in her usual lounge spot, in the living room on the floor and in front of a blaring TV. He was relieved to see no packages. Just the regular teenage mess of magazines and junk food.

A news brief interrupted her television show. She muted the sound, but Tully asked her to turn it back on when he saw that it was a press conference at Saint Francis Hospital in Chicago. There wasn't anything he didn't already know. Two doctors and a CDC guy fielding questions and keeping to the basics. In the corner of the screen was a picture of Markus Schroder. It looked like a wedding shot and included his wife. The guy looked like an ordinary joe. An accountant, they were saying, for a Chicago firm. Tully didn't recognize him. He'd batted the name around his brain all morning and couldn't place it. Even now as he studied the photo there was nothing he recognized about the man. Then Tully glanced at the wife. There was something familiar about the eyes. Did he know her?

"It's so sad," Emma was saying.

"Did they say the wife's name?"

"Yeah, something with a *V*. Vera, maybe."

Vera Schroder. No, the name didn't mean anything to Tully, either.

"Gotta go, sweet pea. Remember everything I said, okay?"

He was back on the road again. He got Maggie's message and revised his route. It would take him more than forty minutes to UVA. He was looking for a radio station with more news from Chicago when his cell phone rang.

"This is Agent Tully."

"Conrad's mom got one of those cute little packages filled with money, too." It was Caroline again and even more angry. "What the hell's going on, Tully?"

The realization hit him and it felt as if Caroline's words had injected ice water into his veins. He could see everything so clearly.

He had recognized Vera Schroder. And now he remembered where. It was a photo from a newspaper clipping that his roommate had insisted he keep tacked on their bulletin board to motivate him. A distraught young woman, devastated at finding her parents dead in their home after taking cyanide-laced Tylenol. Only, her name wasn't Schroder then. It was Vera Sloane. She was George Sloane's sister.

CHAPTER
78

University of Virginia

UVA at Charlottesville was Maggie's alma mater, so when Professor Sloane told her to meet him in the Old Medical School Building she knew exactly where it was. She also knew from her alumnae newsletters that the building was now used for faculty offices. Other than offices, it housed research laboratories and clinical-training facilities. Fall break made it possible for her to find a quick parking spot.

Maggie had worked with Professor Sloane only once before, but she knew him from teaching at Quantico. His forensic-documents class used to follow her criminal-behavior class. Cunningham frequently called on Sloane as a consultant when documents were a part of a case. She wasn't surprised that Tully and Ganza hadn't pressed the professor when he gave them what sounded like a quick assessment.

Tully and Sloane rubbed each other the wrong way. She knew it from the tension the two men gave off just being in the same room. She was hoping she could get information out of Sloane that perhaps Tully wasn't able to.

The front door to the Old Medical School Building was unlocked, though there was no one in the halls. She took the elevator to the basement, and as soon as she got off she could hear what sounded like monkeys screeching at the end of the hallway. Doors were closed and secured with key-card locks. A few signs indicated most of the rooms down here were research labs. One had a QUARANTINE sign posted.

She continued to search for what could be Sloane's office. Unsuccessful she headed down the other direction despite the screeching. Her cell phone started ringing and she grabbed it out of her pocket.

"This is Maggie O'Dell."

"It's Sloane," Tully said, and he sounded out of breath.

"I'm looking for him now."

"No, you don't understand—"

That was all Maggie heard before she felt the blow to the back of her head.

CHAPTER
79

Tully couldn't believe he hadn't seen it earlier.

He barreled down the Hwy-20 exit off of I-95. It would take him forever to get to Charlottesville. Maggie's cell phone was going to voice message. Had Sloane already done something to her?

Now, of course, it all made sense.

He remembered George Sloane asking where he was when the box of doughnuts was delivered.

Sloane had said, "If I remember correctly, you can't resist a chocolate doughnut."

Chocolate doughnuts were Tully's one constant obsession. He went through stages. Oreo cookies, licorice and once upon a time jelly beans, but chocolate doughnuts were a mainstay. But that wasn't what should have set off the trigger. Sloane had also said, "So terrorists are delivering their threats at the bottom of doughnut boxes now?"

How did he know the note was at the bottom of the box? Only Cunningham, Maggie, Ganza and himself knew that. You'd never assume a note to be at the bottom. Sloane knew because he placed it there.

And why would Caroline and her fiancé be targeted by the Ebola mailer unless her old sweetheart, who had still been in touch with her as recently as July, was somehow involved?

Her old sweetheart, Indy aka George Sloane, had gone a bit berserk the last time she had chosen someone else. It had even gotten him thrown out of the FBI before he finished training. As a result he became a forensic-document expert, still working with the FBI but always on the outside, working on the fringes. Working on every major case but never getting the credit he thought he deserved. George Sloane had always wanted to be a feebie, not a professor.

How many other packages had Sloane mailed?

And Maggie was with him right now. Unable to answer her phone.

Maybe Tully was wrong. Maybe she wasn't in danger. It was possible her cell phone was just out of range. Maybe there was no reason for Tully to panic.

Tully told himself this as he continued to punch down on the car's accelerator.

CHAPTER
80

University of Virginia

Maggie's head throbbed. High-pitched fingernails on a chalk-board brought her back. Her eyes fluttered, blurry images, swishes of green. The air was foul, something rancid, sweaty fur, animal feces.

She recognized the screeches from down the hall. Only, they weren't down the hall. They were closer. She opened her eyes, kept them open, willed them to focus. Then jerked to consciousness.

Beady eyes stared out at her. Green fur flicked and swirled. Razor-sharp claws scratched out between the metal bars of cages. She was in the middle of a small room lined on both sides with cages of screeching monkeys.

She tried to bolt upright and fell back. Her wrist was anchored to a corner table, strapped tight with a plastic tie.

She pulled and yanked at it, but it dug into her skin. Her movement only made the monkeys scream louder and bang around inside their cages, slamming their small hands against the bars or reaching out.

Maggie tried to calm herself. To steady herself. *Keep quiet. Don't move.*

With her free hand she patted down her jacket pocket and wasn't surprised to find her cell phone gone. So was her Smith & Wesson. She looked around the room to see if there was anything she could use to cut the plastic tie. There was nothing but monkey cages. Pellets of food and monkey feces scattered across the floor around and even underneath her. She rose to her feet, keeping her movements slow and easy. She couldn't stand upright with her wrist bound to the metal table.

She searched the room again for anything she could use. This time she noticed the two end cages and a chill slid over her. Both the doors were flapping open. That's when she saw a flick of a long green tail slip out from behind the table by the door.

Instinctively she grabbed at her shoulder holster, again, before remembering it was empty.

Then she saw a second ball of green fur out of the corner of her eyes. This one was sitting high up on top of the cages and he was staring down her.

Okay, so there were at least two monkeys loose. Sharp claws, sharp teeth. Somewhere from her data bank she remembered that they spit, too.

Don't look them in the eyes. Stay quiet and calm. Don't move.

She'd figure something out. But she needed to stay calm. Breathe. She scanned the room again, moving only her eyes.

That's when the lights went out.

It took everything she had inside her to not scream. When she felt the first brush of fur against her face she automatically jerked away. She gasped and gulped for air before making herself stationary again.

Quiet. Be still. Don't show your fear.

She was dripping wet with sweat and fear. How could they not sense that? But something told her they wouldn't attack unless threatened. That's when she felt the second swipe across her cheek. Only this time it was claws, not fur.

CHAPTER
81

University of Virginia

Tully had been to Sloane's office only once before, but it was easy to remember where it was. He bragged about being in the basement of the Old Medical School Building, where no one bothered him. Leave it to Sloane to brag about a basement office and make it sound like a privilege.

Tully noticed a parking sign for George Sloane right out front. One of those anniversary signs the university rewarded professors after so many years of service. An SUV was parked in the slot. An SUV with government plates. Tully shook his head. The guy had his own parking space, a government-issue vehicle. He had tenure at a reputable university and he still wasn't happy.

Tully didn't waste time with the elevator. He found the stairs.

Sloane's office was closed. The door locked. Tully pounded anyway. He pulled out his Glock and started checking doors left and right despite the key-card security pads. All the while monkeys screeched at the other end of the hall.

He stopped and stared at the door that held behind it screaming monkeys and he hoped to God he was wrong about what the monkeys were screaming at.

"It took you long enough," George Sloane said from behind him.

Tully turned slowly to find Sloane in the hallway, several syringes in his hand.

"I saved some of the virus just for you." He held up one of the syringes as he slid the others into his jacket pocket.

"Where's Agent O'Dell?"

"She's smarter than you…" Sloane smiled. "She found all my references. You didn't get any of them, did you?"

"Does it matter? Or are you still trying to compete with me?" Getting under George Sloane's skin might be the only way to set him off. Did he really want to set him off?

"You were never competition. Now, Razzy, I could understand when Caroline slept with him. But I knew she'd never marry him."

Tully kept his finger on the trigger. The monkeys kept screeching at his back. Sloane wasn't unnerved by them at all.

"I spent years planning this, months rehearsing and finding the perfect patsy. Every step was deliberate, an intricate piece of a total puzzle. I outwitted everyone, just like I did twenty-five years ago."

"The Tylenol murders. That was you?"

"I had to get rid of my fucking family. They were in the way. They kept after me to come home and run the family business. Nagging me. Never understanding why I wanted to be an FBI agent. Caroline was the best thing that ever happened to me. I was clearing a way for us to be together and she was off fucking you in Cleveland." His face turned red at the memory.

"And yet you still wanted her."

He stared at Tully, a blank stare, surprised that Tully knew.

"You still wanted her and you lost her again," Tully said. "But not to Razzy or me. She had a chance to choose you again, after all these years, and she chose someone else."

Sloane shrugged, pretending it didn't matter. Tully watched him jerk his head from side to side. His eyes darted around as if to shake the memory. When he finally looked back up at Tully he was George Sloane again and not that boy Indy who'd had so many idealistic hopes and dreams.

"Seems it's you who has a choice now," he said with a grin. And he pointed to the door behind Tully. The door the monkeys were screeching behind and now thumping around.

"Saving Agent O'Dell or taking me down."

Tully's stomach slid to his feet. He was right. Maggie was trapped behind that door.

"You can't shoot me," Sloane told him, waving his arms up and down as if giving Tully a free shot. "You don't have the guts."

Tully raised his Glock. "You forget. I was always a better shot than you."

"Yeah," Sloane said, holding up the syringe with one hand while his other hand reached for the wall, flipping a light switch Tully hadn't seen. The entire hallway went black. "Are you as good a shot in the dark?"

Tully swiped at the walls on both sides of him. No switches. He couldn't see anything, The basement hallway was pitch-black. There were no red lights that marked smoke detectors. There were no exit signs. Not even a slice of light beneath any of the doors. Doors that Tully already knew were all locked and required key cards.

He tried to stay calm. He tried to focus, to keep his breathing slow and his heart from pounding in his ears. He needed to listen. How could he hear over the monkeys screaming behind him?

He thought he heard a squeak on the floor directly in front of him. Was that possible? How far away? A foot? Maybe two?

He took a deep breath. Didn't Sloane use an aftershave? Or was he smelling monkey urine?

Tully braced his back against the wall, staying in one place. Sloane would expect him to move away, back away. He waited for his eyes to adjust to the dark, closing them tight and opening them again. He still couldn't see anything but total black.

One thing was certain. Tully knew he was coming.

Sloane had probably memorized how many paces it took to get down this hallway. Maybe he'd even made sure all the exit signs would not light up. He said he'd rehearsed everything. Did he have time to rehearse this, too? If so, he'd be able to stab the needle in before Tully could get off a shot.

Their training taught them to aim for the heart. Sloane would remember that. In fact, he'd count on Tully doing just that. Tully had to think quickly. He had to act fast.

He slid down the wall so that he was crouching. And despite the pitch-black, Tully tried to imagine Sloane crawling toward him. He raised his Glock and started firing. He fired low, shot after shot, left to right, a steady stream of bullets. He heard a yell, maybe a thump. He stopped.

Silence.

Even the monkeys had gone silent.

Tully stood up, put his hand on the wall and walked the length of it, swiping at the wall until he found the light switch.

He was right.

George Sloane had been on his hands and knees only ten feet away. How else could Tully explain the head shot that left his old friend dead in the middle of the hallway?

He turned back toward the door. The monkeys had started screeching again. He could hear them rattling against their cages. The door was locked. Key-card pass only. His Glock would have to do, one more time. The monkeys were silent a second time.

It was completely quiet when he eased into the doorway. Out of the dark corner he heard Maggie repeat Sloane's welcome, "It took you long enough."

CHAPTER
82

Wednesday, October 10, 2007
Newburgh Heights, Virginia

It was too beautiful a day for a funeral.

Maggie sat out on her patio and watched Benjamin Platt in her backyard, throwing a Frisbee to Harvey. He had taken off his cap and dress blue uniform jacket and rolled up his white shirtsleeves. Still, he looked so official with spit-and-polish black shoes and his necktie still in place.

She slipped off her leather pumps and leaned back in the wicker chair, closing her eyes and wishing she could numb the emotions still churning inside her. The entire time she had watched the casket make its way from the church to the plot at Arlington she kept hearing a voice in the back of her head saying, *"I can't believe he's gone."*

When she opened her eyes again, Platt and Harvey were

joining her. Platt dropped in the chair beside her and Harvey dropped on the floor at her feet.

"You okay?" he asked. "No more nosebleeds? Headaches?"

"No." She shook her head. "It's funny how stress works."

"You've been through a lot. But your blood continues to test negative. And," Platt said as he reached out to touch her cheek, lightly brushing a finger over the scar that had almost healed, "you're a very lucky woman that that monkey wasn't infected."

She reached down to pet Harvey, pulling away from Platt's touch when she really wanted to return his gesture. *Too soon.* What was wrong with her? Too soon could quickly become too late.

"Chicago's Saint Francis is open again," Platt told her. "This morning I talked to Dr. Claire Antonelli. She was Markus Schroder's doctor. It's amazing that she never contracted the virus."

"But they ended up with three cases of Ebola."

He nodded. "The chief of surgery who operated on Schroder. A hole in his glove. Two nurses who took care of Schroder. All of them are responding well to the vaccine. It could have been much worse. There could have been hundreds."

She glanced at him and smiled.

"What?" he asked.

"So says the new commander of USAMRIID."

"It's not official."

She didn't push it. He had already told her he might not

accept. He loved his work. And although he seemed pleased with Commander Janklow's resignation, he had told her he had no desire to replace him.

"I'm a doctor and a soldier, not a politician."

She certainly understood. She loved her work, too. Exposure to Ebola and being locked in a room with monkeys hadn't changed her mind about being an FBI agent. Risk was part of the job. That's what she'd tried to tell R. J. Tully. He had been at risk every second in that dark hallway. He had acted in self-defense and that's what the review board would corroborate. Cases like this, personal cases, left scars. Unfortunately, Tully was learning that.

Risk was a part of the job, Maggie told herself and knew deep down that's exactly what Cunningham would say. *God, she couldn't believe he was gone.* And all because of one man's petty revenge.

George Sloane had used all his experience and expertise to get back at three men he thought he had lost the love of his life to: R. J. Tully, Conrad Kovak and Victor Ragazzi. While he was at it, he'd take out the woman herself along with his sister, who twenty-five years ago had survived his first attempt to get rid of his entire family.

And because of what Sloane had learned in his profession—that the victim of a crime can often point a finger at who the killer is—he sometimes chose victims indirectly connected to his targets. All of his planning had left Mary Louise Kellerman without a mother and Rick Ragazzi and

Patsy Kowak still fighting for their lives, their friends and families quarantined.

What a waste of brilliance George Sloane was.

"Do you have to get back to USAMRIID?" Maggie asked, not wanting to sound like it mattered, then thinking, why not let him know it mattered? She wanted him to stay. She enjoyed his company. Lately she looked forward to it, even catching herself putting aside things in her mind that she wanted to tell him, that she wanted to share.

"I think I put in enough hours recently to warrant taking a day off. What did you have in mind?"

"Are you as good at preparing dinner as you are with breakfast?"

"I think I can scrape up something."

"How about a beer before you get to work?"

"Sounds good."

Maggie left him with Harvey and padded barefoot back into the house. She had two Sam Adams bottlenecks grasped in one hand when the doorbell rang. She had invited Tully, Emma and Gwen to stop by so she didn't even bother to check the peephole.

She pulled open the door to find a young man holding out a pizza box for her.

"Must be the house next door," Maggie told him. "I didn't order a pizza."

He shifted the box and glanced at the name and address on the receipt that was taped to the top of the box.

"Maggie O'Dell?"

"Yes, that's right."

She stared at the box, suddenly suspicious of another food delivery until he added, "Italian sausage and Romano cheese? It's already paid for, lady."

He handed her the pizza and left.

Maggie closed the door. She held the box in one hand and stared at the receipt. Next to "ordered by" was N. Morrelli.

Italian sausage and Romano cheese. She smiled. Perhaps Nick Morrelli did know her. And he certainly didn't give up easily.

CHAPTER
83

Benjamin Tasker Middle School
Bowie, Maryland

Ursella Bowman didn't mind returning from vacation in the middle of the week. It meant she had only two days to clean up the mess her substitute had left for her before she could recuperate on the weekend.

She walked into the mailroom and immediately thought she'd need that weekend much sooner. There were postal-storage bins stacked and the electronic meter had been left on the floor. Why in the world didn't that woman have any respect?

Ursella started picking up empty boxes and sorting un-deliverable mail that needed to be returned. She shoved a collection cart to the side and noticed a six-by-nine padded manila envelope that had gotten stuck between the cart and the wall.

It was addressed to Benjamin Tasker Middle School and it looked like a child's block printing.

Ursella shook her head as she slipped the envelope into the principal's mail slot. She hoped it wasn't something important.

* * * * *

TRUTH OR FICTION?

Notes from Alex Kava

While I was writing *Exposed* an outbreak of Ebola occurred in the Democratic Republic of Congo. The World Health Organization had more than four hundred suspected cases in the region, but as of this writing it hadn't been twenty-one days—the time Ebola takes to incubate—so the total confirmed cases and deaths were not yet known.

Could an outbreak like this occur in North America or Europe? Some experts believe it's only a matter of time. All it would take would be one infected person to get on an airplane. That speculation brought us closer to reality on May 24, 2007, when a man infected with tuberculosis got on an airplane in Atlanta and flew to Paris. He boarded yet another flight to Prague, then flew to Montreal and drove himself back to the United States to turn himself in to the CDC. Imagine if he'd had Ebola.

As an author I'm constantly asking questions like this. My research includes digging up the answers and nagging a lot of people who know such things. Sometimes it's difficult to recognize where the facts stop and the fiction begins. If the reader can't tell, then I've done my job.

I use real-life details in all my novels, but this time I wanted to let readers know what some of the facts are.

The Tylenol murders in Chicago during September 29 through October 1, 1982, remain unsolved to this day. There were seven known victims. One of them was a twelve-year-old girl named Mary Kellerman from Elk Grove Village, Illinois. However, to my knowledge there were no victims in Terre Haute, Indiana.

A scientist and bioweapons expert named Dr. Steven Hatifill, who worked at USAMRIID for a period, was considered by the U.S. Department of Justice to be a "person of interest" in the investigation of the 2001 anthrax attacks. Charges were never brought forward.

A vaccine for Ebola does exist. As mentioned in the novel, it was developed by research teams from Canada's National Microbiology Laboratory in Winnipeg and Fort Detrick's USAMRIID. The report of the findings first appeared in the *Journal Public Library of Science Pathogens,* January 2007. It has not been approved by the FDA as of this writing.

The U.S. Army Medical Research Institute of Infectious Diseases (USAMRIID) at Fort Detrick, Maryland, really does have frozen samples of all the Level 4 biological agents I mention in the book. My apologies for taking any liberties in using the facility for my setting. Suggestions and assertions I've made are entirely mine and not any of the staff's or anyone associated with USAMRIID. I have only the utmost respect for the facility as well as for the scientists and doctors who do amazing work there.

The same goes for the University of Virginia. And as far as I know there are no live macaque monkeys in the basement of the Old Medical School Building on UVA's campus.

Though undocumented, there have been stories about

monkey traders using the islands in Lake Victoria as dumping grounds for sick monkeys and then going back to retrieve those same monkeys to make up shortages in future shipments.

There are many other facts sprinkled throughout *Exposed* including those about criminal cases. The phrases in the note found in the doughnut box are actual phrases used by the Beltway Snipers. The impression "Call Nathan R" was found on a letter from the Unabomber. Ted Bundy was arrested in Pensacola, Florida, on Davis Highway in a stolen VW. For any of you who find this sort of trivia as fascinating as I do, I'm including some of my research resource materials.

RESOURCE BOOKS

23 Days of Terror, Angie Cannon and staff of US News & World Report, Pocket Books, 2003.

Amerithrax: the Hunt for the Anthrax Killer, Robert Graysmith, Jove, 2003.

The Hot Zone, Richard Preston, Anchor Books, 1994.

Identifying and Understanding the Narcissistic Personality, Elsa F. Ronningstam, Oxford University Press, 2005.

Inside the Criminal Mind, Stanton E. Samenow, Ph.D., Crown Publishers, 1984, Revised Edition 2004.

Physical Evidence in Forensic Science, Henry C. Lee, Ph.D. and Howard A. Harris, Ph.D., Lawyers & Judges Publishing Company, Inc., 2000.

Profilers: Leading Investigators Take You Inside the Criminal Mind, Edited by John H. Campbell and Don DeNevi, Prometheus Books, 2004.

Sniper: Inside the Hunt for the Killers Who Terrorized the Nation, Sari Horwitz and Michael E. Ruane, Ballantine Books, 2004.

Unabomber: A Desire to Kill, Robert Graysmith, Berkley, 1998.

Virus Hunter: Thirty Years of Battling HotViruses Around the World, C. J. Peters and Mark Olshaker, Anchor, 1998.

PERIODICALS

"Anthrax Q&A: Signs and Symptoms," CDC, June 2, 2003.

"Ebola Vaccine Shows Promise as Treatment," *Toronto Star,* January 21, 2007.

"God at Work Among Ugandan Refugees on Isolated Lake Victoria Island," Sue Sprenkle, Baptist Press, June 25, 2001.

"Interim Guide for Managing Patients With Suspected Viral Hemorrhagic Fever," CDC, May 19, 2005.

"Portrait of a Poisoner," *Time*, October 18, 1982.

"Renovated High-containment Lab Offers More Effective Research Space," Karen Fleming-Michael, U.S. Army Medical Research and Materiel Command, February 1, 2007.

"Why They Kill: The World of the Mass Killer," Jeffrey Kluger, *Time,* April 30, 2007.

'Somewhere out there is a monster and he's even more hideous than me'

On 17th July convicted serial killer Ronald Jeffreys was executed for the murders of three innocent boys. Three months later, the body of another boy is found butchered in the same style.

Cold-blooded copy-cat or the real thing— there's a killer on the loose and someone will atone for his sins…

www.mirabooks.co.uk

BL_273_APE

The line between good and evil can be crossed in a SPLIT SECOND

They called him the Collector—and now he's on
the loose again…

Criminal profiler Maggie O'Dell had been instrumental
in putting Albert Stucky, the notorious Collector, away, so
named for his ritual of collecting victims before disposing of
them in the most heinous ways possible. Since then, O'Dell
has lost her edge, tortured by the nightmares and
guilt for the ones she couldn't save.

But as the death toll increases, Maggie becomes the FBI's
best hope to hunt this man down. Only she can see into
this psychopath's twisted mind. And Albert Stucky
wouldn't have it any other way.

www.mirabooks.co.uk

A group of young men commit suicide in a secluded cabin.

A politician's daughter is found raped and strangled—her clothes piled neatly next to her body.

Special Agent Maggie O'Dell is assigned to both cases and, as she delves deeper, she finds a connection—Reverend Joseph Everett, the charismatic leader of a religious cult, bent on seducing the lonely and vulnerable into his fold.

Maggie's involvement becomes personal when a member of her own family is seduced by Everett's slick illusions. But the soul catcher wears many faces of evil and the case is nowhere near as simple as it seems.

www.mirabooks.co.uk

BL_275_TSC

In the tomb-like silence of an abandoned quarry, someone is trying to hide their dirty little secrets...

When Special Agent Maggie O'Dell receives a concerned phone call from Dr Gwen Patterson about a missing patient, she agrees to look into the woman's disappearance.

At first she dismisses Gwen's fears, but then a graveyard of bodies is discovered in rusted barrels buried in a rock quarry.

Is there a link between the missing patient and the horrifying murders?

www.mirabooks.co.uk

BL_276_ATSOM

GARDEN OF EDEN OR KILLER'S PARADISE?

A panicked answering machine message is the last
Liz Ames hears from her sister Rachel.

Liz heads straight to Rachel's home in Key West
and within hours of her arrival a man jumps to his
death. Then a teenage girl is found murdered.

The ritualistic style of the killing is hauntingly
similar to that used by the notorious 'New
Testament' serial killer—now on death row.

Could these deaths be related to Rachel's
disappearance? Is a copycat killer
at work?

www.mirabooks.co.uk

BL_279_DR

'THERE ARE MANY OF US AND WE ARE ALWAYS WATCHING'

When Avery Chauvin returns home after twelve years, she starts hearing rumours about The Seven—a mysterious group protecting the tight-knit community against moral decay.

Soon the events of the past and present take on a terrifying new meaning—a woman is found murdered, an outsider disappears and neighbours go missing in the night.

Uncertain who to trust, Avery faces the truth: that in this peaceful town a terrible evil resides, protected by the power of silence…

HARLEQUIN®MIRA®
www.mirabooks.co.uk

BL_280_IS

THEY CALLED HIM THE SLEEPING ANGEL KILLER...

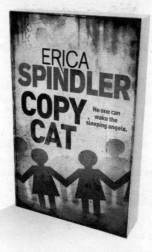

Five years ago, three little girls were murdered in their beds, posed like sleeping angels by a twisted killer.

With no witnesses and no clues, Detective Kitt Lundgren was forced to look on helplessly—taunted by a psychopath proud of his 'perfect crimes'.

Now the Sleeping Angel Killer is back. But there's something different about this new rash of killings—a tiny variation that opens terrifying new possibilities...

www.mirabooks.co.uk

BL_283_C

HARLEQUIN®MIRA®
www.mirabooks.co.uk

The mark of a good book

At MIRA we're proud of the books we publish, that's why whenever you see the MIRA star on one of our books, you can be assured of its quality and our dedication to bringing you the best books. From romance to crime to those that ask, "What would you do?" Whatever you're in the mood for and however you want to read it, we've got the book for you!

Visit **www.mirabooks.co.uk** and let us help you choose your next book.

★ **Read** extracts from our recently published titles

★ **Enter** competitions and prize draws to win signed books and more

★ **Watch** video clips of interviews and readings with our authors

★ **Download** our reading guides for your book group

★ **Sign up** to our newsletter to get helpful recommendations and **exclusive discounts** on books you might like to read next

www.mirabooks.co.uk

HMIRA_WEB